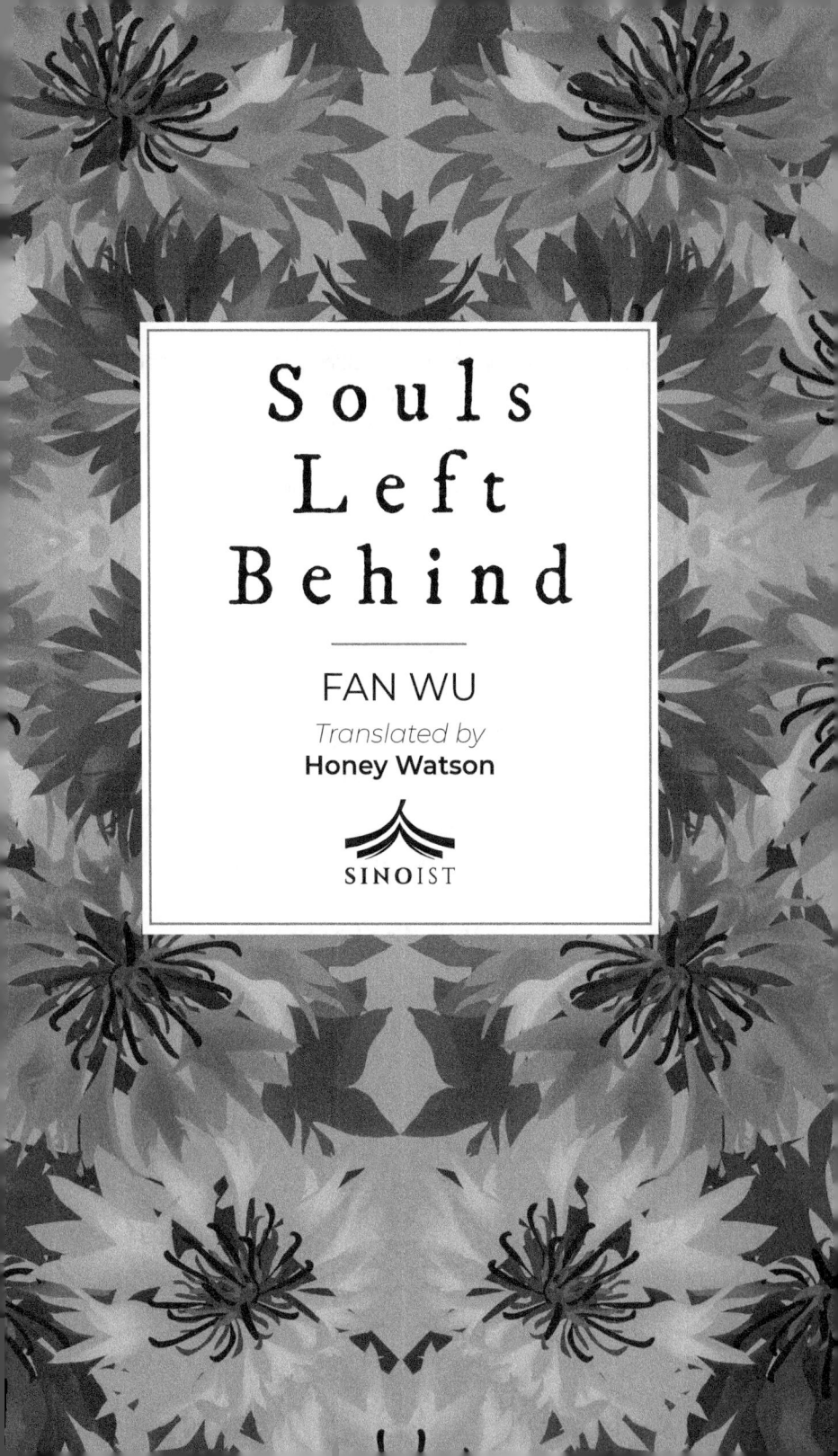

Praise for the Author

FEBRUARY FLOWERS

"Subtle and deftly paced, it's ultimately a story about sheer awakening"
OBSERVER (UK)

"[Fan Wu] enters the past as it was lived, in real-time and without the props of hindsight"
***FINANCIAL TIMES* (UK)**

"Her style is deceptively simple, her prose confident, clear and precise"
***THE BULLETIN* (AUSTRALIA)**

"Fresh and original"
***THE AGE* (AUSTRALIA)**

"The author's control of her subject matter is impressive"
THE ASIAN REVIEW OF BOOKS

BEAUTIFUL AS YESTERDAY

"Fan Wu is an exciting storyteller with an original take on the disarray of family history and, ultimately, how we manage to define ourselves"
AMY TAN* author of *THE JOY LUCK CLUB

"A fascinating and heartrending account of the conflicts and misunderstandings that exist between Chinese immigrants raised during different regimes"
***BOOKLIST* (USA)**

Souls Left Behind

Fan Wu

Translated by
Honey Watson

Sinoist Books

Published by Sinoist Books (an imprint of ACA Publishing Ltd)
London - Beijing
info@alaincharlesasia.com ☎ +44 20 3289 3885
www.sinoistbooks.com

Published by Sinoist Books (an imprint of ACA Publishing Ltd) with special thanks to The Mothers' Bridge of Love (MBL) and Sino-UK Arts and Cultural Bridge Ltd for their help in the making of this book. Their encouragement and support will help many to the discovery the hidden histories of our world.

Author: Fan Wu **Translator:** Honey Watson **Editor:** David Lammie

Original Chinese Text © 被遗忘的灵魂 *(beiyiwangdelinghun)* 2023, Guangdong Flower City Publishing House, China

ALL RIGHTS RESERVED. NO PART OF THIS PUBLICATION MAY BE REPRODUCED IN MATERIAL FORM, BY ANY MEANS, WHETHER GRAPHIC, ELECTRONIC, MECHANICAL OR OTHER, INCLUDING PHOTOCOPYING OR INFORMATION STORAGE, IN WHOLE OR IN PART, AND MAY NOT BE USED TO PREPARE OTHER PUBLICATIONS WITHOUT WRITTEN PERMISSION FROM THE PUBLISHER.

English Translation text © 2023 ACA Publishing Ltd, London, UK. A catalogue record for *Souls Left Behind* is available from the National Bibliographic Service of the British Library.

This novel is entirely a work of fiction. The names, characters and incidents portrayed in it are the work of the author's imagination. Any resemblance to actual persons, living or dead, events or localities is entirely coincidental.

Hardback ISBN: 978-1-83890-597-2
Paperback ISBN: 978-1-83890-557-6
eBook ISBN: 978-1-83890-558-3

Sinoist Books is honoured to be supported using public funding by Arts Council England.

1

The room was full of people, but the guest of honour was nowhere to be seen.

Earlier that morning, Anne had been busy in the kitchen. Though she had ordered fresh flowers and a cake, and had arranged for a meal to be delivered, she still felt as if she had forgotten something. Then she remembered: she should make dumplings. When Maman was still alive, Anne had helped her to prepare Baba's favourite dumplings for his birthday every year, rolling out the dough, mixing the filling, wrapping them. But many years had passed since then.

She found a Chinese cookbook in the same place Maman had left it. Touching its yellowing yet still glossy cover, she imagined her mother bustling around the room. Anne could almost see her standing by the sink, humming a tune while washing her hands, swaying her head to the rhythm of whatever music was playing.

David entered the kitchen as Anne was kneading the dough. He was a tall, rosy-faced man with a sturdy posture – yet Anne could tell that he had aged quickly in the three years since

Maman's death. He had begun to stoop and lost his appetite. At dinner the night before, he had eaten only half a bowl of noodles and a few greens. Where, she wondered, was the man who could boast of polishing off three big bowls of noodles no matter what?

Today, he was neatly dressed in a light blue dress shirt, black trousers and loafers. It was the first time since Marguerite's funeral that he had worn such formal attire.

"Wow, you're looking great today!" Anne reached out to hug her father, giving him a kiss on each cheek before returning to the dough. It was too moist, needed more flour.

"One has to dress well on one's birthday," David said with a smile, suppressing a wince at the sudden pain in his thigh caused by an old shrapnel wound that still bothered him from time to time in autumn. Worried that his daughter might notice his discomfort, he pointed to the pile of bowls on the table and said, "Ah, dumplings! Since when have you been a chef?"

"Since it's your eighty-fifth birthday feast, of course! I'm going to make it extra special. Pierre and the kids will be here before midday to help me as well." She began to count on her fingers. "The Bernards, Mr and Mrs Wang, some of your tai chi students, a couple of former colleagues... Heavens, that's sixteen adults and six kids! I should make at least a hundred of these!"

David looked lovingly at his daughter. Marguerite was approaching forty when she became pregnant with Anne, who had her mother's wide forehead, high nose and curled eyelashes along with his dark brown eyes, black hair and thick eyebrows. She smiled just like Marguerite too, with a gentle rising at the corners of the mouth and a shallow dimple appearing on the right cheek.

His eyes dampened at the thought of his wife. He took a dust cloth and, bearing the pain in his thigh, began to wipe the framed family pictures on the kitchen wall. After those, he moved on to the frames in the other rooms. This had become his daily routine since Marguerite's passing. He would sometimes repeat it several times in a single day. He then watered the flowers on the balcony, taking particular care to inspect the leaves and blossoms of a large red geranium for pests.

Anne gazed silently at her father through the window. She knew that her mother had picked out that geranium herself the year she died. When she brought it home, it had been in a tiny pot with no more than a single scarlet orb blossoming from its side. Now its tendrils spread halfway across the balcony, draping a curtain of flowers over the side of the balustrade.

David returned to the kitchen and asked, with an air of hesitancy, "Are you sure you want to have this party? It's so many people. Let's just invite Mr and Mrs Wang."

"Ba," she replied, her eyes widening, "we've already sent out the invitations! It's too late to change your mind."

"I just don't want you going to any trouble. You so rarely get to enjoy a relaxing weekend, and you came here last night just for me."

"There's no need to be like that with your own daughter, I'm happy to do it. Anyway, Ba, I need to go out and get some more chilli sauce, there's none left in the fridge and I know you like it with your dumplings."

"I'll go. I like to get out for a walk every morning, otherwise there's just no life in a day."

"I'll come too."

"No need. Someone should stay at home, what if a guest were to ring?"

Anne knew her father well enough not to press him. "If you insist. But be careful on the stairs and when you cross the road." Two years earlier, David had been knocked over by a cyclist in the street. He had been OK, nothing broken, but it was unlikely that he'd be so lucky again.

"It's like I'm five years old! Your father is perfectly capable of looking after himself. Look, isn't the house in order? And I'm in great health! I was still going lake swimming in the winter all through my seventies. When your Maman was alive, she would always say-"

"She would say that my Ba was made of iron," Anne chipped in.

To show his daughter how well he was, David flung out his hand and strode to the door like a marching soldier.

She followed him, ready to help him with his coat, when a new idea came to her.

"Wait a second, Baba," she said, rushing back to his bedroom to find a certain dark blue jacket in his wardrobe. Maman had bought it for him years ago. She had watched Maman putting it over his shoulders countless times as they prepared to go out together, but since her death, she had not seen him wear it even once.

She smoothed the collar down after helping him put it on. He smiled but said nothing.

Anne closed the door behind him. She realised then that she was playing Ma's role, and couldn't help but let out a faint smile. The expression was immediately followed by a tingling in her eyes.

Baba had been refusing to celebrate his birthdays since Maman died, but this year she had made sure to have a party and had rearranged her monthly lunch with her best friend Clara for the occasion.

She returned to the kitchen and, feeling the elasticity of the gleaming dough that she had pinched between her fingers, smiled happily to herself.

2

THE STREETS WERE ALMOST EMPTY. Everybody who had to go to work was already there, and this was neither a commercial district nor a tourist attraction.

Seven or eight years earlier in the late 1970s, property developers had taken a fancy to the area and covered it with a dozen or so new residential and commercial buildings of twenty or thirty storeys each, spreading the word that the 13th arrondissement of Paris would become a popular place for housing investment. Parisians did not flock to it as they expected, so there were no more shops or restaurants. Then, just as it seemed the property developers had no choice but to count their losses, hundreds of thousands of refugees arrived. Fleeing the Vietnam War and suffering many hardships along their path, they came to France all the way from Cambodia, Vietnam and Laos. The French government housed many of them in the vacant 13th arrondissement homes. In just a few years, the district's population skyrocketed. Migrants also came from China, mostly from Wenzhou, including many stowaways, who began to work there and open businesses once they saw the cheap rent and small but growing Chinese population. When David and Marguerite had first considered moving to the 13th arrondissement from the Latin Quarter after retirement twenty years earlier, they had no idea it would someday become a little Chinatown.

It had rained the previous night. Sycamore leaves had soaked together where they fell, looking like animal prints in their clumps on the ground.

David dropped his spirited act the moment he was out of his daughter's sight. His pace slowed and his head drooped. He had not wanted this party, but how could he refuse Anne when she was so excited?

The pain in his thigh lessened. His coat felt warm and comfortable on his back.

"I'm not leaving you, David," said Marguerite in his dreams last night. "We swore a vow to be together forever." She lifted her face to look at him, her thick curls like layers of white, rippling waves on her head. He buried his face in her hair, smelling the early summer sunlight, seeing them walking hand in hand through the forest as a young couple.

He dreamed of her every night these days.

He spotted an empty bottle, a cigarette pack and a half-eaten ham sandwich discarded in a wet napkin on a roadside bench. The type of person who couldn't stand to see littering, he furrowed his brow and placed them one by one into a rubbish bin a few metres away. Then, he paused a moment by the open glass doors of the Atlas Café, looking around inside and remembering its previous owner, Monsieur Dreyfus.

Monsieur Dreyfus had been a short, bald fellow with glasses and a smile that would fold his eyes into narrow creases. After beginning to study tai chi with David, Monsieur Dreyfus had stopped calling him Monsieur Zhang and started to call him Master Zhang instead. Dreyfus had inherited the cafe from his wife's parents ten years previously. It had been a small establishment back then, with only four tables in total.

Five months had passed now since Madame Dreyfus had found his body in their bathroom. He had killed himself, leaving behind a single line: "I can finally sleep peacefully." He had not even reached sixty! Before Dreyfus' passing, David had spent every morning chatting with him over his usual order of tea and a croissant. His wife sold the cafe after his death.

The aroma of freshly baked bread and rich coffee poured out into the street. David's stomach grumbled, but he decided against breakfast.

He continued in the direction of the supermarket, remembering the times when he would walk along this road with Marguerite. She would be on the right and he on the left, her hand resting gently in the crook of his arm. She walked with her head high and her shoulders back, making her seem taller than her five-foot-two frame. She liked to wear dresses, especially those with floral patterns. She even wore skirts in winter, pairing them with brown or black stockings beneath a knee-length coat and leather shoes.

He subconsciously raised his arm, as if hers were still there to receive it.

A public park lay ahead of him. It was small yet refined, adding colour to the grey streets and sky with the last of its rose blooms. Through it, he followed a stone path that he and Marguerite had walked together innumerable times.

There was heavy traffic at the intersection between

Avenue de Choisy, Avenue d'Ivry and Rue de Tolbiac. Over the past few years, many new shopfronts had been added to the area, along with many Asian faces. David felt both happy and sad about this development. On the one hand, it was much easier to buy Chinese products, and he had many more opportunities to speak his native tongue. On the other, all this change had happened so quickly that he felt he had become a stranger in his own home.

He stood for a while on the street corner. Chen Ji Supermarket was right there, but he found he did not want to go inside. He thought that he really should not have let his daughter organise this party. His heart palpitated at the mere thought of so many people crowding his house, filling it with noise. Curious guests would examine his photographs, asking all sorts of personal questions as if he had invited plainclothes detectives into his home. The children would certainly make a mess of things, too.

They often had friends over when Marguerite had been healthy, but her death had taken his desire for visitors. He had no guests other than Mr and Mrs Wang, who would sometimes stop in for a chat. He was used to isolation, at liberty to eat or sleep whenever he felt like it, content to spend much of his day in reverie about the past. For people who live to such an age, time ceases to feel like a long, continuous flow of water, but rather more like memories, each condensed into a block of stone. Some large, some small, some shiny, some clouded, some clear-edged and angular, others contouring softly. All you had to do was hold on to each one, studying them without missing a single dent or line.

There was a stall in the area, operated by a man in his thirties. His table was lined with a plastic sheet, on top of which he had arranged a display of cheap leather belt bags, pieces of African jewellery and a row of blue cornflower brooches made of cotton.

David headed over and stood in front of the stall. "I'd like two flowers, please," he said.

He and Marguerite would wear commemorative flowers, the bleuet de France, each year as it approached Armistice Day. He pocketed the two he had just bought, thinking that he would put Marguerite's on her grave on 11 November.

He let his hand linger over the flowers, recalling the year before Marguerite's death when they had worn their brooches to the town of Compiegne, where the Allies had signed the armistice with Germany. She had been so cold when they came out of the Armistice Museum that she was trembling. She was always cold in those years, freezing in winter no matter how many layers of clothing she wore. David would massage her feet before bed, believing in the Chinese medical saying that cold begins in the feet.

That day at Compiegne, he had unbuttoned his own heavy overcoat and hugged her into it. She stopped shivering, resting her face on his chest with her arms wrapped around him. He bent his head to her, kissing her hair and forehead. In his eyes, she was still just as beautiful and enchanting as ever.

When he released the cornflowers, his fingers discovered that there was an unfamiliar piece of paper in his pocket beside them. He pulled it out, producing what turned out to be a tiny envelope in Marguerite's favourite shade of light green. The words on the front read, "To My Dear Delun".

His hands began to tremble. He turned away, not wanting the stall keeper to see him like that, but the other man's attention had been drawn away by a middle-aged woman in a pink suit who had also come to browse his wares.

David opened the envelope and extracted a small white card on which a shaky hand had written in black ballpoint pen: "Two-Horses, Green Garden Retirement Home". Beneath that was an address and phone number. There was no mistaking that it was Marguerite's handwriting. He could also see that she had taken a great deal of effort to write those two lines; the letters varied in size, and some she had gone over twice to deepen the colour. She must have written it in her final days. Her usual handwriting had been so beautiful, with all the grace of a ballerina on stage.

David slowly returned the card to its envelope, his eyes full of tears. Marguerite, Marguerite, he said in his heart, why would you do this? How much effort did it take you to find that address?

He stood for a moment, letting the tears subside. Then, a loud rumbling began suddenly in his ears.

He turned to face the direction of the noise, but there was nothing to be seen. He asked the stall keeper, "What was that noise just now?"

The man looked confused. "What noise do you mean, sir?"

"Just now, like thunder."

"Yeah? I didn't hear anything."

"Delun..." David thought he could hear a faltering old voice in his ear, his father speaking his Chinese name in his own native accent. He had not been back to his hometown since he was seventeen years old. Nor had he seen his parents or younger siblings ever again.

He felt a tugging at his heart, knowing that his father's voice was as much a fantasy as the phantom thunder.

His feet turned mechanically in the direction of the supermarket. He stopped at its entrance.

A backpacker in a worn-out canvas sun hat walked by. He was tall and long-limbed, looking not yet twenty with a round, sun-browned face sporting a week's worth of stubble. His backpack was a full metre tall, bulging with its contents and topped by a red sleeping bag. He was still smiling despite his heavy burden, looking straight ahead as if he could see his own glorious future.

David thought of his own journey at the age of seventeen, and a long-held impulse surged to the forefront of his mind. He had to see his old friends today. He had to!

He lingered for a while, then strode right past the supermarket. He turned right at the crossroads, joining with the flow of people to the other side of the street.

3

Fireworks shook the sky with colour and sound for a full hour, leaving the smell of gunpowder in the air.

A crowd of onlookers pushed around Wuping Town's most illustrious mansion, the Zhang family residence. Children weaved through the throng, picking excitedly among the unexploded firecrackers on the ground, checking their fuses for sparks before stuffing them into their pockets. There were also a few children playing with the red silk which had been draped over the great stone lions that stood on either side of the mansion's door, peering up through the smooth fabric. Despite having already lost most of their leaves, the black branches of the nearby apple trees still made a striking contrast against the blue sky.

The older residents were all saying that this was an auspicious date, so it was no wonder that the town's two wealthiest families – Zhang and Lu – had chosen today to wed. Gold gets gold and wood gets wood, isn't that the way it always is?

Xie Changqing, the Zhang family housekeeper, sauntered from the vermillion double-door inlaid with copper studs. The crowd of children surged to take the special wedding sweets from the basket he was holding. Changqing was usually stern and haughty, but today he was wearing brand-new clothes and a smile, even joking and patting the children's faces on his masters' happy day.

The children did not disperse after getting hold of their sweets, but waited by the door in the hope of catching sight of Miss Lu in her bridal sedan. They sang a ballad as they did so:

A yellow dog is very yellow.
Behind the yellow dog stands a blue-tiled bungalow,
Inside, a Shandong girl embroiders love:
A pair of ducks, a pair of geese,
A pair of rabbits on the hillside,
A pair of oxen grazing green grass,
A pair of children laughing aloud.

I was also waiting beside the door for that sedan, surrounded by a cluster of people congratulating me, offering their words of good luck for my marriage. I had no choice but to force a smile and bow my thanks, but my gaze drifted to those apple trees, fantasising that I could be alone among them.

I had returned home from school the previous year, and ever since then regretted yielding to my parents and submitting to the humdrum of a life spent keeping accounting records. How much rent had we taken in, how much tea or medicine had we sold? In Wuping Town, you could not get hold of blood-pumping literary publications like *New Youth*,[1] nor was there anybody to talk to about the merits of

Goethe or Dostoevsky, nor any friends at all. Everything was so old-fashioned, so outworn. It was like everybody there lived their lives under a thick layer of sand.

If it hadn't been for my father suddenly coming down with tuberculosis, his non-stop coughing all night, and my mother's constant pleading, I would never have cut short my education in Qingdao, and I certainly would never have agreed to the marriage that my father had arranged with the Lu family back when I was just fourteen years old.

I had met Miss Lu once, after I had returned from Qingdao. My father and I had been visiting the head of the Lu household. The Lu family owned a rice emporium, a general store and several country estates. When a maid raised the bamboo curtain to bring tea, I caught a glimpse of Miss Lu hiding behind it with her maidservant, trying to steal a glance at me. She and the maidservant had giggled and fled the moment that her father began to scold her for this mischievous behaviour. The townspeople all said that not only was Miss Lu elegantly beautiful, skilled in the four old arts of painting, calligraphy, chess and lute-playing, but that she was also incredibly kind and generous. But the wife I had hoped for was a woman of the new age, someone who had been through school, someone I could talk to about current affairs.

Now it was too late to say anything. The bride price had already been paid to the Lu family, all the arrangements had been made: a wedding canopy, a banquet, a lion-dance troupe and monks from Jade Buddha Temple who would chant their scriptures.

"Sir," Changqing called to me, "the bride's sedan is coming!"

He needn't have told me. I could hear the drums

approaching, banging and clattering, every thump like a hammer against my heart, making me feel as though I had to gasp for air.

The send-off party that had come to accompany the bride appeared at the end of the green cobbled paving stones, a distant streak of red developing into an impressive scarlet throng as they approached. Firecrackers rang out again, and grey smoke obscured the houses on either side of the street. The crowd poured towards the sedan.

For the next seven or eight hours I was a mere puppet, with beaming faces flashing constantly before me. My parents, my father's two concubines and my three younger siblings among them. The ordeals of the ceremony, the banquet and all the traditional *naodongfang* teasing that newlyweds are subjected to went on until it was completely dark.

Quiet finally returned to the Zhang household. Other than the sound of the servants' footsteps and low whispers as they tidied, there was only the occasional bark of a dog.

I was sitting on a stool by the side of a peachwood table at the window. A newspaper rustled in my hands as I read by the faint light of the lantern and wedding candles, but I couldn't concentrate on the words. My bride sat on the edge of the bed, still in her red veil with its dangling ornaments of pearl and gold. The bed's curtains were raised, and a silk quilt had been laid out for us behind her – embroidered with mandarin ducks and the hundred-boy *baizitu*, all symbols of happiness and prosperity.

She stood, swaying gently, then sat again with a soft sigh. I looked at her, or more precisely, at her red embroidered shoes. Her feet were about half the size of my palm, like a triangle *zongzi* rice cake that Mother would make for the Duanwu Festival.

I had imagined my wedding night countless times, imagined the caress of a woman's body – but the thought of the deformed feet within those embroidered shoes made me sick with disgust.

I had managed to prevent my parents from binding my two younger sisters' feet, but they had still tricked me into marrying a woman with bound feet regardless of my strong opposition. My mother had sworn to me just the day before that Miss Lu had natural feet. She and my father may have been genuinely fond of my bride, but they were even fonder of the Lu family property. My father had been saying all along that we were living in uncertain times, with warlords fighting all around, and so the rice business was a better guarantee than tea or medicine.

The sounds of the night watch drifted in. I said to myself that the least I could do was to untie her veil and see what she looked like. But I was unable to do even that.

I put down the newspaper, stood and said quietly, "I'm going out for a minute."

She said nothing.

I went to the doors, pulled out the wooden fastener and opened them. I truly did not know what I was going to do, but everything in that room suffocated me.

"When are you coming back?" she asked, her voice soft and sweet. That was the first time I had heard her speak. I turned around to look at her, my eyes falling again on those embroidered shoes.

"I won't be long." I closed the doors behind me.

I followed the cloisters into the atrium. The room gaped like the mouth of a behemoth, cavernous and empty. I looked back to see golden lettering still gleaming across our plaque in the dim, shadowy light.

I came to our garden, with artificial mountains and an arching stone bridge. I stood at the bridge's apex to watch the koi in their moonlit pond. The sound of my footsteps had roused them from their rest beneath the rocks. I smiled bitterly; was I not just the same as these fish, spending their whole lives in the same stagnant water?

I descended and passed through a small bamboo forest to the study.

Once I had opened the door, I spotted the bike that I had ridden back from Qingdao. When I was still a student, my classmates and I would often ride around after class, racing each other wherever there was space. I always won, thanks to my long legs. I would stand on the pedals, head lowered, the wind whooshing past my ears as I pedalled, looking for all the world like I could take off into the clouds. How happy we were!

I thought of Lin Yumei, one of the few girls in our class. She had a round face, short hair, long eyelashes and a laugh like the trickling of a forest spring. She would play basketball and shuttlecock with the boys and joined in our bicycle races. In class, I would steal glances at her profile or the shape of her calves below her skirt. She always wore white stockings, but it was still enough to send your thoughts racing. When she turned to look at me, I would quickly avert my eyes and pretend to have been listening to the teacher. She caught me once. She smiled, and I was out of my mind with it for a week.

Thanks to the planning of some of the boys, one day after one of our bike races, I finally got the chance to walk alone with her by the sea.

No, I scolded myself. I must not think like that any more. She's gone. I pulled my bicycle out from behind the door, twisted the handlebars and then checked the tyres. I had taught my little brother to ride just a few days earlier, so they were still full of air.

I was struck with the desire to ride the bicycle. I took off my wedding attire and, wearing only my silk underclothes, rode to the back door, where I lifted the heavy bolt and left. There was not a single soul on the street outside, and the moonlight cast a soft, silvery glow over the slate tiles on the ground. I shivered as a cold wind hit my face.

I rode through Dragon Bridge Road, Elegant Water Street, Jade Flower Road, then arrived at the road leading from Wuping Town to Qingdao. It was a wide road with beggars sleeping on rice-straw mats at its edge, surrounded by all their worldly possessions. One of them looked up at me, then lowered his head and went back to sleep.

The road was uneven, but not too bumpy for the bicycle. It led between harvested cornfields where wizened straw lay like rows of exhausted, sleeping soldiers. A stray dog followed me for a while, running until it had to lie down to pant. It watched me into the distance with mournful eyes.

I was using my full strength, my grip like a vice on the handlebars, my feet whirling on the pedals. My body was drenched in sweat, but I did not want to stop. When I turned around to look behind me, Wuping had already become a moonlit shadow, an image from an ink painting. Ride, ride, faster, further, I told myself, find Lin Yumei. No, she is no longer yours to dream of. She's living the high life in Shanghai. Her fingers once caressed your face, your lips. Her warm breath once made you tremble. All that is in the past.

The moon floated high, illuminating the path stretching

between smooth fields ahead. I pedalled madly, hurtling along until I reached a turn where a loose rock sent the bike flailing and me along with it. Sharp rock cut through my silk clothing, ripping holes in the sleeves and trousers. I lay there, looking up at the sky with stones digging into my back, and sobbed.

A dog began to bark in the distance, and then the ground trembled. I stopped crying and stood, looking over to a forest in the sound's direction.

A dusky black train emerged from a cloud of smoke less than a hundred metres away, the rest of its giant body winding like a dragon along the tracks behind it. I could feel the dust stirred by its movement, smell the choking fumes of its engine.

I stared with eyes wide. I just had to admire its sheer power, I felt that it could overcome everything in its path, that the coal in its firebox was heating my young body, too.

How I wanted to catch up with that dragon, follow it to cities full of crowds and noise!

I looked back and saw only the endless wilderness.

I picked up my bicycle, undamaged. I wiped the blood off my legs and arms, then put one foot on the pedal.

4

I OPENED MY EYES to find the sun already high in sky.

I didn't ride much further the previous night. A tyre had burst, forcing me to abandon the bike, so I walked until I was cold and thirsty. I happened across a collapsed hut covered in straw, and had made a den for myself with the abandoned thatch.

The thought of my parents' worried faces was a dagger in my heart, but my mind was cold and relentless, asking me: Do you want to go back there to be a pharmacy manager, spending all your days by an abacus? Would you really be happy spending the rest of your life with a woman with bound feet?

I told myself that my answers were obvious, I would go back in two or three weeks, and perhaps my parents would be so worried I'd leave again that they would persuade the Lu family to annul the marriage. Maybe they would even let me continue my studies.

I returned to the main road in the direction of Qingdao. I

had an acquaintance there who owned a pharmacy and would surely be willing to find me a place to lay low.

I arrived at the city gates around noon.

There is a large market near the gates, bustling with dozens of stores. You can buy noodles, fruit and vegetables, odds and ends, general goods, have your fortune read, anything you can think of. I hadn't a penny in my pocket, but the smell of food cooking still drew me in.

"Meat pancakes! Crispy and fragrant!" I followed the pedlar's sonorous voice to a stall where pancakes spluttered with oil atop a charcoal stove, the scent of them overwhelming my senses. The shopkeeper called to me warmly, an apron wrapped around his waist. When he saw my appearance his expression fell, and he waved me away while mumbling, "Just my luck, another opium junkie!"

I realised then that I could not go to see Mr Wu looking the way I did. There was a pawn shop not far away, and I had a Swiss watch in my pocket that my father had bought for me in Shanghai. I went into the shop and emerged again with ten silver dollars packed into my pocket. Afterwards I bought a shirt, a cheap brown suit and a pair of leather shoes. The clothes were a little tight, but would do. From the clothes store, I went to a restaurant and ordered a couple of pancakes along with a few side dishes.

After I had finished eating, an explosion of drums and gongs came from outside.

I followed the sound out of the restaurant, arriving at an open space near the market. It was filled with people, a mass of bobbing heads. I pushed my way into the crowd and squeezed to the front. Once there, I saw five red-belted men putting on a performance. Two banged drums while another struck a gong, one danced and the last spoke *kuaibanshu* in quick, rhythmic tones in the intervals between the drumbeats, rattling bamboo clappers in his hand.

> *Brothers gather round, come hear what we've found.*
> *Three years abroad, a huge reward.*
> *France invites you to her land, Europe needs a helping hand.*
> *But what of those you love, and familiar skies above?*
> *The years flash by, but let me tell you why.*

He rattled the kuaiban clappers in his hand, then continued.

> *This calamity begins with assassins, who came to put down the Austrian crown.*
> *Seeing opportunity and acting with impunity,*
> *The German troops' mobility surrounded France on land and sea!*

A burst of drums and gongs rang out before he started to speak again.

> *Good nations of Europe, they joined in the fight,*
> *America came too, brought all of her might.*
> *But the war's ferocity has caused a great calamity,*
> *Soldiers cannot plant the seeds, the fields lie empty full of weeds,*
> *It's plain for all of us to see they need our help to keep them free.*

Pap-pap-pap, the kuaiban reached a crescendo to the crowd's applause.

Our nation is their friend, shall ministers we send?
Do not be ridiculous, their uselessness is hideous.
To show our friends our decency we men must act with urgency,
Unite ourselves for them to see and work the land with dignity.
Brothers crowd around let's go, let China's reputation grow,
Then the world will come to see, our strength and grace in years just three!

At that moment, the gongs and drums rang an animal cacophony, the dancer nimbly stripped off his jacket, summersaulting shirtless over the ground. He used his foot to kick up a set of wooden sticks, which he juggled and chopped, sweeping and stabbing in an endless storm of fluctuating motion.

The audience cheered and applauded. Someone by my side said, "Wow! I wonder what martial arts school he's from."

"Yeah, he's a decent performer," someone from behind added coolly, "but that's not going to stop a Western bullet."

I turned to listen to the conversation. It was between three men, around the same age as me and likely students from the look of their clothing.

One of them was small and lean, wearing gold-framed spectacles on a face soaked with sweat. Clearly a little taken with the excitement he said, "Let's all... let's all sign up to go to Europe!"

"They're at war!" exclaimed one of his companions.

"But the poster says we wouldn't be sent to the front, just the rear."

"Isn't China neutral in this, though? If we allied with the Anglo-French side, wouldn't that just be like declaring war on Germany?"

The man in the gold-framed spectacles removed them, then wiped the sweat off his forehead with the back of his hand before replacing them on his nose. "I've had terribly long debates regarding this issue with Mr Wang. He believes that China should stand idly by, whereas I myself believe that we should support Britain and France in declaring war on Germany and Austria. As victors, we would be able to abolish the twenty-one demands imposed on China by Japan, thus enhancing our international standing."

"And how do you know," asked the one who had praised the martial artist's skill, "that Britain and France will win?"

"They are both formidable naval powers! Germany and Austria will not be able to beat them. Haven't you been paying attention? These recruitment and translation agencies are civilian rather than military, the Chinese government has been smart about that. See, the whole recruitment is a civil activity, nothing to do with the government. Germany can try to start trouble, but our government can just say that they have no part in this. From Britain and France's point of view, this is like China sending coal in a snowstorm – doing the thing most needed at the most difficult time. They are both suffering heavy losses at the front, and so by hiring foreign labour at the rear they can spare their own soldiers from having to build military bases and doing logistical work, which means more of them for the front lines. That is to say, frankly speaking, Duan Qirui's government has declared war without declaring war at all."

The one who had said that martial arts were no match for bullets raised his voice. "Looks like all that reading of yours has paid off. I agree. Also, won't this give us the chance to see Notre-Dame or the River Thames? Life is short, and a man should see the world. We're being given an opportunity to see all the continents' scenery for free – we'll actually be paid! Besides, we're all studying to change the Chinese attitude towards women's education. Neither of our sisters has had the opportunity to study here, but over there, women could attend colleges as early as the seventeenth century. When we arrive in Europe, we'll be able to study those advanced ideas and technologies, then bring them back to China."

The one who had praised the artist nodded his head repeatedly. "Let's go tomorrow!"

The man in the spectacles leapt up and waved his hands. "Notre-Dame, here we come!"

This said, they looked ready to leave, so I called out to them. "Friends, all this about Britain and France hiring labourers over here – what's going on?"

The spectacled man explained for a while, then pointed in the direction of the city wall. "There are job advertisements all over there."

His companions urged him along, saying that class was starting any minute.

I found the wall with its posters, black ink on white paper saying that British and French representatives were in Qingdao and Weihaiwei hiring labourers and translators to go to Europe with full board for three years, and the recruits would have the opportunity to terminate their contracts after just one. They would not participate in the construction of military engineering facilities, and would only work at the rear in locations at least sixteen kilometres from the front line. The income for labourers was a franc a day, which would be paid monthly.

I'll come back after a year, I said to myself, and by then the marriage will naturally be annulled. I'll start a new life according to my own ideas.

I smiled. Everything around me seemed so beautiful at that moment. The atmosphere was bustling and lively, vibrant with pedestrians, vendors, performers, rickshaws and cars. In the distance, a flock of gulls swept across the grey-blue waters. Cargo ships sailed over the waves among them, packed full of containers. They glided along as if the whole world belonged to them.

5

David pondered his heart's troubles as he walked, stopping to rest briefly when the pain in his leg was too much. It was only on arriving at the train station, sweat beading on his brow, that he realised he could have travelled there by bus or subway.

A train ran twice daily to Noyelles-sur-Mer, and he had arrived in time to catch the ten o'clock service. He found a phone booth, hesitated, then picked up the receiver. He inserted the coins he had counted out and dialled his home number. Halfway through, he pressed the cancel button and redialled a different number, delighted that he could still recall it by heart.

Mr Wang picked up the phone, his leisurely personality audible in the relaxed tones of his voice. David breathed a sigh of relief. If Mrs Wang had been the one to answer, then she would have bombarded him with questions.

David boarded the train twenty minutes later and found himself a seat by the window. The rows around him were empty. This suited him; he could immerse himself in his own world.

The city faded away to be replaced by quiet rural scenery. The sun pierced the clouds, shining over yellow-green meadows interspersed with woods and colourful farmhouses.

The train arrived at noon in Noyelles-sur-Mer, a small station with a solitary brick building that resembled a cottage. The village had a population of about eight hundred. At its centre was a triangular flowerbed surrounded by grey bricks. On one side was a darker-grey stone carved with the village's name, on the other a collection of road signs varying in size and colour.

His destination sat on the village periphery, twenty minutes by foot if he walked quickly.

He walked between the plastered walls of red-roofed farmhouses, admiring the plants, flowers and ornaments in the front gardens. Nearby, black-and-white dairy cows grazed in thicket-lined meadows.

It had been years since he had last visited.

After several stops to rest, he finally reached the cemetery. He bowed deeply before the traditional Chinese-style arch, then pushed open its ornate, wrought-iron gates, so carefully that one might think he was afraid to startle the souls inside.

What a sombre world. More than eight hundred white stone tablets arranged in neat rows, flowers or plants in front of each. When Old Henry – a thin man with a goatee who lived in the nearby village – was still alive, he had come every week to tend to the cemetery. Nobody paid him, he just did so of his own accord. Each time David and Marguerite had visited, they also stopped by Henry's house to chat for a while. Whenever Henry saw them, he would talk about his memory of fighting in the Battles of Somme and Verdun, all the while combing his beard with a slow motion of his fingers.

After Old Henry had died ten years earlier, several villagers had taken responsibility for looking after the cemetery on his behalf.

David walked between the gravestones, stooping from time to time to wipe dirt off the tablets. Some of their words had already been eroded by wind and rain, but most were still clearly visible. Each bore the name of the deceased in Chinese vertical script at the centre, his place of birth to the right and a eulogy carved in Chinese and English at the top.

A noble thing, bravely done
Though dead, he still liveth

The bottom part of each stone read: "Chinese Labour Corps", followed by the deceased's ID number.

"70710, 48979, 56543..." David whispered the numbers. He saw the flesh and blood behind each cold, impersonal Arabic numeral. He had dug trenches and carried shells with these men. They were his brothers. He had worked, chatted, played and laughed with them.

"58909", David muttered his own number. He had been addressed by it countless times in his dreams.

He dug the two cornflower brooches from his pocket and kissed one before setting both in front of a tombstone. He felt that Marguerite would be pleased to have travelled here with him again.

Tired and closing his eyes, he rested against the low wall at the rear of the cemetery. He exhaled a satisfied breath, as if he had returned to a home long missed.

6

A**NNE GAZED BLANKLY** at the dishes on the table. The meat had become flaky and dry after long exposure to the air. The dumpling wrappers she made had hardened, too.

Her father had still not returned. It had been so long that she had already gone to look for him at the supermarket, but none of the employees had seen him. She had even tried all the small shops along the road, asking after him, worried that he might have been hurt in traffic. The owners had all shaken their heads: no, they had not seen such a person; no, they didn't know of any accident. A street pedlar said that a man fitting her description had bought two brooches, then headed across the street; he seemed in a hurry, as if he had to be somewhere urgently.

Could Baba have fainted in a corner somewhere? Or perhaps he had run into an acquaintance, chatted with them until he lost track of time?

She regretted not having gone with him earlier.

The doorbell rang. She took a few steps to the door, but her heart sank when she heard children laughing outside. It wasn't Baba. Her two children, Noah and Sophie, came rushing in followed by her husband Pierre. Pierre was carrying a large cake box, Noah a bouquet.

After hugging and kissing them all hello, she told them that David had not come home since he left for the shops that morning. Pierre suggested that they go out to look for him together.

At that moment, the telephone rang: Mr Wang was on the line. Anne knew him well. Since she had been a child, her father and Mr Wang had been best friends, often chatting and taking walks together.

Mr Wang said that David had just called, saying he would be back around five o'clock that afternoon. Anne asked him if he knew where David was, but he did not.

Is Baba playing a prank? Anne felt hurt and worried at the same time.

"Did it seem like something was wrong with Ba when you spoke to him?"

"No, not at all. He sounded fine."

"Why didn't he call home?"

Mr Wang said that he did not know, then added, "David also said that if he wasn't back by five, just go ahead and eat. He said there was no need to worry."

After the call, she and Pierre decided to stay home and wait for David. She went back to the supermarket to buy hot sauce and fruit before teaching the kids how to make dumplings, trying her best to relax while fervently hoping that her father would come home before five.

Five o'clock arrived, as did all the guests. The meal she had arranged from the restaurant was delivered too, but still no trace of David. Anne and Pierre fussed anxiously around their guests, encouraging everyone to eat and saying that David would be back at any moment. Half an hour passed by, then an hour, but David had still not returned.

Anne told everybody to go home, promising to let them know as soon as she heard from David. The guests all comforted her, saying that he would be fine. The Wangs said he would definitely be back soon, he had probably just gone somewhere to forget his cares.

After seeing out her guests, Anne called the police's missing persons hotline. She was so distraught after answering the operator's questions that she slumped on the sofa, face in her hands. Pierre held her, saying that maybe David had gone to see friends, was enjoying himself too much in their company to remember the time.

Noah and Sophie's voices clamoured from David's bedroom.

"I found it!"

"Give it!"

"No!"

Sophie chased Noah out of the room. He was holding something that looked like a bracelet in his hand. They ran from the living room to the kitchen then back to the living room again, where Noah dived onto the sofa to use his mother as a shield.

"Stop fighting, let me see," Anne said.

Seeing Sophie grab at his arm, Noah handed the object to his mother. Pierre also peered over to look. It was an open-clasped copper bracelet. It seemed old and roughly made, bearing only engraved numbers. The copper around the numbers was much brighter than the rest of the metal.

"58909," Anne mused to herself. She asked her children where they had found it.

Sophie said it had been in a wooden box by her grandfather's bedside.

"There's red velvet in it!" added Noah.

Anne was familiar with that box having seen it often as a child. Her father doted on her but had forbidden her to touch it. In her curiosity she had tried to open it several times, but she could never find the key. When she asked her mother, she just smiled, saying she did not know where the key was either. Anne had forgotten all about the box's existence since she had grown up. If not for the children bringing her the bracelet now, she would not have remembered it at all.

"Where did you find the key to open the box?" she asked them.

"I didn't see a key," Sophie replied. "It was unlocked."

"Looks like it's from China," said Pierre. He took the bracelet in his hand and inspected it carefully.

"I've never seen either of my parents wear this," Anne said. "It seems Ba touches it a lot. Look how shiny the area around the numbers is. What could they mean?"

"Maybe it's from an antiques market," suggested Pierre. "Didn't he and your mother really like going to them?"

"Maybe. But why would he treasure it so much to keep it in that box?" She went on to tell Pierre about her memory of the box when she was a child. "Baba must have opened the box recently and forgotten to lock it afterwards."

Restless and needing to act, she and Pierre went into David's bedroom to seek clues as to his whereabouts.

The bedroom was very simply furnished: a double bed, a desk, a chair and a row of bookshelves. On the walls, Chinese landscape paintings hung alongside Western art and Marguerite's own paintings. There were framed photos of family and friends and also of David and his colleagues at the La Grange machinery factory. After Maman had died, Baba did not move anything in the room for a whole year. Then one day he got up early to sort everything, donating or selling the furniture, leaving only Ma's wardrobe untouched. The apartment seemed empty afterwards.

Anne sat on the bed studying that Chinese lacquered box. It was the size of a shoebox, its patterned lid faded with age. She opened it. Inside there lay a leaf-shaped brooch decorated with a small pearl and neatly folded paper that looked like yellowing old letters. She recognised the brooch as her mother's favourite piece of jewellery.

She opened the paper carefully. It was filled with extravagantly flowing Chinese calligraphy that she could not understand. She sighed. She would have to wait for her father's return to know what it said, if he were not upset that she had seen it at all.

The thought dawned on her that she knew very little about her father's past. The thought hurt her. All she knew was that he was originally from Shandong Province in China, that he came to work at a French factory when he was seventeen and then decided to stay after meeting her mother.

She jumped to her own defence: I've always been too busy to ask! I was a diligent student, then I had work and the kids.

But another voice spoke at the same time: Is it really because you didn't have time? Or did you just not want to know – not then, not even now?

"You must be an alien!" The memory of Gaston's voice came to her from nowhere. He was her classmate at primary school, a big boy with a mean face. He always laughed at how she looked, saying that she was slant-eyed, her face flat as a pancake.

"My eyes *do not* slant, and I *do not* have a pancake face," she yelled back, beside herself with rage.

"Your dad's a slant-eyed freak, so of course you're a little slant-eyed freak too," he said. The whole class burst into laughter.

She rushed at him and kicked his stomach, tangling into a fight. He made her nose bleed and gave her a few bruises – but she got him back knocking out one of his front teeth.

When she cried at home later, Maman crouched down and took her hand. "Don't cry. Hold your head high. Be proud of who you are."

She remembered those words whenever Gaston or the other kids laughed at her. Yet she often found herself staring blankly at her reflection in the mirror, wishing for some fairy godmother to change it.

"My love, what are you thinking?" Pierre asked.

"Oh, nothing. I'm just worried about Baba. I have no idea where he is."

Anne waited all night long, but David never returned.

7

THE LABOUR CORPS REGISTRATION OFFICE was crowded. The middle-aged man behind the desk, wearing traditional black robes and glasses, was an employee of the Huimin Company whom everybody called Mr Liu. He was soaked with sweat but too busy to even wipe his forehead. "Next," he called, his voice hoarse.

Someone told me excitedly that three hundred people had signed up just the day before. Today, he predicted, there would be at least another five hundred. He had heard that there was one village in which every man was planning to enlist.

That didn't surprise me. Many parts of Shandong had been experiencing a drought since the previous year, the crops had been suffering.

It was an unusually warm, breezeless day. The air felt sticky, as if sweat was fermenting within it. Dozens of seagulls circled low, searching for scraps of food on the ground and letting out long, melancholic cries. Their screams mingled with the voices of the crowd, infecting everyone with a sense of unease.

I was disgusted with it all. Most of the people closing in around me were poorly dressed and giving off foul odours, a few of them wearing long braids. They made a boisterous racket, just like a flock of ducks. How could I be mixed up with these people?

A man with messy hair and a filthy neck squeezed in front of me, opening his mouth to reveal a yellow-toothed smile. I held my breath and stepped back.

Finally, it was my turn.

Mr Liu's expression softened as he looked me up and down. "Can you speak English or French?" he asked. "That way you can be a translator."

I gave him my honest answer. "I can speak a little English, but not well. French not at all."

Disappointed, he leaned back and said, "Then don't go. I can see from one look at you that you're the son of a wealthy family, that you've enjoyed a comfortable life. The war in Europe is serious, the labour hard and dangerous, the place unfamiliar. If you become sick, you could die there." He lowered his voice as he continued. "A lot of the people who are there now regret it, and they can't come back."

"I can do it. I'm capable."

He pointed to the crowd. "Have you seen this lot? Most of them are illiterate. They are dock workers, rickshaw pullers, farmers, soldiers. You're not one of them. You won't last."

I assured him that I could handle hard labour.

He shook his head, as if laughing to himself about my naivety. He took a form and wrote my name, age and place of birth, telling me to take the form with me for a medical examination. The examiner's office was in a makeshift canvas tent around a hundred metres from the registration office. There were three or four hundred people already there, split into different groups and lines. Mr Lu, a Chinese man wearing a Western suit and hat, put me into the line near the entrance. It was strangely quiet despite the crowd, probably because people were curious about what the medical exam would involve, or perhaps because they were behaving themselves since it was the first time they had been required to stand in a queue. Even those who were chatting were doing so quietly.

After a while, Mr Lu led our group out of the tent and into a room next door that had been arranged like an office with a mahogany desk at its centre. The friendly-looking medical examiner was wearing a British military uniform under a white coat, with a stethoscope around his neck. Mr Lu told everyone to strip for the examination.

My face reddened at the instruction. I had heard about boys and girls swimming naked in my Western literature classes. I had also heard Mr Yu explain the art of nude sculpture in ancient Greece and Rome when he had returned from overseas. According to him, nudity was not shameful, it embodied naturalism and human beauty. Still, for as long as I could remember I had never been naked in front of anyone.

Everyone else had already stripped and was starting to joke around.

"Look 'ere, we'd be better off in a whorehouse!" called out a broad-shouldered man with a scar on his forehead. A mountain range of muscles bulged across his arms.

The line stirred up a burst of laughter.

"We can sleep with whoever we like when we get back with all that money. Twelve dollars a month!" replied a long-braided fellow.

A middle-aged man with a square face spoke next. "I grow crops, ne'er been to a doctor in my life. Why they so special? Gonna keep an eye on 'im."

The young man with the scar replied, "He ain't gonna do shit. They just wanna see if we've the muscles for carryin' their cannons."

"You haven't even got hair on you yet. It'd be enough for you to carry off some woman, never mind a cannon!"

The scarred young man did not respond but instead walked up to the mahogany table and, bending at the waist, lifted it off the ground. It must have weighed more than two hundred kilograms.

There was a round of cheering, even the doctor smiled and nodded.

I undressed myself, thinking of the Louvre and the Seine, recalling a tune from Bizet's *Carmen* that I had heard on the family gramophone. France, here I come!

Half an hour later, the first medical examination was complete. Only six out of the twenty people present had passed. The others were either too short, suffering from tuberculosis or bronchitis, or had breathing problems or rotten teeth. The man with the square face had not been admitted because of trachoma in his eyes. He became indignant at the diagnosis at first, protesting that his eyes were fine. But then he began to sob, saying that the fields had been consumed by locusts, there was nothing to eat back home.

I was one of the lucky ones.

Mr Lu took those of us who had passed the exam to a clearing behind the examination room. There, a group of naked Chinese were standing by a dozen large wooden basins filled with water, washing themselves with towels.

They were in high spirits, talking and laughing. One sang a rhyme that he improvised as he went.

"To Europe we go, where silver coins will flow, eating meat and wine, we'll be living so fine..."

These men were my height or taller, but were more robust and tanned suggesting a life spent outdoors.

Pointing to a barber standing to the rear of the wooden basins, Mr Lu addressed the man who had the long braids and said, "Go get your hair cut!"

The man looked surprised and said, "You jus' wanna chop off a life's worth of growth?" Then, seeing the look of impatience on Mr Lu's face, he added, "Hair's a gift from your parents, it's unfilial to cut it!"

"Either keep your hair and stay in China," Mr Lu retorted, "or cut your hair and go to France. There are plenty out there who'll take your place!"

The long-haired man seemed dumbfounded, but he lowered his head in obedience.

There and then, I felt that was it. Whatever was going to happen to me would happen. I was no longer the young master of Wuping's rich and powerful Zhang family, but a man who relied on his own physical labour for his meals. All the pain and suffering of the labouring class were now mine to share. Strangely, I felt proud. I had cast off the bonds of marriage, the expectations of my parents. I was free. "Laughing aloud at the skies, I walk out of my house; a man like me is destined for greatness." The line from a poem that had inspired me so much in my high school years was ringing in my ears once more.

At seventeen I felt my body's strength was still growing, as if my muscles were leaves and branches that would erupt through my skin.

After we bathed there was another examination, then those of us who had been selected went to press our fingerprints onto our contracts. Each digit individually, followed by all five together. We were given clean clothes and a copper bracelet with a number on the side, which we were told would serve as our identification. We would use it to collect wages, food, clothing and work assignments.

The moment they gave me that bracelet, I almost tossed it to the ground. I had a name. My name was Zhang Delun! The first syllable, "de", means morality and kindness. The second, "lun", means human relations and order. When I was born, my father had made generous donations to the temple and asked the town's literati to come up with that name. He wished that I would grow up to be virtuous, with deep-seated ethics regarding others. I was not some number.

I suppressed my anger, swallowed my pride. I recalled a teacher once telling us that weak countries have no power in matters of diplomacy.

My compatriots were unconcerned, weighing their own bracelets in their hands and guessing how much they could sell them for. A few had never been given decent names by their parents, and some might even have been named after their family's livestock.

The bracelet was heavy and cold on my wrist, reminding me somehow of the two stone lions flanking the entrance to my family home. When I was little, I climbed on their backs and pretended to be the great Song Dynasty general Yue Fei riding into battle. The servants would all watch me anxiously, worried that I might fall.

Now I really was like Yue Fei, travelling thousands of miles to war. But he had fought for his own country, whereas I was going to do hard labour on behalf of somebody else.

The thought of those stone lions made me anxious. I twisted my neck as if it had been caught in rope. No, I couldn't go back now.

A British private stood nearby, smoking silently. He seemed wilted, demoralised beneath the sun. Even the gun on his back seemed to be asleep. When he saw me looking at him, he sprang to life. He gave me a vicious stare, raised his eyebrows and opened his mouth as if to laugh – but instead spat out a wad of mucus.

I turned away. From then on, as far as the British or French were concerned, I was no longer Zhang Delun. I was 58909.

For the next three weeks, life rotated around me like the image of a galloping horse cast by a shadow lamp. The other labourers and I had drills every day at the temporary British base. We practised marching, climbing and crawling in sections made of fifteen men. We were just like soldiers, except without the weapons. Dozens of us boarded together in the barracks at night. I had never been so exhausted in all my life, sleeping the instant my body hit the mat. Though life was monotonous, it was exactly what I needed. I could temporarily forget my troubles.

Labourers ran away every day, but our numbers remained the same. There was always a steady flow of people to take their places. After all, you had bread at every meal, sometimes even meat or fish. On the first day, I ate a bowl of noodles and a bread bun for each meal, but a few days later I still didn't feel full after three bowls.

One Friday morning after drills, our leader declared that we would be leaving for Weihaiwei the next day. From there, we would set sail to France.

8

THE *MANCHESTER* was a modified German transport ship with two levels of windowed cabins. Almost two thousand of us boarded amid the yelling of armed British soldiers. I was in uniform, as were most of the other labourers, but some recruits from Tianjin were still wearing their own clothes.

The deck filled quickly. *"Wang xia zou!"* an Englishman with a beard and a beer belly called to us in shoddy Mandarin. "Go down! Room down there!"

"That's storage space," said a few labourers in unison. Then someone added jokingly, "You want us to flatten ourselves?"

"You lot, you won't leave China for another week – no, make it a month!" Pointing at the bearded man, he continued, "You don't get paid until you get to France."

The labourers standing at the entrance to the storage room exchanged glances, and then they followed the ladder down below.

I was lucky enough to find myself a place on deck, near the right rail. The ship's whistle sounded. The gongs and firecrackers of the lion-dance ceremony rang out, and the *Manchester* set sail. Men on deck rushed desperately to wave to their loved ones on the docks, watching the wharf fade as if they could hold onto it with just a look.

Nobody had come to send me off.

The sky was dusky and overcast. Mist hung low over the waves. I felt cold droplets on my face even though it wasn't raining. I turned towards the southwest, in the direction of Wuping. I begged my parents' forgiveness in my heart.

A lad by my side nudged me with his elbow. "Don't be sad, I didn't have anybody say bye to me either."

When I turned to face him, I recognised him as the same young man who had lifted the mahogany desk in the medical examination room. I had not seen him for two weeks. He seemed taller, and his short hair had been shaved off to reveal a shiny bald pate.

He noticed me looking at his head and smiled bashfully. "I'm just too lazy for hair! I don't wanna wash it, so this way I won't get lice."

"What's your name?" I asked him.

"Well, I've never had a mum or dad but I got the nickname 'Two-Horses' when I was pulling rickshaws. 'Cause I'm as fast as two horses, right. So everyone just calls me Two-Horses."

"And why do you want to go to Europe?"

"Well, I'm pullin' the rickshaw one time and there's one of them foreign devils what speaks Chinese. He was really nice, and he 'ad this book with all these pictures in it. So, I decides to be brave and asks him what the pictures was of. He puts it in front of my face and it's this beautiful house with a fancy car. I asks him where it was, and he says it's France. Then he asks me what I wanna do with my life, and nobody's ever said that to me before, so I says, well, I like cars. They're faster than this rickshaw, and they've got a horn and everythin'. He said if I went to France, then I could be a driver. I've been thinkin' on that picture ever since. I can't read, but one day I pulled the rickshaw to the city gate and saw those notices. Someone told me France was recruitin' labour, so I signs up." He laughed. "I saw you in the medical exam. You," he said, pointing to the other people standing around, "aren't like the rest of 'em."

"It doesn't matter what we were like before, we're the same now." Speaking to him was making me feel better.

"Why you goin', then?" he asked.

"Just like you, I want to see the world."

"Yeah, good. In Europe you should take me when you go places, I've got no other skills really, but I can be your bodyguard. I'm not showing off, I've studied kung-fu. One time when I was pullin' the rickshaw, a bunch of scumbags tried to rob me, I had 'em pissin' their pants in no time." He struck a martial pose and opened his eyes wide, making me laugh. "See this scar on my head? I got it then. I can also talk to birds. I used to go sing in the forest and listen to 'em when I weren't pullin' the cart. Listen to this if you don't believe me." He puckered his lips and let out a string of crisp, clear birdsong that sounded so much like an oriole that people looked to the sky.

"How old are you?" I asked.

"About sixteen or seventeen. Said eighteen when I signs up. I'm big, people believes I'm twenny-eight even."

I laughed. "No they don't, you don't look twenty-eight."

"I can sing opera too!" Saying that, he used that low voice to sing a passage from the Peking Opera, *Wu Song Fights the Tiger*:

Ah! Flash, flash, it leaps to the sky,
Just like that, in the twinkling of an eye.
A man-eating beast,
And it's mine to defeat.
Show me your power,
And I'll show you who's strong.
Tiger, tiger, meet Wu Song!

He struck a heroic pose at the last line. I applauded, feeling in a much better mood.

The sky darkened not long after we set out to sea, looking like it might erupt with rain and thunder at any moment.

Lieutenant Colonel Wilson stood on a wooden crate to address us. He was the Brit in charge of transporting the labourers and had been responsible for our group of more than three hundred men back in the camp. He had been in China for a few years and spoke pretty respectable Chinese. Whenever we encountered him in camp, we had to salute. If you failed to do so fast enough, he would forbid you from eating supper or make you stand to attention for however long he fancied. As he stared at you, the corners of his mouth would twitch to the side, as if he was wondering what to do with you. We heard that he was dissatisfied with his position. He had been sent straight to China to manage labourers after graduating from the military academy, instead of playing a heroic role on the battlefields of Europe. He never smiled and always walked bolt upright, so everyone called him Woody behind his back.

"You coolies have already begun a great journey," he began, smiling unexpectedly. "Over the next few years, your hard days in China will become only memories, and the sun of Western civilisation will shine upon you..."

As he said these words, someone behind me loudly began to recite Du Fu's ancient poem, *Spring View*: "The mountains and streams of a broken nation still stand, / Springtime cities in bloom across the land." A few labourers joined in, their different accents blending to form a beautiful theatrical effect. I joined in, too. "Tears splash on the petal of a flower / Birds mourn farewell and hearts all cower."

That changed the mood on deck, and the neat lines fell into disorder. Some sat, scratching their itches, while others rushed to the railings to watch the scenery.

Woody's face turned livid and, with his hand on the pistol at his waist he shouted, "Who started it?"

"I did," said a man of about forty years old, his voice loud yet calm. As he emerged from the crowd, I saw that he was a handsome chap with narrow eyes and a strong jaw who hadn't been far ahead of me when we were boarding. I had noticed him then not only for his tidy clothing and woollen hat, but for his firm, resolute steps and his eyes looking straight ahead. Now, I recognised him as the man who had danced the martial arts performance the day I signed up.

"Boss Cai, a wise man does not fight against impossible odds," shouted the man beside me, his hands cupped to amplify his voice. Seven or eight people stood fast behind Boss Cai, staring angrily at Woody. More joined them.

The bearded man stomped breathlessly from the control cabin. Before reaching Woody, he waved his hands at the crowd, smiling and saying, "*Meishi, meishi*, it's OK, it's OK. Everybody relax."

Woody's hand remained on his pistol as he stared at Boss Cai, his posture betraying the desire to shoot.

The bearded man stood between Boss Cai and Woody, saying to the latter, "Colonel Wilson, why the bother?" He began to mutter in English, his smile becoming a shake of the head. He sighed, pointed to Boss Cai, then shrugged and spread his hands.

My English was mediocre, but I could catch fragments of what he was saying. What he meant to say was that the lieutenant should not waste his time fighting with these ignorant Chinese coolies, a bunch of kids who don't understand the rules. He was arguing that they needed to focus on the task at hand. Their only responsibility was to take the Chinese to France and collect their payment.

Woody let his hand fall from his pistol, and he abruptly left the deck. The two soldiers behind him took deep breaths, then indicated that we were free to move around.

"Boss Cai, you've gort some guts," said a man standing beside him, in the 'r' accentuating tones of a Beijing accent.

Boss Cai smiled, but he did not respond. He walked over to the rail and looked out to sea.

I asked the man with the Beijing accent how he knew Boss Cai. He said that Cai was the leader of their troop in the training camp.

"He's a fair man. Everyone likes him except the foreign devils. They warnted to get rid of him," he said, lowering his voice, "but they were worried the Chinese would protest. He's not a big talker, only says a word if he hars to."

"I 'eard 'e ran a martial arts school in Tianjin," added somebody else.

"Don't tarlk crap," replied the man with the Beijing accent. "He was a university professor in Beijing! He went orff somewhere but came back after his wife died. He couldn't teach any more and was out of money, so started painting arnd writing calligraphy. His calligraphy, so beautiful! Loads of people gort him to write their letters home when we were in camp."

"You don't know shit! He's rich. How can you make that money by painting and writing?" someone else chimed in.

The Beijinger retorted, "If he's so rich then why's he going to Europe?"

"Who knows! Aren't you from the same place? Why don't you ask him?"

"I did, he didn't answer."

Someone joined in again, "He has to 'ave been rich, otherwise why would everyone call him 'Boss'?"

The Beijinger smiled. "People call him boss becaurse of the way he acts, idiot! Look at how he walks. No matter how hard we tried, we couldn't copy him!"

I looked curiously over at the figure of Boss Cai. At that moment, Two-Horses squeezed over to me and happily tugged my hand, wanting me to come over to see a pod of dolphins that were following the ship.

What a sight! I had been out at sea a few times with my classmates, but I had never seen dolphins chasing the waves like that. They competed and jumped together, calling to each other, their grey backs roving up and down like layers of tumbling mountains as they leapt.

For a few moments, surrounded by smiling faces and with all those different accents mixing together, it felt like we were a group of holidaymakers.

9

"Look, the butterfly couple came back to say hello," Marguerite whispered in his ear, one hand gently stroking his sun-warmed hair. She was particularly fond of his thick, dense hair, sometimes affectionately calling him "*mon petit lion*".

They lay together on a hillside. The grass popped with white daisies and the tall trunks of grey-barked elms cast shadows here and there. He turned to kiss her cheek. The breeze blew a whirling current through the shadows, making him feel like he too was about to take off. Close by, three stone farmhouses slouched against the hill.

They were less than a mile away from the factory, a habitual after-work meeting spot that they would walk to separately so as not to attract the locals' attention. He was always the first to arrive, bolting up the hillside like a sprinter. Then he would wait, watching the path in expectation. When he saw her approach, he would hide behind some rocks or trees and leap out at her, giving her a fright.

He kissed her before turning his contented gaze to the

two butterflies looping and diving in the air above them. It was surely the same pair that had visited them ten minutes earlier. They were beautiful, with nimble black bodies between azure wings with a white-splattered black border.

He told her the Chinese legend of the lovers Liang Shanbo and Zhu Yingtai, who were reincarnated together as a pair of butterflies.

Sighing softly, Marguerite said, "Let's become butterflies after we die, too. So we can be together forever."

Suddenly, as if struck from the sky, the butterflies dropped towards the ground. He jumped to catch them and they floated lightly into his palm – then passed straight through, becoming grains of white dust that the wind scattered away. He turned, and Marguerite was gone. The world fogged around him.

"Marguerite! Marguerite!" David cried out, extending his hand to her but finding only cold rock. He opened his eyes, realising that he had been dreaming. He rubbed his eyelids, and the scenery before them became clear again: white tombstones, the clipped grass in front of them.

He felt relieved, knowing that he was still in the cemetery on the outskirts of Noyelles-sur-Mer. He used his cuff to wipe away the cold sweat on his brow. He shivered despite the afternoon sun slanting across his body. He struggled to stand but was unable to move, as if all his joints had rusted over. His head, his back, his arms, his legs, everything ached.

He wrapped himself tightly in his coat, as if it could give him strength, and began to feel better.

He looked at his watch, already half-past four. He had missed the last train back to Paris and would not make it home in time for his birthday party.

What was he going to do? He began to panic, what was

he going to say to his daughter and son-in-law? And the guests? Should he call Anne and let her know where he was? If he did that, she would want to know why he had come here in the first place.

All these thoughts surged through his mind like the tide, then receded in just the same way. The rows of tombstones seemed to gaze back at him with earnest, sorrowful expressions, as if to say, "Brother, where have you been all these years? We've missed you. Do you still recall those days when we were all together?"

No, he told himself, he could not go home. He had to continue this journey. Not just for himself, but for his dead brothers in the labour corps, and for Marguerite. He fished the nursing home's address out from his coat pocket and inspected it. Two-Horses was still living there, he had called them at the train station to make sure.

The journey to Noyelles-sur-Mer had begun on a whim, but now he knew that it was only the beginning.

He remembered what Marguerite had said to him in her hospital bed. "This is part of your life, you can't blot it out." The cancer had already reached her liver. Constant coughing had made her throat raw, her voice hoarse. Her swollen abdomen was hard as stone; if he touched it accidentally, she would shudder with pain. The doctors said that she had a month left.

Her hand was frail, cold. He had taken it and pressed it to his cheek.

"Promise me," she said, and she squeezed out a little laugh.

Fighting back tears, he nodded.

The tombstones interrupted his reverie. "Your brothers will cheer you up!"

David struggled upright, flexing his hands and feet to replenish some strength. He touched the liver spots on his hands, the blue veins bulging beneath his translucent skin, and smiled in self-deprecation. Perhaps this would be the last time he could ever travel alone. Perhaps in a few years he might need a wheelchair. Perhaps he would not even be able to remember his own name.

I'm sorry, Anne, he thought. I'm very sorry.

His feelings were overtaken by an incredible sense of urgency to travel onwards. He forced himself to calm down and think, reckoning that two weeks should be enough. He would sleep here tonight. If his old friends had been sleeping in this place for more than half a century, then he could join them for one night. It was not too cold, he would be fine in his coat. He had bought himself a bottle of water and a sandwich before boarding the train. It would be better if he had a sleeping bag...

He smiled at that thought. He and Marguerite had often been seized by the impulse to go camping when they were young. They had been so free and unrestrained, leaving their footprints and laughter behind in wilderness, forests and streams. Out there, they were free from criticism, the prying of others. Amid the crisp, chirping birdsong, David could forget feeling guilty about his own family back in China and just give himself fully to the joys of love.

He closed his eyes and sank back into the memory of Marguerite.

10

THE MOONLIGHT SHONE with a silvery gleam over the distant earth. The train hurtled onward, shaking icicles from the trees standing sentinel along the tracks.

I pressed my face against the wooden slats over the window, peering out through a thumb-sized hole.

It had been four days since the *Manchester* brought us to Victoria Island, where we quarantined before being permitted to disembark onto Burrard Pier, Vancouver. From there, we were led directly onto a train.

Barring a few brief stops in the wilderness, we had been on that train for three continuous days and nights. The thin winter clothing provided to us was no match for the cold coursing into the unheated train through poorly sealed windows on all sides. It was so cold that it felt as if the wind had burrowed into your body and solidified into ice. We only had straw mats for beds; no better than sitting in snow. I constantly rubbed my hands and feet together to stay warm, but still shivered uncontrollably if I stopped. When I managed to curl up into a ball and fall asleep, I would dream all night long. I dreamed of my parents, of the red candles on my wedding night, of my new bride shedding tears behind her veil. I dreamed of our drills at the training camp, of our ship – fragile as a leaf on the huge, swelling waves of the Pacific Ocean. I would often wake, gasping for breath, until, to my relief, I realised that I was on that swaying train.

Back in Qingdao, an interpreter at the training camp told me that he had overheard the British officers saying that Chinese labourers were being taken on this new route via Canada to escape the German submarines. He also said that the Canadian government's regulations usually demanded an entry fee, but it had been waived after an agreement between the Canadian government and Britain and France. The windows had been boarded up out of fear that the local media would report our arrival.

I was grateful for the crack in the window beside me. Even though the stunning view came at the cost of letting the cold in, I could see vast snowfields and forests, endless mountain peaks, clifftop glaciers, blue lakes and all sorts of wildlife. One day, I spotted a small herd of moose emerging from the forest. The largest of them stood almost two metres tall, proud and graceful with its head held high. Another day, I caught sight of a lucky Arctic fox holding freshly caught prey in its mouth. It ran across the snowfields, lovely and spirited. I also saw elk, bighorn sheep, even a snowy owl flapping its wings across the sky. They made me happy, made me forget the cold, forget that I was like a prisoner.

Sometimes Two-Horses and the others would borrow my *baodi*, my treasured place, beside the window. They would press their heads together, taking turns to look out through that tiny little gap. Most of the time there was nothing to see but the vast snowfields, which didn't interest them. Who wants to look at snow? The snow back home was much prettier, they said. But I liked it. As I gazed out I could imagine that I was strolling along, leaving a trail of footsteps in the powder instead of being trapped inside that hideous carriage.

Getting off the train to relieve ourselves was the ordeal we awaited most anxiously and feared most ardently. The British soldiers would unlock the doors and direct us to a designated space, watched by armed soldiers the whole time. Lowering your trousers to reveal your bare buttocks in a crowded place is humiliating enough, but on top of that was the knee-high snow and biting cold air that seemed to suck away the last remnants of the body's heat. But those moments were also precious, allowing me to raise my head to the sky, even inspiring me to recall a few lines of ancient poetry in my heart. The sun, moon and stars always stir one's thoughts. When we were lucky, the sun would be up in the sky. Everyone would be overjoyed even though its light was weak and without heat. We turned our heads towards it like sunflowers.

The train began to slow. Through the crack, I saw we were approaching a small train station. A group of white women stood beneath the lamplight, wrapped in winter clothing and thick scarves. They held up banners, bunting and baskets in their hands. We began to accelerate just as I thought we might stop. They passed in a flash.

"There are people welcoming us!" I called out, excited, warmth spreading over my frozen face. The train had been travelling too fast for me to read the banners properly, but I had made out the English words "Welcome" and "China", which was enough for me to guess that they were there to greet us.

They must have been Canadian. Heaven knows how

they knew we were going to pass that tiny station. They might have imagined countless heads behind the train's windows, people crowding to wave at them behind the glass. Perhaps they thought that when the train stopped, they could share fresh bread and snacks from their baskets to the sound of our cheers. They couldn't have imagined that the train would have been sealed shut with wooden planks.

I pictured them fighting through the snow in order to reach the station, their disappointment as they left with their food untouched. But how exciting it was, the sudden realisation that there were people who cared for us in this alien land!

I had woken the whole carriage with my cry, and now everyone was trying to talk at once. The two guards in their thickly padded uniforms peeked in and, seeing nothing wrong, went back to their slumber. For them, this duty was no different from watching over livestock. They had nothing to worry about unless the cattle were trying to harm each other or flee.

I told everybody what I had seen: the women, the banners, the baskets.

"Delicious food..." Two-Horses leaned against me, feebly repeating what I had said and extending his tongue to lick his dry, cracked lips. He was sallow and emaciated, his stomach unaccustomed to the type of food we had been given on both the train and ship. We protested, but we were still only given rations of stone-hard bread and stinking cheese.

While on the ship, Two-Horses and I had done our drills together, we had eaten and slept beside each other; we had become sworn brothers. Because I had been to school, he called me "Ge" – Older Brother – to show his respect. The first time he said it, he was elated, saying that he had never had family before. I was thrilled too. Now I had a little brother, and my life was less lonely.

The carriage was crowded with people, some sitting, some standing, some lying down. Everyone looked a little haggard, resigned even, after almost a month on the Pacific Ocean. You may as well make the best of it, as the saying goes. What else could we do? We could hardly jump off the train and run away.

We couldn't know what the future held for us, but we had a hunch that our days in the Qingdao training camp were the most comfortable we'd see for a long time. But even with that thought, we didn't want to complain. After all, the train was at least on solid ground, unlike the *Manchester*. Many of us were farmers, used to the soil. If the ground was solid under foot and the smell of soil was in the air, farmers felt safer and more relaxed.

Someone asked, "Mr Zhang, why were they welcoming us?" People had been addressing me like that since they found out I could read. At first it made me feel guilty, undeserving, but they didn't stop. I got used to it after a while and began to play the role of a schoolteacher – answering questions, reading their letters from home to them and helping them write some back.

I paused and then said, "Perhaps their children are away fighting in Europe. They know we're on our way to help them."

Many nodded.

Someone else asked, "Do foreign devils fight other foreign devils, then?"

Immediately came a response, "There is nothin' foreign devils love more than fightin'. The moment they see other people with somethin' good, they want it for themselves.

They came over to China when they saw our tea and our silk."

Someone laughed. "You think they invaded just for tea and silk? It's more'n that. They seen our minerals, our antiques, our land, the strength of our poor workers. They're after all it!"

A man who had wrapped his clothes around his neck to keep out the cold spoke up next, "Seriously, though, this war, who's the good guys and who's the bad guys?"

This question had probably never occurred to most people in the carriage. It fell quiet.

After a while, someone raised an uncertain voice to say, "I guess the British and the French are probly the good guys."

"You cannae just guess," came an immediate retort. "We don't even know why they went to war in the first place. Maybe they're just bullying Germany cause they reckons they're stronger. Maybe it's devil fighting devil, and neither's any good."

A man huddling in the corner shouted, "Who cares why foreigners go to war? If the Germans were paying us, we'd be working for them instead."

The man who had wrapped his neck did not agree. "If we helped the bad guys, wouldn't we be bad guys too? I'm a Buddhist, we don't do that kind of thing."

"Whoever pay us is who're the good guys!" This answer had a lot of people nodding in agreement.

"Delicious..." muttered Two-Horses.

Old Shuan, who loved to sing, was sitting beside Two-Horses. Hearing Two-Horses muttering, he sat up, wiped his nose with his sleeve and sang:

Delicious, delicious, truly delicious!
Spring onion pancake, sesame biscuit,
Peanut cake, peach pastry,
Cakes as small as a copper coin,
Cakes as big as a tray...
Delicious, delicious, truly delicious!
Delicious, delicious, truly delicious!
Mountain garlic, Qingdao buns,
Steamed bread, Jining meat,
Jellied noodles, donkey meat,
Endless dishes, endless flavours...
Delicious, delicious, truly delicious!
Delicious, delicious, truly delicious!
Eat until the corners of your mouth flow with oil,
Eat until your body is soaked with sweat,
Eat until your belly is a drum,
Eat until you are so satisfied,
Eat until you don't even want to marry the emperor's daughter.
Delicious, delicious, truly delicious!

The carriage all cheered. Someone called, "Again, again!"

Another person yelled, "Come on, let's have a little wine too!"

Many people raised imaginary glasses and downed them in one gulp. A man named Da Zhuang, about twenty years old, had a few glasses of the imaginary wine. Then he covered his face and wept.

"He must be hungry," someone commented.

"Nah, he misses his wife," suggested somebody else.

"If I 'ad a wife, I'd be cryin' an' all," added another.

"Knock that off, just makin' wild guesses. I misses our family ox," said Da Zhuang, in sobbing disbelief.

"If someone gave me a warm blanket right now," said a man named Hu Hezi, "I would slave away for them like an ox for as long as I live." He was the tallest among us and his clothes appeared noticeably smaller on him. He was six foot three but always walked with a slight hunch that made him appear shorter. He had his hands tucked up his sleeves and an old formal hat that did nothing for the cold. After speaking, he broke into violent coughs. A dim kerosene lamp hung above his head, its light giving his skin a deathly, greenish-black hue. He had started coughing two weeks earlier. The Western medicine that the doctor had given him was doing nothing to help.

Someone else said, "If it weren't for the bad harvest, the locusts, drought and all that stuff over the last two years, I never woudda left Shandong."

"If it wasn't for the famine, I would never've left Hebei either," answered another. "My county, Ningjin, it's great. Everywhere you go there are arches to remember all the famous people from around – we calls it Phoenix City. It was the *baodi* of the Yao Emperor, y'know. Plus, I have so many relatives there."

"What use are relatives?" someone else cut in. "When you leave the house, your fate's with heaven."

"Before signing up, I never left my village!" said another. "We were on that ship in the Pa-whatever-it's-called Ocean." He made a broad gesture with his arms. "It was so big..." He shook his head as if he still could not believe that he had made the journey. Unable to articulate the enormity of it all, he repeated himself. "So big..."

"It's Pa-ci-fic!" someone explained to him.

Everyone started to talk about the month we spent on the ship.

"It shouldn't be called that. Sounds too much like Peace-ific. Should be called War-ific, that's how it feels."

"Always rainin'. Makes you mouldy. And the waves, one after another, like walls. It's a good thing the ship was so strong, otherwise we'd have been smashed to bits."

"And the smell. Like a ghost hauntin' your nose, can't get shut of it. Awful!"

"You were such a little bitch about it, couldn't stand up without vomiting." Someone laughed.

"You threw up too! Worse than me, even, and the whole time moanin' 'Oh God, oh God', like some whore."

"Even if there 'ad been some whore, I wouldn't have 'ad the strength to do her. I'd barely the strength to breathe and wish I was dead. What about those foreign bastards, though, you wouldnae think they were tougher than us to look at 'em but they're not afraid of the waves, are they! Smoking and drinking plenty, what a life."

"You can't compare us with them. Think what they was eatin' and what we 'ad. If we 'ad wine and meat every day and big rooms on deck, we'd look like immortals too."

"Y'all remember our brother who jumped overboard?" someone asked.

Of course everyone remembered. I saw him jump. It had been a rare sunny day, that Saturday. We had been at sea for almost two weeks, so most of us had our sea legs. We were halfway through lunch when a man wearing an unfastened coat suddenly stood up and leapt over the rail. By the time we rushed to throw the lifebuoy, he had already vanished in the foam of the ship's wake.

The train entered a tunnel, and our voices were drowned out by a great rumbling echo.

"Let's talk about somethin' happy," someone suggested when we emerged from the tunnel. "Talk about, er, what are you gonna do when you get your money?"

A few people started answering at once. Some said they were going to build a house, others give it to their parents, or get a wife, or spend every day eating meat and drinking wine, or gamble. The mention of gambling piqued a few people's interest.

Gambling was forbidden aboard the train, and we had no mah-jong or cards anyway. But a gambler will always find a way to play. Someone had a few rocks in his pocket and used them to make a game. One of the guards saw them at it but didn't say anything.

Before I enlisted, I would never have imagined that I would associate with such people, but now it was as if we labourers were connected by blood. I sometimes reflected on the luxury that I had been born into, and it felt like a past life. Looking at the blisters on my hands, the calloused skin and swollen joints, I knew I had become a different person. I felt as if even the blood flowing through my body had changed.

I turned my head to look at Boss Cai. He seemed asleep, sitting beside a window with his head tilted against the wall and his eyes closed, but I knew he was awake. He had a piece of straw in his mouth that was moving as he chewed. I had tried to chat with him a few times when we were on the *Manchester*, hoping that we'd become friends, but he didn't like talking. Other than when he was eating or sleeping, he spent all his time in meditation, watching the sea. He could sit there motionless for hours on end, detached from everything around him.

Old Shuan began to sing *sixian* four-string opera, his voice forlorn. He coughed every few lines. The carriage fell quiet, and many expressions showed longing or a sense of loss. Our homes were already so far away. Who knew how many months or years would pass before we saw them again?

"On the Pacific, we think of Ma and Ba. We sold our lives for three hundred dollars…"

After a while, the singing stopped, and everybody became drowsy.

Two-Horses was sleeping curled up against me, his mouth partly open, the pain of hunger on his face. I flexed my arms and feet, then began to read my books by the light of that sole kerosene lamp. A few days before we boarded the ship, I had bought myself an English-Chinese and a French-Chinese dictionary. I secured them in my coat like treasure and took them out to study from time to time.

Early the next morning, the bodies of Hu Hezi and one other worker were removed from the carriage. They had frozen to death in their sleep.

11

WE REACHED HALIFAX on Canada's eastern coast three days later, where the train stopped beside a steamship. We were given no time to see the city, just to board the ship, bound for Liverpool.

Named the *Julius*, the ship was converted from a captured German transport vessel. It was much bigger than the *Manchester* and cleaved the sea like an axe, sending a massive wake cascading behind it.

After our morning drill, we stood on deck looking at our convoy of eight merchant ships – too far from us to see what they were carrying – and two American-flagged warships. Old Man Wang from the kitchens said he had overheard two Chinese translators saying that last week, a German submarine had attacked a ship called the *Athos*. The *Athos* had sunk in the Mediterranean, killing more than five hundred Chinese labourers who were on board. France and Britain had naval escorts for their goods now, fearing it would happen again. The other ships were either French or British, too.

A storm raged for a whole week. We wore lifejackets day and night, even when we slept. We had rice or steamed buns to eat at first, but the portions shrank until they were replaced with rations of hard, mouldy bread. Many of us slept all day to conserve energy. We were so exhausted that we could sleep for five or six hours just sitting on the cold steel deck with our heads on our knees. I was faint and dizzy, listless, my mind churning like the ocean's waves. I didn't want to think about or do anything.

Rumours spread that the ship was suffering a smallpox outbreak and that the British were secretly tossing sick Chinese overboard. Panic ensued and anyone who felt unwell no longer dared to ask the translators for a doctor. Yet another rumour spread that we had been targeted by a German torpedo boat – which explained why the ships were zigzagging – and that the American warships had been firing depth charges to drive them away.

At one point, Two-Horses managed to find a small bottle of brown liquor. He and I took small sips, the liquid scorching our mouths as it became a ball of fire moving down our throats and into our bellies, making us cough and splutter. Even though it was unpleasant, the alcohol roused our spirits for a while, giving us a short-lived burst of energy. More important, it made us feel alive.

We arrived in Liverpool after ten days, boarded a train and rode all night to Folkestone, a town on England's southeast coast. The journey took us through Manchester, Birmingham and London. I looked out through a gap in the closed window curtains along the way – the train was kept dark for fear of attack from German aircraft – to see dimly lit factories on either side. After a night in Folkestone, we took the ferry across the English Channel to the northern coast of

France. Our destination was a village near Calais named Loyelle.

At last, our feet were on the ground again. Many of us forgot about the hunger and cold, squatting excitedly to scoop thaw-softened earth into our hands, comparing it with our native soil, discussing which crops it could support. Some even put it into their mouths to taste its flavour.

The British officers and soldiers, also exhausted from the journey, stood around smoking in twos or threes, their whips tucked under their arms.

Dozens of villagers stood by the roadside watching us, their hoes, shovels and other farm tools in hand. There was no curiosity, no happiness, nor disdain in their eyes. Only numbness. Their clothes were rags hanging listlessly from their frail bodies. They didn't look much better than we did.

There was a sign at the village entrance where someone had written in Chinese, "It is forbidden to cross this boundary. Trespassers will be punished harshly by law."

A boy of seven or eight peered out at us from behind his mother, snot dripping from his nose. When a labourer spotted him and called out an excited *'bonjour"* in the French he had just learned from a British soldier, the boy hid behind his mother's skirts.

The road was muddy and potholed, some of the craters huge. The occasional brick-and-tile farmhouses on either side of the road seemed full of dust, as if they had just emerged from the ground. Everywhere we looked were bombed houses, burnt tree stumps, shell casings, abandoned farmland and barbed wire. A bloodied strip of cloth lay tangled in the wire. It looked like the village had recently been a battlefield.

No hens clucking or dogs barking. No children's laughter. It wasn't like a village; it was like a tomb. I was surprised that these villagers had not already left.

We had not gone very far before arriving at a large tented area surrounded by tall trees and shrubbery. The tents had been divided into several areas by two-metre-high barbed wire fences. Each section housed twenty or thirty domed tents with camouflage patches of yellow and green, a few rectangular wooden buildings among them.

Woody and his soldiers divided us into groups. I was assigned to a tent with Two-Horses, Boss Cai, Old Shuan and another ten or so people.

The tent was dark and damp, smelling of mildew. When my eyes adjusted to the dim light, I saw a pile of straw mats and wooden planks: our beds. There was no other furniture – not even a stool, let alone a source of heat.

Old Shuan had often stayed with Two-Horses and me when we were aboard the *Julius*. He was a 28-year-old man from Hebei who had served in the army and had later gone with his family to Shandong, where he earned a living as a street performer. He could sing Peking, Yu and Lu operas, and was good at improvising songs. Despite his youth, wrinkles scored lines across his forehead. I had also made some headway with Boss Cai. One day, he had taken the initiative to say hello to me and we talked for a while – mostly me speaking while he listened. I still knew nothing about him, except that he had grown up in Beijing. The four of us went to put our things in the same corner.

Shortly after entering the tent, we were called to form lines in the open space outside where we were divided into companies, platoons and sections. Everyone who had been in our tent was put into the same section of fifteen, led by two foremen wearing armbands with a single yellow stripe. One was a Chinese man named George who had worked for a foreign bank in Shanghai and had already been there for about a month. The other was a tall, slim British soldier named Edward, who could speak only a few simple sentences in Chinese. We even had an interpreter, a red-haired Canadian with a freckled nose who spoke fluent French and Chinese. A little older than me, he introduced himself to us as a Christian who had been sent by The Youth Christian Church's branch in Tianjin, where he had lived with his missionary parents as a child.

After dismissal, we lined up to get haircuts and have tailors patch our clothes and resew buttons. Those with worn-out shoes went to the cobblers, who were chosen from the labourers based on their past professions. Knowing that our long journey was finally over and smelling the rice and meat being cooked in the kitchens, we came back to life despite our exhaustion. Outside, we walked around and exercised, soaking up the weak heat from the pale sun.

Two-Horses fished a pinch of tobacco from his pocket and began to pack it into his handmade wooden pipe with the utmost care. "A little treasure," he said, then like a magician produced a box of matches from his other pocket. "Last one, hope it lights." Ever since starving on the train in Canada, he had acquired this almost supernatural ability to obtain commodities like alcohol, salted meat and tinned fish. He said that he had befriended Old Man Wang from the kitchen, who even wanted him to marry his daughter in China! He had always been an optimist, and now the look on his face was even more vivacious. Even if the sky were to collapse on his head, you bet he would greet it with a smile.

After smelling the tobacco and lighting the pipe, Two-Horses happily took a pull and handed it to me. I had

71

secretly smoked cigarettes with my friends in my student years, and my father had since taught me how to use a pipe, but I hadn't touched tobacco for a while. I closed my eyes to inhale, and, mimicking Two-Horses, slowly exhaled a puff of smoke, my heart rate calming as if a gentle breeze had passed through my mind. I passed the pipe to Old Shuan, who smoked and handed it to Boss Cai. Cai handed it to the next man without smoking.

"What's they up to?" asked Two-Horses.

I looked in the direction he was pointing and saw George taking a large, black lock to the door in the perimeter of our barbed wire fence and shutting it fast. An armed British soldier ran to stand guard on one side.

"They're worried we'll run away," I said, thinking to myself how ironic it was that I had come to France in search of liberty.

"These fuckin' foreign bastards!" said the man beside Old Shuan. It was Da Zhuang, the man who had cried about his family ox when we were on the train. He had a thick Henan accent and sometimes spewed out words I couldn't understand. With a big square head atop a big square chest, his hands and feet resembling thick wooden planks, he was worthy of his name: big and strong.

"But George is Chinese," said Two-Horses.

"Aye, an' he's a foreigner's dog! Don't you see 'ow he bows and scrapes for 'em? He don't deserve to be called Chinese."

Old Shuan pulled out his blackened *kuaiban* clackers from his pocket and began to sing, "After a thousand miles we arrive in France, a difficult unbearable road. Now that we're strangers in a strange land, who knows what tomorrow will hold?"

A distant rumbling began, lasting for some time. After a few moments of silence it began again, this time seeming much closer.

"Thunder?" Two-Horses looked up. "But it's a nice day."

Boss Cai responded, his voice calm. "It's artillery fire."

"I never seen a cannon," said Da Zhuang. "It yells jus' like our ox." He mimicked the sound of cattle lowing. "Jus' like the ox. It could plough ten *mu* in one day![1]" He sighed, his expression grief-stricken. "Such a good ox, 'ow could you get sick and die? It were fine that night, but then in the morning..."

Old Shuan looked disdainfully at him. "You're gonna compare a cow to a bomb? It'd blow you to pieces."

"I thought that when we gets to France everything'd be pretty as a picture," said Two-Horses. "But it's not as nice as Qingdao, is it?"

"You think this is France?" Old Shuan said. "There are loads of beautiful places in France, but these foreign bastards won't send us to 'em."

"Even the lice is smaller than in Qingdao," Two-Horses muttered, pinching a shiny black louse from his cuff and sending it to the underworld with a snap of his teeth.

Everybody laughed, and I felt itchy all over. It went without saying that I had also been invaded by lice. I scratched for a moment and then said, "When the contract expires, we'll go to Paris to visit the Champs-Élysées during the day, and then take in the view from the top of the Eiffel Tower at night. We'll try some genuine French cuisine. We can rent a car. Two-Horses, you can sit up next to the driver, if we give him some extra money maybe he'll teach you to drive."

With a longing expression, Two-Horses said, "I'd give him all the money I 'ad."

"Ey then, 'ow you gonna pay Pock-Face Wang the bride price for 'is daughter?" Da Zhuang joked.

Two-Horses lifted his head proudly. "If I can drives, then obviously I'll have cash. When the time comes, I can drive 'er home with me."

The image of Miss Lu's red veil and her tiny feet wrapped like *zongzi* in those embroidered shoes flashed before my eyes. I had sent letters both to her and my parents before we boarded the *Manchester*, but I did not know whether they had received them. How was my father's illness? Was my mother drenched in tears every day? I hoped Miss Lu did not react too strongly to my leaving, perhaps even taking her own life.

My mind muddled, I stood and walked towards the tent.

"Ge, what's up with you?" Two-Horses called from behind. "When you gets a wife, I'll drive 'er to you as well!"

12

DAVID HAD BEEN GONE FOR A DAY before Anne called the editor-in-chief of *Women's City Weekly*, the magazine she had founded ten years earlier. She asked the editor to take charge of operations in her absence. The kids had been restless, so Pierre had taken them to the zoo while Anne stayed back at David's apartment to wait for him.

She stood looking out over the balcony. The left side was filled with plants and flowers, while the right was occupied with her parents' chairs: Baba's rattan armchair, Maman's wooden one, both from the antique market. In front of them stood a small wooden table with a glass surface on which rested a white porcelain teacup. Her father had forgotten to return it to the kitchen; there were still dried tea leaves at the bottom.

As Anne touched the two chairs, her earlier unease was replaced by a feeling of warmth. She had a hunch that David was off somewhere reminiscing about the past, somewhere she had never been herself.

She looked down at the street: the busy tables outside the

cafe, a young man hurrying out of the florist with a bouquet of red roses, a couple playing with their baby in a pushchair.

Did Baba often sit here and look out? How had he been coping with the loneliness since Ma's death?

Her mind conjured the image of her father kneeling on the ground, carefully examining the red geranium. It was then that it occurred to her that he had probably not wanted that birthday party. She always thought that the occasion might offer her father some relief from the pain of losing Maman, but now she realised that it might have had the opposite effect. She had been bringing Pierre and the kids to visit him every week since Ma's death, but she really hadn't spent that much time with him. Preoccupied with children or work, she was absent-minded whenever they spoke.

She was always busy. When driving, when walking around, even when cooking or showering, she would be thinking about work. Revenue and profit, quarterly plans, customer satisfaction, the magazine's circulation... Her schedule was always packed. To her colleagues and clients, she was dynamic, competent, inexhaustibly energetic. But deep down, she knew she worked so hard because she was insecure. She hadn't told anyone about that sensation, not even Pierre or her best friend Clara. She felt that her success in her career was the way to earn respect, the way to become truly French.

She had wanted to expose this part of herself to Pierre, but faltered every time the words came to her lips. He was an architect whom she had met ten years ago when she was trying to attract advertisers for the magazine. Pierre was not the problem; he was an understanding and supportive husband. She was the problem.

The phone rang. Anne dashed into the kitchen and picked up the receiver.

After a moment's silence, her father's voice came through. "Anne, it's me."

Anne was overjoyed. "Baba, where are you? Are you OK?"

"I'm fine." Ba's confident, clear voice reassured her.

"Where are you? I'll come and get you."

"Ah, I, I'm quite far away. I thought you might still be at our place, so I called to let you know not to worry, not to come looking for me."

"Far away?" Anne's tone intensified as her anxiety returned. "Ba, are you kidding me? It's dangerous for you to be going on long journeys alone at your age. Where exactly are you? If you want to go travelling, I'll come with you."

"I want to go alone."

Anne bit her lip, reminding herself to stay calm. She knew how stubborn her father could be. She softened her tone, trying to persuade him to come home. "Ba, how long are you going to be?"

"Erm, I'm not sure. Maybe two weeks."

"Two weeks!"

"I need a break."

"A break where?"

He did not answer.

Anne controlled her temper before continuing, "Ba, wait for me there. We'll go together."

"My train is leaving any minute, I have to go."

"What? You're at the train-"

But he had already gone.

Anne stared helplessly at the receiver, then called the police station to say that her father had just called but to ask that they still look for him anyway. He would have to stay in a hotel, and the police would be able to find his whereabouts when he gave his name to a check-in desk. The officer agreed to do so, but she knew they would not go to any great lengths. Crime rates were rising, and the city's police force was overwhelmed.

After calling to update Pierre, she decided to pay a visit to Mr and Mrs Wang. She called to make sure they were home, in an apartment just a block away.

Mrs Wang opened the door. She was wearing a deep green velvet cheongsam with a dark floral pattern, her hair in a bun and her lips painted red. Mrs Wang dressed up whenever she left home or had visitors. She reminded Anne of her own late grandmother, who used to stay with them for a week or two at a time when she visited from Lyon. Like Mrs Wang, she also paid great attention to appearances. Mr Wang, on the other hand, looked very casual, with a loose woollen cardigan over slacks and slippers.

Mrs Wang invited Anne to sit in the living room, while Mr Wang served tea and refreshments. Anne was not a tea drinker but accepted it anyway. She knew this was a habit among older Chinese people.

Their home was very Chinese in style: mahogany furniture, lamps on the ceiling, blue-and-white porcelain in the entrance hall and landscape paintings hanging on the walls. By comparison, her parents' home reflected a mixture of Eastern and Western cultures.

After Anne had sipped her tea, she told them that David had called. "Where do you think he's going?"

Mr and Mrs Wang looked at each other. Mrs Wang said, "We spoke about this last night. Your father often told us that he wanted to travel, to go somewhere to relax. But whenever we invited him to join a tour group with us, he'd say that he didn't want to go. Strange, isn't it? Even if he has finally decided to go travelling, why so suddenly? Why not after his birthday party?" She looked at her husband. "Anything to add?"

Mr Wang shook his head slowly. "This is an unusual trip for David. I think he's going to a few different places. Otherwise, why would he have bought all those maps?" He had forgotten about the maps until now. It was Mrs Wang who had played detective and got him to repeat David's every word to her just before Anne's arrival.

"Did Ba mention going anywhere to see friends?" Anne asked.

"He didn't."

"Was there anywhere Ma was particularly fond of?" she asked, thinking that perhaps her father might go to a favourite spot of hers when he missed her.

"When your mother was alive," Mrs Wang said, "she would often speak highly of Lyon."

Anne had been born in Paris but visited Lyon with her mother as a child. She had also travelled there for work as an adult, and still did so occasionally. Though her mother was nostalgic about the city, her father barely mentioned it and always excused himself from their visits, saying that he had to work.

"Honestly, your father doesn't talk to us about his past," Mr Wang said. "Even if it's brought up, it's just a few words here or there. But he likes to hear me talk about Chinese affairs, political matters, food and living, all that, always asking lots of questions." He paused. "There is one thing, though." He looked at his wife, as if not sure he should continue. She nodded, so he went on, "The year your mother died, we visited China. After we returned, we tried to persuade your father to join us for another visit. He's from Qingdao and I'm from Yantai, about two hundred kilometres apart, so we're practically neighbours. I said, David, the Cultural Revolution is over, China has opened itself up to the West and the government is encouraging overseas Chinese to visit friends and family. He was tempted, you could tell from his expression. But every time I brought it up, he shook his head and said again and again, 'I can't, I just can't go back'. Then he changed the subject. It looked like it really weighed on him."

"He definitely said that he *can't* go, not that he did not *want* to," explained Mrs Wang, being careful to highlight the difference between the two.

Anne felt that this was an important point, but she could not figure it out. "Baba's an orphan," she said. "He doesn't have any relatives in China."

Mrs Wang said, "Yes, he told me that as well... Anne, please don't take offence at this, but I don't think he seems like someone who spent his childhood in an orphanage. We have had deep discussions of classical Chinese literature, he's so knowledgeable that he has to have attended a good private school in China. Not only that, but he has a great depth of knowledge about tea. He knows where the best leaves come from, and which tea goes with which tea set. My family had a tea shop, so I know a good many things – but he knows more than me! There's a saying in English, 'born with a silver spoon in his mouth'. If you ask me, your father is that type, born into a wealthy family. He says he's an orphan, but I don't think it's true."

"You don't know that!" Mr Wang interjected.

Hurt, Mrs Wang retorted, "Have you not said the same

yourself? You also said that his every move and gesture resembles that of someone born into a rich, old-money family."

Anne remembered the letters in her father's wooden box. She had considered bringing them for Mr Wang to translate but had abandoned the notion, fearful of invading her father's privacy.

At that moment, Mr Wang's eyes lit up as he suddenly remembered something. "A few years ago, your dad mentioned that he had an old friend who was living in France. What was his name..." He lowered his head and thought for a moment. "Yes, it was *Er-Ma* – Two-Horses! From the look on your dad's face when he spoke about him, I think that he really seemed to miss him."

Er-Ma? Anne repeated the name in her head. She had never heard Baba mention him.

13

THE TRAIN HAD BEEN MOVING for some time, but David's heart was still pulsing with anxiety. He had not been away from home like this for six years. He looked out like a restless young man as fields, orchards, farmhouses and telephone poles flashed by. It had already gone eight in the morning by the time he woke from his peaceful sleep against the cemetery wall. The pain in his leg wound had subsided too, either a blessing from heaven or a sign that his body was suddenly full of energy.

To David's surprise, the carriage was packed – there was some sort of event going on at a station ahead. His was the only Asian face among the passengers, and many of them had stared at him when he boarded. They were probably just curious, but he remained uneasy, their eyes like thorns pricking his side. He had lived in France for sixty-eight years now, but would often encounter this kind of "welcome" when he left Paris. The attention was worse if he was with Marguerite. Only a few of the stares would be overtly unfriendly, but even a sidelong glance reminded him that he would always be a foreigner.

On their thirtieth anniversary, he and Marguerite had made reservations at an upscale restaurant in Paris. The place was decorated with crystal chandeliers, silver candlesticks, gold-plated cutlery and fresh flowers in tall vases. He wore a grey suit with a red silk tie, while Marguerite was the picture of elegant simplicity in a floor-length lilac dress and the pearl brooch that had been his gift to her. As they drank their pre-dinner cocktails, a finely dressed woman wearing a crucifix approached and said to them, "This is not the sort of place for you. You had better dine somewhere else."

The surrounding diners all stopped to listen. The manager and a few waiters also looked silently on. There was a trace of a smile on the manager's face.

In the same way one might be aware of a stray bullet on a battlefield, David was always wary of the malice that could be stirred up by his appearance. But once they had entered this restaurant, its high and refined atmosphere led him to drop his guard. Now his first impulse was to grab Marguerite's hand and leave, dragging her into hiding in some secluded corner as he had done when he was still a young man in love.

The impulse turned to rage. He wanted to slap the woman. But of course he could never strike a woman, nor even open his mouth in reproach. His upbringing simply would not allow it.

He could only leave in silence, as he had done many times before when facing such behaviour while he was out by himself.

He looked to Marguerite for help, ashamed of his inability to protect her, his helplessness and his timidity.

Marguerite rose to stand behind David, putting both of her hands on his shoulders before turning calmly to the woman. "I have loved my husband Delun for half a century. He has worked in France since he was seventeen years old. He has built railways and operated cranes. He has designed and built heavy machinery. He works hard. He is kind and generous. He pays his taxes. He has built a family here and is as true a Frenchman as anybody here. China is his home, and so is France."

David gripped her hand on his shoulder. Hers trembled slightly with adrenaline but was full of strength nonetheless. He calmed as she spoke.

She did not shout, but her manner was as if she were addressing a crowd from a stage. Her gaze swept the room, finally returning to the woman in front of them as she said, "You and I are about the same age. As both a French national and a human being, I am ashamed by your ignorance and your vulgarity. May your god have mercy on your soul." To the manager, she continued, "My husband and I deeply regret choosing your establishment. Its marble serves only to conceal its filth."

It was clear that nobody had expected this of her. There was a stillness over the room. The silence was interrupted by an uneasy cough, then whispers.

Marguerite held her head high as she took David's arm, the two of them leaving the restaurant at their own pace. They mingled into the crowd outside, weaving beneath the bright streetlights of the sprawling cosmopolis. They walked silently arm in arm until they crossed the pavement, when Marguerite suddenly burst into cheerful laughter. "Delun, that woman was so angry, her whole body was shaking!"

She had that ability to dispel pain. She had once said to

David that in this life, nobody could escape physical or mental anguish. So instead of languishing in it and letting it eat you, you had to smile and joke at yourself along with it.

They spent the rest of their evening on the bank of the River Seine, enjoying pastries from a little bakery and chatting away until after midnight.

Times had changed, of course, with more immigrants coming to Paris and other parts of France every year. David now had many friends and acquaintances who had been born and raised locally. Nonetheless, he still occasionally had to face those sideways looks, those contemptuous glances.

How he longed for Marguerite's company!

He was sitting in the aisle seat beside a young man in his early twenties with a plaid scarf and a few curls of hair hanging over his forehead. He was wearing headphones, dozing off against the window.

David pulled out his newly purchased maps, a leather notebook and a ballpoint pen. He arranged them on the small wooden table in front of him, its surface mottled with animal stickers from children who had sat there before. No matter where he went, he liked to buy and study local maps, a habit he had started when he was young.

He had already planned a basic route before boarding, and now he had to iron out the details.

He remembered how he and Two-Horses had once studied a shabby old map in the moonlight, the night quiet around them. Half the map was missing, and the one remaining was full of rat-chewed holes – but this did not lessen their interest. They were sitting in the trenches, cushioned by branches and vines. The boundless, starry night stretched away overhead. "Ge, if we catches a boat 'ere, go by the Cape of Good Hope, we gets to India, then Australia, Iceland and Brazil..." Two-Horses let his imagination roam free, stringing together all the different countries he could name.

He could still see Two-Horses' gleaming eyes, his nose twitching with excitement as he spoke.

The man beside David opened his eyes. He watched as the old man's finger moved across the map. Unable to contain his curiosity, he removed his headphones to ask, "Where are you going?"

David turned to him. "You mean where am I going on this train?"

"It seems you're going to a few different places."

"Yes. Probably four or five cities and a few smaller places."

The young man's friendliness dispelled David's unease, and he pointed out his destinations to him one by one. Relax, he told himself, weren't most of his interactions with French people like this? You could talk to strangers with ease when travelling alone. Getting on the same train, sitting on the same row, aren't those the kind of lucky occurrences that bring people together?

"Is this little village the place you're going to today?" The young man looked at him doubtfully, then said teasingly, "Do you have a lover there?"

"*Mon amour*..." David tapped his heart. "Lives in here."

The young man understood. "There are so many beautiful villages, why do you want to go to that one?"

"I once worked there, many years ago."

The young man pointed up and down David's map, saying that he had cycled to all those places. "I can guarantee that all the places I just pointed out would be more fun than that village."

David smiled at his earnestness.

What could he say? Should he tell him that a barbed wire-fenced labour camp near that village had been his first foothold in France? Should he tell him about the nights he had spent curled up there weeping, longing for home? Or perhaps he could tell him about the sign that forbade Chinese from entering at the village's gate? When all that happened, he had been even younger than the man now sitting beside him.

14

DAVID STILL HAD TO TAKE THE BUS after disembarking. He had not known how to find the bus station, but a stranger led him there personally out of concern that he might get lost on his own. The morning sky was overcast, threatening rain, but the sun kept peeking out from behind the clouds. Its heat and the air's humidity made for an afternoon so comfortable that David almost wanted to doze off. A green vineyard cascaded down the slope opposite the station, rising and falling along a flattened ridge of growth. The black and purple grapes had already been harvested, and several workers in grey overalls were clearing weeds and rebuilding broken stakes in preparation for winter.

Of all the sights in the French countryside, the vineyard was among David's favourites. He and Marguerite had visited Bordeaux Castle, Alsace, Provence and the vineyards of the Rhône valley. Beneath her paintbrush, she had captured them, complete with all the unique qualities of the seasons and weather. In one watercolour that still hung on their bedroom wall, the juice of a ripe purple grape soaked David's fingers as he held it.

The workers busy with their tasks made David think that he was not unlike a harvested vineyard himself. Now all that was left to do was to clean up the twigs and leaves, then go tidily to rest. The future would bring new life to the vineyard, just as it would reunite him with Marguerite. He was not religious, but he was fond of the Buddhist position on reincarnation, that life and death were successive and interdependent. He had wilfully added his own position that no matter in what world and in what form, he and Marguerite would have another life together. Human, animal or plant – they would be together.

The bearded driver drove quickly, with only a few passengers on his bus. It was half an hour before David arrived at Loyelle, where he was the only one to disembark.

To the right of the main road, a dirt path meandered into the distant woods. The village itself, made up of orange-roofed white farmhouses and a stone church with a grey spire, lay between the road and the forest. Its trees were shorter and sparser than in his imagination, and there were more houses. Perhaps the trees of his memory had been felled to build the houses, and the ones he was looking at had been planted later.

In his reminiscence, he could hear his companions' footsteps falling heavily over the frosted earth, hear one of them calling *"bonjour"* to the watching villagers in Chinese-accented French. Had he lifted the soil to his nose like some of the others, had he even tasted it? He could not recall. What he remembered was the feeling, his heart brimming with expectation for his new life in a foreign land. He had not yet seen the camp, did not yet know that it was surrounded by barbed wire fences with sentries on patrol.

He stepped cautiously onto the dirt road as if it were a river with currents to sweep him along with it. He took the path towards the woods. Subconsciously, he looked to the side of the road as he passed the T-junction that led into the village. Of course, there were no longer any signs prohibiting entry to his race.

Two hundred metres from the woods, the road narrowed. It became a footpath with weeds and wildflowers on both sides, sometimes wandering through patches of low, unkempt vegetation that then receded to reveal the path again. With fewer than twenty households, how many villagers frequented this path?

The area that had once contained the barracks was now densely packed with trees. It was silent but for leaves and birdsong. Sunlight dappled across David's feet, and large moss-covered stones lay scattered among the trees. The path vanished. He raised his head to see a thick canopy of greenery obscuring the sky.

He rested on one of the smooth rocks, tired but not enough for him to need a lie-down. His feet were not bothering him, even though he was surprised they had carried him this far. Perhaps his body had longed for this trip as much as his soul. His stomach began to growl, so he took his time enjoying a flattened ham sandwich and a bottle of water from his bag.

Five or six metres ahead, a large solitary rock about a metre high stood between two towering trees. It was covered with green moss and shaped like an ancient Chinese ingot with raised sides around a concave centre.

He set down his half-eaten sandwich and walked like a

man bewitched towards that rock, then squatted down and began to gently scrape the moss from its surface. An etching of a bamboo forest appeared beneath his fingers. Time had erased areas of the image, but most of the thick-knotted bamboo and its sparse leaves were clearly visible. This had been his own work one homesick evening, carved with a small, sharp rock. That night, surrounded by people playing chess, gambling, singing or telling jokes, his mind had been far, far away.

What, he wondered, is history? Is it just the process of scraping moss from stones, to see what lies beneath? If the moss goes untouched, then it's as if the history it conceals had never even existed.

15

AFTER MORE THAN A WEEK spent building the road in Loyelle, our 12th Battalion boarded canvas-canopied trucks and arrived two hours later at a town called Arras. It was even gloomier than Loyelle.

We formed lines to pass through a town centre that had been battered with bombs. Of some buildings only half a wall remained, with carvings and twisted balcony railings the only testament to their former size and grandeur. Broken lampposts and debris sprawled across the overgrown weeds of what had once been an urban garden, among them a crucifix blackened by fire. The stiff body of a dog lay beside it.

I can't say what the air smelled like. A suffocation of gunpowder, smoke, rotting meat and petrol.

An old woman passed by, spectral and dishevelled with blood at the corners of her mouth. She was dressed in black and carried a woven suitcase. Her eyes remained fixed ahead as if she were staring down the gates of hell.

We passed some stone ruins, where another woman

emerged from underground with a child in her arms. Her long, brown hair was filthy and clung to her chest, but her face was smeared with rouge and powder. The contrast was dramatic, her pale face like plaster around her bright red lips. She must have lived in the cellar. I quickened my pace as she winked at me, fearing that she might approach.

When we reached our destination, we found that our so-called camp was a stretch of level ground amid broken tiles and ruined walls. We could slip into the cellar through the gaps in the rubble in case of an air raid.

We set up our tents after clearing some more of the debris. Dinner consisted of bread and a tin of beef, onions and potatoes. We were so exhausted after eating that we fell asleep, still fully clothed, the moment we had spread our military blankets on the ground. The tent rumbled with snores.

I awoke suddenly in the middle of the night, the image of that burnt cross fixed in my mind. It seemed as though it was still burning, the flames engulfing me along with it. I tossed uneasily on my blanket, gasping for breath.

My classmates and I had once visited a Catholic church in Qingdao out of curiosity. Inside it there was a giant cross, from which hung a Westerner, half-naked with a crooked crown of thorns and blood flowing from his body and mouth. Startled, we hurried out. Our teacher told us later that the crucified man was Jesus Christ, a Jew from the Middle East.

Curious, I asked if he had atoned for all the world's sins with his own death. The teacher nodded. But we don't believe in God, I said, did he still atone for our sins? The teacher nodded again and spent hours introducing the concepts of the Bible. I have forgotten much of what he said, but I remembered the words of a hymn he taught us. I sang the hymn under my breath, feeling a little reassured. I stared wide-eyed at the moonlit tent, imagining that my prayer had floated into the sky.

"This too shall pass," I heard someone whisper. It was Boss Cai, separated from me by three other men.

I did not respond, but his words relaxed me. I went back to sleep.

We were awoken before sunrise four hours later. Several foremen handed each of us a brown canvas bag containing fifteen tins of meat, six packets of biscuits and a box of matches. They also told us to take blankets and toiletries, saying that we would be gone for days.

"What are we going to do?" someone asked. There was no reply.

We walked in darkness for more than an hour, our path beset by craters, collapsed houses and charred trees. Some craters were large enough for a dozen people to lie in. Standing in the centre, even a tall man like me could not touch the sides.

There were bodies, too. Blood leaked from the neck of a decapitated war horse, dyeing the soil a dark, blackish red. Another, even more disturbing, leaned against a tree stump as if sleeping with its head bowed. Circling the other side, we saw that its stomach had been pierced, viscera flowing out of the wound. A man beside me put his hands together in prayer and said, "Amitabha".

The sky had brightened enough by the time we reached our destination that we could see blue-grey smoke billowing around us, as if something was on fire. We were nearing the front lines of battle. The whispers among us became loud protestations. We stopped walking.

"Didn't our contracts say we wouldn't be goin' to the front?" someone asked.

"We never came to fight!" someone else added, the crowd voicing their support.

Woody urged his horse to the front, an armband with triple yellow bars on his left sleeve. He dismounted and spoke to Tom, our translator. Though we had thought that Woody would leave us after we arrived in France, somehow he had stayed and remained our commander.

When Tom wasn't eating, sleeping or serving officers, he spent his time with us. He told us about his childhood in Tianjin, that he loved *jianbing* pancakes, chestnut soup and making figurines out of mud. He smiled whenever he spoke about God, and though people laughed at him and said his Western God could never know what the Chinese wanted, he still repeated Bible stories with great enthusiasm. Everybody loves stories, so a friendship blossomed rapidly between us.

I was too far from Woody to hear what he was saying. He and Tom seemed to be arguing, Woody kicking a tree stump, Tom raising his hands in disbelief. Eventually, Tom seemed to give in. Frowning and morose, he climbed onto a tree stump to address us.

"Colonel Wilson says we are still sixteen kilometres from the front, still in the rear. Today's task is to dig trenches. The German air force has suffered heavy losses under British engagement, so we are in no danger of their return for now." It seemed like he regretted having to tell us that lie.

The crowd quietened, but nobody moved.

Boss Cai stood out of the crowd and announced, "We're already here, we may as well make the best of it." He stepped forward; the crowd followed.

After leaving our baggage in an area two hundred metres ahead, each section began to dig trenches with the tools we had just received. There were already trenches in the ground, but bombs had ruined their structures. Half of us were assigned to repairs, while the other half worked on extensions.

We all worked under the instructions of the foremen, some of whom carried guns over their shoulders and leather whips in their hands, as if they were ready to suppress a revolt at any time.

Our section was responsible for repairing bomb damage. I had already begun to feel the haze of war in Loyelle, but it was not until my canvas shoes sank into the mire of those trenches that I truly understood how close we were to battle.

The trench before me was about three metres deep, snaking through the earth like a long black reptile. Its sides were packed with sandbags, earth bricks and corrugated metal sheets. There were recessions for shelter in its back wall. Within those recessions were wooden shelves, places for sitting or sleeping and wire to hang your belongings. A few even had wooden planks for beds. Behind me, an explosion had formed a crater now filled with yellow, turbid water that vibrated under our footsteps. Loops of barbed wire jutted out of its surface here and there. The walls on both sides had been blown out.

Staying there made you feel no better than a rat.

"Wow," called Old Shuan, using a stick to toss a hoop of wire out of the tunnel. "These is a lot bigger than them trenches I fought in."

Two-Horses looked sceptically at the shovel in his hand and said, "These Brits, why can't they even make a shovel right?"

They were oddly constructed, comprising a short wooden handle and a wide head fixed at a right angle, like a combination of a Chinese spade and a pickaxe.

Old Shuan smiled. "It's you who don't get it! This kinda shovel doesn't take space, it's made specially to dig quick in the trenches. Plus, the Brits sharpen the edge so if the enemy ends up down here, you can use it to send them straight to heaven."

Da Zhuang sighed repeatedly as he looked up and down the endless trenches. "Local god's gonna be 'eartbroken we've dug so many 'oles without crops."

I spotted a scrap of paper in the wet mud. When I stooped to pick it up, I found it was a half-burned photograph showing a large family, their heads burnt out except for two five- or six-year-old children. Their expressions were blurred, but they seemed happy. One was carrying a lamb. I used my sleeve to wipe away the mud and put the photograph into my pocket. I don't know why I did that, I just felt it should not be left there all alone.

We worked hard under Edward's supervision. Looking not yet twenty, he had a long, pale face, light brown hair, straight eyebrows and eyes so deeply set that they seemed to be hiding from the world. His left foot was slightly lame, which appeared to bother him – he tried to keep his body as steady as possible when he walked. He did not talk much, but was friendly, often greeting us in Chinese, unlike the other British soldiers, who were arrogant and quick to shout at us. I noticed that he did not speak with them much. When they were chatting and smoking together he would be off to the side, smoking alone. They seemed not to like him either, treating him as if he didn't exist.

George had been resting outside the trenches. When he

saw Edward working with us, he seemed embarrassed. He jumped in for a few symbolic shovelfuls of dirt, then said he was going to inspect progress elsewhere.

We had been unwilling to dig the trenches at first, but once we began, we exerted all our strength. We pitied the soldiers who had fought there and would fight there still. It did not matter that we had never met them and could not speak the same language, our fates were tied together.

Our progress was particularly rapid thanks to Old Shuan's experience as a soldier and Edward's personal demonstration of the technique. To show off his strength, Two-Horses removed his coat and slung a sandbag onto his back with one hand. As he walked, he swayed his hips and danced *yangge*, one hand on the bag, the other on his waist.

"Two-Horses," someone teased. "You're gonna 'ave to marry an elephant! No woman can 'andle all that strength."

I sensed myself becoming stronger, but when I tried to lift a sandbag with one hand, it didn't budge. "Ge, you're a scholar, stick to the pen!" Two-Horses laughed. My face went red with effort. Even with Two-Horses' help, I still struggled to get it onto my back. It was like carrying a little mountain.

Da Zhuang taught me how to shovel the soil quickly and economically. He said that the earth has a soul, you have to follow it, talk to it. He had a special affection for the land, even if it was French. He said he was born in a mud pit, that he had loved to put mud in his mouth even when he was still being breastfed. He needed to feel dirt in order to rest at night. His mother had made mud balls for him to hold as he slept.

We stacked the side of the trench that faced the enemy with sandbags and added wooden supports to its exterior.

We repaired the bunkers on the back wall and filled in the puddles with dirt, even installing a wooden platform to drain the water after we did so.

Boss Cai was the oldest, but he worked no less. We tried to stop him from carrying sandbags, but he ignored us. Da Zhuang whispered to me, "Boss Cai reminds me of my ox."

Old Shuan said, "I guessed right, he has to have been a martial arts master. Y'know the saying that skill's better than strength? Boss Cai's using them kung-fu skills to move sandbags. He walks as if the bag's empty."

Woody came to inspect our work around noon. George returned a few minutes before he arrived, wiping mud-stained hands over his clothes to give the impression that he had been working all along. Woody told him that our team had done the job quickly and well. Grinning, George said that despite the formidable nature of the task, our section was more than up to it. I turned to look at Edward, who was leaning against the wall, his sweat streaming over an unconcerned expression. I wanted to kick him, make him say something.

We spent our break in the trench, eating our tinned meat and stale bread. Woody and the foremen sat at a makeshift table outside the trench and enjoyed a meal from the chef, smoking and drinking all the while.

Two-Horses was sitting on a sandbag, his shirt soaked with sweat. He asked me what George had said, so I told him what I had understood from the conversation. He tore a piece of bread and stuffed it into his mouth. Through chews, he said, "Why don' Edward do nothin' 'bout that lyin' son of a bitch?"

"I'm wondering the same thing," I said.

Da Zhuang gulped a mouthful of water from the

canteen, belched, and said, "Summin' went wrong with that guy in his ma's belly."

"I quite like him," Old Shaun said. "Which of the Brits talk to us other than him? Never mind work with us." He turned to face Boss Cai. "How d'you see it?"

Boss Cai still looked as dignified as ever, sitting on a filthy sandbag and covered in mud. He held a biscuit in his hand as if it were a book for his lecture. He put the biscuit into his mouth and chewed carefully. After swallowing, he replied, "He is troubled."

"Boss Cai," said Old Shaun, "if it doesn't offend you, I want to ask why you came to Europe. Me, Two-Horses and Da Zhuang all came for the money, Delun to see the world. And you?"

Boss Cai picked out another biscuit but did not place it into his mouth. He smiled faintly. "You probably don't know much about the Western invasion of China in 1900 and 1901."

"The teacher taught us a little about this in school," I said. "We also saw a few photographs of foreign soldiers in Beijing and Tianjin."

Boss Cai nodded. "In September, a German named Waldersee led his army into Beijing and Tianjin. By then, the two cities had already fallen to other invading armies. But Waldersee still had some fight in him, so he invaded the surrounding areas. His army was ferocious and brutal. They killed everyone indiscriminately. Even the elderly, women and children. The people took to calling German soldiers 'Huns' because of their savagery. Later, the Qing government surrendered and signed a treaty with the eight coalition forces, agreeing to pay them more than four hundred million taels of silver."

"Four hundred million!" Two-Horses shouted. "We'll be payin' that 'til the end of time!"

"I fled from Beijing to Shanhai Pass," Boss Cai went on. "But Germans hung their flags over the tower walls there, too. After that, I went to Baoding."

"So you hate Germans?" asked Old Shuan.

Boss Cai did not answer.

George wandered over, trying to ingratiate himself with us a little after seeing that we were ignoring him. "I just spoke with Lieutenant-Colonel Wilson. Tomorrow everyone in our section will be given three more tins of food and two more packs of biscuits."

Nobody paid him any attention. He squatted beside Da Zhuang and one of the others and said slowly, "You know, Edward is a deserter." He paused and, seeing that we were all watching him, took a pack of cigarettes out of his pocket and handed them around. The appeal of the cigarettes was too great, and everyone took one except for Boss Cai. We lit up with his lighter, and soon the trench billowed with smoke.

"He wanted to go home, so he shot his own foot," George continued. "The military doctor exposed him, saying there were gunpowder marks and burning on the wound. The bullet entry point and gunpowder residue were on the same side, in his instep. The army was going to execute Edward, but instead decided to send him and the others who had tried the same trick to no-man's land between the French and German forces. Either the Germans would shoot them, or they'd freeze to death. Edward's lucky, still breathing a week later. Somebody felt sorry for him and brought him back, then a priest begged for his life. I don't know how such a coward was sent to the labour camp."

Oh, I sighed to myself, that's what it's about. Perhaps

Edward feels inferior to the other soldiers, so he doesn't want to be around them. Or perhaps he's always alone because they despise and reject him.

I was disgusted with George for using Edward's past like that. "George," I said. "We all like Edward. Please don't say such things. He is no coward."

"What's up with wantin' to go home?" protested Two-Horses.

George scoffed, "If all the soldiers went home, who would fight the war?"

"Wars are all started by the rich," said Old Shuan. "They want more money, more land. What poor man wants to fight?"

"It ain't that I wanna fight, but I does wanna gun," Da Zhuang said. "Used to 'ave all these acres o' land, but a man from the village who knew people in the local army fancied it, so he says it's his family inheritance. Gotta fake deed 'n everythin'. 'E said if I didn't givvit, then he'd 'ave me in jail. If I 'ad a gun..." He pretended to take aim and turned to George. "Bang! I sends him straight t'see Yama, King o' Hell."

Spooked by Da Zhuang, George made some excuse to leave. We all laughed loudly, and even Boss Cai cracked a smile.

We worked until dark. At dinner we were so tired that we didn't know what we were eating. We were just mechanically stuffing things into our mouths.

While we were still eating, a mob of dreadful grey rats emerged from the trenches, squeaking greedily, sending goosebumps all over my body. They were all so fat. How could have they become so fat in such a barren wasteland?

We beat them off with our shovels, stamped on them

and whipped them ferociously with our coats. Soon their bodies piled up. But for every one killed, more scuttled out. They weren't only after our food, but ran up our legs. Their disgusting, slippery tails swept across my neck and face. I hit at them as I jumped. If I had been moving even a little more slowly, I'm sure they would have eaten me alive.

They seemed to admit defeat after a while, suddenly hitting a retreat. I stomped on one that was too slow to flee. It struggled desperately, screaming, then abruptly went still. When I tried to lift my foot, I found that my whole leg had cramped and stiffened, like a piece of wood outside my body. It took me a while to massage it back to life.

Our section alone killed at least a hundred rats. We stayed to bury them despite our cramps and exhaustion, digging a mass grave outside the trenches beside the barbed wire. Two-Horses kept looking back as we left, as if afraid that the dead rodents could emerge from their pits for revenge. He said he feared nothing in heaven or earth other than rats. A fortune teller had once told him that rats had a vendetta against him from a previous life, and so he must avoid them at all costs in this one.

We slept in the trenches that night, laying sandbags and wooden planks on the ground as beds. One man fell asleep the moment he sat down, his body askew and his head lolling as if his neck were broken. Most of us slept in the bunkers on the back wall, some spacious enough to sleep seven or eight men. Two-Horses was afraid there would be rats inside, so we slept outside together. It wasn't too cold, thankfully. A coat and blanket provided adequate protection against the elements.

I don't know how long I slept before the cold woke me. I

opened my eyes to see snowflakes fluttering down like butterflies in the charcoal sky.

Trancelike, I found myself back in my childhood. My siblings and I were laughing and playing in our garden one early winter morning. There was snow everywhere: hanging from the bare tree branches, spreading across the stone bridge, piling up over the rockery. The *lamei* wintersweet flowers were blooming in shades of red and yellow, astonishingly bright and fragrant. We started a snowball fight, picking up the fine, fresh snow with our little hands frozen red, squeezing the powder into balls. Sometimes we were too hasty, and the snowball would fall apart in the air before reaching its target. Whoever got hit would not give up, but launch one back at their attacker straight away.

Tired of the game, we pushed open the heavy wooden doors to the rear of the garden and walked out into the street. The stalls were already busy, the sound of men hawking their wares reverberating in our ears. The stalls we lingered at the longest were of course the ones selling toys or sweets: kites, slingshots, spinning tops, wooden swords, chicken-feather shuttlecocks, red and green paper windmills, sugar-coated hawthorn and sugar figurines, all of these plus a few things we had never even seen before. We took out all the copper coins from our pockets and fussed over what to buy. We sang on the way home, skipping and jumping, the sweat on our faces gleaming in the sunlight.

I stuck out my tongue to catch a snowflake. Cold, a little sweet.

"Damn it!" said Two-Horses, sitting up. "This cursed weather, is it gonna freeze us all to death?" He saw my expression and said, "Ge, what you smilin' for?"

"Am I smiling?" I grinned and laughed.

He rubbed his eyes sleepily. "Let's find somewhere sheltered to sleep. Rather get bit by rats than freeze to death."

We found a bunker that wasn't too wet. It even had a thin layer of rice straw and wooden planks overhead.

I slept soundly, perhaps with that smile on my face the whole time.

16

IT RAINED AND SNOWED CONTINUOUSLY for three days. The trenches were so thick with mud that sometimes your foot would emerge from the bog without its shoe.

We did not stop working, every day from dawn until dusk. Our bodies were soaked despite our raincoats, and many people developed itchy, painful patches of prune-coloured frostbite on their hands and feet. Their sores swelled and made it difficult to wear shoes. The doctors could do nothing to help, so we used all kinds of folk remedies, rubbing the affected areas with snow, saliva or grass roots.

Sometimes the wounds would break, and pus would pour out to reveal red flesh inside. The slightest touch was excruciating. Some had feet so frozen that they looked like blue-purple turnips, which their friends would place against their own chests to warm them up.

Old Shuan advised everyone in our section to remove their shoes every few hours and massage the soles of their feet to prevent frostbite. We rubbed our hands and bodies constantly to keep the blood circulating. Before sleeping, we would remove our clothes and do exercises under Old Shuan's instruction. Then we got into our straw beds with cold blankets, which that way at least stayed dry.

We finished our food quickly and soon received more: black bread, frozen solid, and canned horse meat that was hard and sour. We wouldn't have touched it if we weren't starving.

"What a sin," said Da Zhuang. "'Ow can you eat an 'orse? 'Orses, dragons and phoenixes are all in the same family, they got God's protection. This is bad luck, this." Many of us agreed, but with starvation as the only other option, we could only wrinkle our brows as we swallowed.

Some of the men began to cough, others ran a fever. The sick talked nonsense in their sleep or cried out in terror. The gloomy weather, muddy trenches, our damp, stinking clothing, the neither warm nor waterproof canvas shoes, and the blisters, rashes and frostbite on our bodies were all unbearable, making us pine for home. We found ourselves unable to work at the same pace as before. Some, after sitting on a sandbag to rest, failed to stand back up. Their legs were just too weak. Some could shovel only a handful at a time. We slowed our pace: a jog became a walk, a walk became an idle. By noon we had accomplished only a fifth of what we had managed the previous day.

Our neighbouring section was known for its harsh discipline. It was led by a Brit named Larry, who employed frequent physical punishment. One day, Larry saw a man resting on a sandbag and whipped him, accusing him of being lazy. The man collapsed with one crack of the whip, shielding his head with his arms. Another British foreman stood nearby watching, his arms folded. The rest of the section stopped what they were doing to watch, but nobody moved.

Two-Horses and I exchanged glances before rushing to the man on the ground. The rest of our section came after us, denouncing Larry. Behind us, George yelled, "Don't get involved!" Edward looked at us with admiration, not daring to offend Larry himself. Not expecting such a reaction from us, Larry retreated a few steps before turning to flee and shouting in broken Chinese, "Reform camp, you!"

Like their commanders, these British foremen could utter only a few simple words in Chinese. They felt it was beneath them to learn what they saw as a coolie language, but they all knew how to say "work" and "reform camp". They probably thought this was enough to deal with the Chinese, and all the rest could be said with whips and bullets.

Nobody in our section had been to the "reform camp", but we had all heard about the horrors inside: people strung up and beaten every day, their bodies scraped with a wire brush.

Tom hurried over to ask what had happened. He looked sympathetic, but what could he do? He was only a translator.

Though we had been in France barely a fortnight, we had learned from earlier arrivals that the British officers not only ignored but encouraged iron-fisted measures from the foremen, telling them to treat us like fathers disciplining stubborn and ill-behaved children.

"I'm sorry," said Tom, with pain and guilt in his eyes.

Before we left for Arras, Tom had learned that I could

speak a little French and English. He chatted with me about this and that, including literature. He had considered me a friend since, and as I watched him apologising one by one to the Chinese present, I knew that he was trying to apologise for the arrogance of all white people.

Softly, he added, "Larry's wife and child were killed in a German air raid last year. That's why he has a foul temper."

I didn't know how to respond. Nothing I could say seemed right.

Woody called the foremen to a meeting that afternoon. We could hear him yelling at them all the way from the trenches. He wasn't admonishing their cruelty, he was saying that we were working too slowly.

On the next morning, the sky finally cleared. The sun warmed our bodies, making us want to doze off. We stripped, some completely, and hung our clothes to dry on the barbed wire and shrubbery outside the trenches. Nobody minded the nudity with no women around, but I kept my trousers on – laughing at my own misplaced sense of propriety.

More of the foremen joined in our labour in an attempt to boost morale. Even George had a try. Woody had probably warned them that their wages would be docked if they failed to quicken our pace. We earned one franc a day, they earned ten.

We devised some labour-saving tactics, for example making a conveyor belt between the trenches from smooth-planed wooden planks, which saved us from having to carry the sandbags. This, and our increased speed, earned us a satisfied smile from Woody.

That evening, we all received an unexpected cup of tea. To tell the truth it was just hot water with a hint of flavour, but we were thrilled to have something hot in our bellies nonetheless. It was then that a group of around two hundred appeared, coming towards us in the same direction from which we'd come. Woody must have known they were coming, he had been looking that way all along.

It was the first time I had seen a company of marching British soldiers. Their faces were gloomy and lethargic. They stumbled like drunks under the weight of their gear. They had rifles, canteens, backpacks and some also carried cookware, shovels or pickaxes. Their long coats had endured the baptism of the elements for so long that their original colour was hidden beneath a layer of mud. Some had unkempt hair, others sported hats of every description. There were metal helmets, military caps, fur hats, cotton caps with earflaps, some just a strip of cloth around the forehead. Their shoes also varied in style, but mostly they wore boots, more effective at keeping out the cold than our canvas shoes.

Five wagons swayed among the ranks, piled high with gear. The exhausted, pitiful horses in their reins walked with their heads bowed. One, a white-chested brown mare, must have realised it was almost time to rest. It raised its head and whinnied.

The soldiers looked at us curiously, and we looked curiously back. Both groups were unbelievably dirty and foul-smelling.

Late sunlight bathed the trenches and bomb craters with a pale orange glow. Its warmth made that war-torn world seem a little more human.

One soldier removed the vest he wore over his coat and sat on the ground with a thud. With that, the brief silence was broken. The other soldiers copied him, putting down tins, bread, biscuits, books, playing cards, metal lunchboxes, glass bottles containing goodness knows what, and other such items. Some ate and drank, others cleaned mud from their rifles and ammunition. Some read or wrote letters, others caught lice, slept, or simply chatted and played cards. None greeted us. It was as if we didn't exist.

Woody sent us back to work after speaking with the newly arrived officer, instructing Tom to tell us that we would be returning to camp after dinner. Woody tried to keep his expression neutral, but it was obvious he was happy to leave that cursed place.

A handful of soldiers jumped into the newly repaired trenches to inspect our work. There was a lad around my age among them, red-haired and thick-lipped. He turned to us, grinned and stuck up his thumb.

Outside the trenches, some of the soldiers began to sing, their songs interspersed with drunken shouts. Many of them played cards while lit cigarettes dangled from their mouths.

"They don't looks like they's goin' to war," Two-Horses said to me while he worked.

Old Shuan hammered a wooden stake into the ground. "Don't look at them all lively now, after the battle's over there'll only be half left. Soldier's life, you have to make merry while you can cos next minute who knows what'll happen? When I was a soldier, the best thing of all was sleep. No matter where, even if I was on the edge of some latrine pit or some rats' nest. As long as there ain't sirens or gunfire, I'd be happy."

Thinking of the photograph in my pocket and the red-haired young man who had smiled at us, I said, "We made the trenches sturdier. Perhaps we've helped them win this battle."

Da Zhuang came closer. "George says the German trenches are big enough to drive a tank through!"

"That guy! When Germans come, he'll be the first to surrender." Two-Horses spat on the ground. "With us lot digging' their trenches, the Brits can't lose. Guaranteed!"

Da Zhuang rolled his eyes. "*Xinqiu*! Your guarantee isn't worth shit."

"What you just call me? What's *xinqiu*?"

"*Xinqiu*! Means stupid, stupid!"

"Yeah, even Douglas Haig wouldn't guarantee that," interrupted Old Shuan.

"Who?" asked Two-Horses.

"The commander of the British Army! They call him 'Butcher of the Somme'." Old Shaun knew a lot about current affairs because he was always asking about the war's progress at camp. Once a soldier, always a soldier.

"What's he called that for?"

"Because so many people dies when he's in command. D'you know how many British soldiers were hurt or died at the Battle of the Somme last year? First day, more'n sixty thousand!"

"Germans is fierce!" Da Zhuang exclaimed.

Two-Horses said nothing, just lowered his head and shovelled.

I noticed that Boss Cai kept looking towards the soldiers outside the trench, as if he wished to join them.

Two-Horses nudged me. I followed his gaze to see that Edward had slunk his way into a bunker to smoke. He was lurking in shadows, the end of his cigarette glowing.

We set off after our usual meal of black bread and tinned horse meat. Some had to be supported or carried because of the frostbite.

Half an hour later, a flare appeared in the sky from the direction of the trenches. It was far behind us by then, looking like a spark flying out of kindling.

"Is they settin' off fireworks?" asked Da Zhuang.

"The Germans have arrived," answered Boss Cai, every syllable like a bullet spat through his teeth.

17

David arrived in Arras at around noon. He walked from the train station to the old town, vibrant with bars, restaurants and boutique hotels. Colourful flowers decorated the streets, adding their fragrance to the October breeze.

He checked into a hotel where he had lunch and a nap before taking a tour bus into the countryside. After visiting Vauban Citadel, he returned to the town and bought souvenirs in a shop on Heroes Square. A corkscrew for the wine-loving Mr Wang, postcards of local landmarks for Pierre, key chains and mini snow globes for the grandchildren, and a stone pendant necklace for his daughter. She had the same taste in jewellery as Marguerite, preferring simplicity. It had been two days since he spoke to her last, he thought. Should he call home this evening?

This was the fifth time in his life that he had been to Arras. The first and second occasions had been as a labourer, the following two as a mechanic sent to help with the reconstruction efforts by L'Usine de machines Faustin. He had contributed to the restoration of the Baroque buildings in the old town centre.

David sat on a wooden bench in a small park, watching all the passers-by. A street artist was performing, and he noticed two lovers kissing on the balcony of a two-storey apartment opposite. Tranquillity all around. No destruction from artillery fire, no charred animals, nobody lost in despair.

He closed his eyes, and an image invaded his mind. A shell crater before him, a blood-soaked hand emerging from the dirt. Its fingers were spread and its knuckles bent, spasming convulsively in its struggle to reach help from those above. Another image. A corpse, its flesh churned into the dirt by tank treads. It crawled with flies, rats gnashed their teeth.

"They're going to eat me! Save me!" He had called out innumerable times in his sleep, and innumerable times Marguerite had wiped the cold sweat from his face and comforted him like a child. "Don't be afraid, I'm here."

He opened his eyes. Sunlight warmed his face. The street artist twirled a hoop, the lovers kissed. Children laughed and played. What, he wondered, is real life? Is it the vivid memory of the past, or the present before your eyes?

A shout came from behind him in Beijing-accented Mandarin, "Watch out! Don't run!" He turned to see a man in his early sixties trying to catch a small child, likely his grandson, who was running around the flowers and shrubbery. The boy hid behind a large tree, giggling, his body shaking with joy. He waited for his grandpa to reach the tree, then ran like a fawn to a rose bush nearby.

"Careful, watch out for the thorns!" He had hardly finished speaking when his grandson clasped his hands and wailed. Though the man was not agile, he rushed to the child and took him in his arms, examining where the roses had caught him, kissing his little hand. Remembering his own grandchildren, David's heart filled with guilt.

The old man spotted David, and asked him in a tone of pleasant surprise, "*Parlez-vous chinois?*"

David nodded and the old man switched to Mandarin to say that he was a retired engineer who had come from Beijing to visit his relatives two months ago. "Call me Old Zhao," he said, smiling. "There aren't many Chinese here, I'm bored to death."

David said he lived in Paris and was here as a tourist.

Old Zhao extended his thumb. "Brave of you!" Then he began to complain. "I want to go back to China but I hate to part with Miguel, it's like being in prison here. I don't understand a word anybody's saying, I can't drive and I daren't spend any money." Old Zhao stroked his grandson's head and continued, "My son and daughter-in-law opened a restaurant, so they leave at five in the morning and come home at ten at night. I try to persuade them to come back to China, but they don't listen. They say they're going to get money and become big names. I said, even if you do, what then? Even if they stay here, they're still Chinese. They'll always be foreigners in the eyes of the French."

David's heart sank as he listened. He felt a cold wind blowing on his face. Old Zhao was right, he thought to himself.

Old Zhao set his grandson down to play with the fallen leaves. "China is poorer and more backward than France, but it's been in a constant state of war for five thousand years and has only become stable in the past seven or eight. Let's take the last hundred years, first there were the two Opium Wars, then the Eight Powers invaded. We didn't fight in the

First World War, but the Japanese invaded and we were roped into the Second. Then there was the civil war been the Kuomintang and the Communists. I joined the army when I was fifteen to fight the Japanese, then the Kuomintang, then Mao came to power and the Communist Party ruled. I finally thought we could be at peace, but political struggles continued one after the other. I was imprisoned for a few years myself for speaking out in the Anti-Rightist campaign in the fifties, and then the Cultural Revolution began. Me, I didn't dare say anything that time and I kept my head down, but I was still labelled a rightist and sent to a labour reform camp in Jiangxi. I returned to my former post and was reunited with my family ten years later." Old Zhao smiled at David. "If you'd have been in China during the Cultural Revolution, you'd have been beaten and lost your life just because you'd lived in France through all this history."

David had read about these events in books and newspapers, and heard about them from Chinese friends. It was difficult to get hold of Chinese books in Paris, but Mr Wang received a big box of them every six months from a trusted source in China. Wang said that he needed the "spiritual nourishment" to help him digest all the cheese and wine.

David was silent for a while before he spoke. "You said that China did not participate in the First World War, but that's not true. China went to war."

That piqued Old Zhao's interest. "Really? Tell me all about it. China declared war on Germany in 1917, but it was just empty talk and they didn't actually send anyone to Europe to help. If China had fought, would the leaders of the Entente have handed over sovereignty of Shandong Province from Germany to Japan in the Treaty of Versailles?"

Certain things can never be fully explained, thought David. Better they remain hidden in forgotten corners.

The park was quiet. Clear and sonorous birdsong warbled in the air. Miguel lifted his head and dashed at a few birds standing on an oak branch. "Careful, don't fall!" Old Zhao shouted after him.

David said, "You go on playing with your grandson, I need to get going."

"OK, safe travels." Old Zhao seemed unwilling to part. "If you have the chance, go home and see it. So much has changed."

David nodded, but when he turned to leave, he found his eyes suddenly full of tears. Home: the word was like a string tugging at his heart, creating a dull ache. He had destroyed his home in China. Not only that, but he had also made Marguerite lose hers in Lyon.

"Delun, why do you want to move to Paris? What for?" Marguerite's question rang in his ears, her eyes full of condemnation and pleading.

Old Zhao watched David's figure as it receded into the distance: Where is such an old man going on his own?

18

AFTER TWO DAYS BACK AT CAMP, our section was one of six deployed by train to Dunkirk. There, we would transport ammunition and repair the railway. The damage at Dunkirk was lighter, with many taller buildings still intact despite evidence of cannon fire. Trams and military trucks ran supplies through the streets, and there were several temporary factories that had already been erected by labourers from Vietnam and India.

It was light work compared with the trenches. We also had slightly better food, even though our stomachs still grumbled with hunger. Meals were mostly just a few thin pieces of meat mixed with potatoes and vegetable leaves, and a soup that may as well have been the water used to wash the pot after cooking. But at least it was hot.

We tried to keep our minds off food, just mechanically stick to our labour. The weather had warmed and we no longer needed our jackets, but even so we would shiver involuntarily, the heat sapped from our bodies.

The camp, near a village named Sair, was enclosed by

barbed wire just like the one in Loyelle – but now there were two layers. Guarded by soldiers, the outermost fence reached two metres high. Within, it had been divided into several areas including accommodation, lavatories, kitchens, a hospital and a prison. The prison was split from the rest with a row of buildings and trees. People were sent there for disobeying orders, stealing or otherwise violating rules. We heard on arrival that it had a dozen inmates. Several of them had tried to desert, and one had strangled another man to death with his belt after a gambling argument.

The British had forbidden gambling within the camp, but our lives were so tedious since we weren't allowed to leave that it became a popular pastime anyway. The British overlooked it, as long as there was no fuss.

We repaired the railway for a week before lining up early one morning to go to L'Usine Bertrand Military Factory. We could see rows of factory buildings even from a distance in the otherwise barren landscape. A long stretch of brown, canvas-covered military vehicles drove past us, loaded with boxes of ammunition.

Beside me, Two-Horses clicked his tongue in admiration and whispered, "See 'em? All the drivers is girls."

"Whaddya expect?" said Da Zhuang from behind him. "Men're at war."

"When can I gets a car then?"

"Get friendly with those women," I joked. "Maybe they'll let you touch the steering wheel."

"Ge, you've been readin' that precious book o' yours, yeah? Teach me some French."

No matter how tired I was, I studied my French dictionary every day. It was a form of escapism. Even if I learned just two or three new words, it was the only way I could make myself feel like I wasn't just some machine. Tom also taught me French whenever he had time. He had an idea to give the labourers French classes and wanted me to be his assistant. Of course, I agreed.

"*Bonjour*," I said to Two-Horses.

He repeated after me.

Da Zhuang laughed. "Sounds like you're sayin' '*bang zhu*'."

It did indeed sound like "tress the pig" in Mandarin.

"'Ow would I say, 'Miss, you're amazin'?" Two-Horses asked.

"Hasn't even met them yet, and he's already lickin' their arses!" said Old Shaun.

I told Two-Horses how to say his line.

Having learned his two sentences, Two-Horses assessed our surroundings. The British soldiers originally by our side had gone to speak with the officer at the front. Seeing this, he began to call out, "*Bang zhu!*"

You had to admire his audacity. According to Old Shaun, Two-Horses was fearless and thick-skinned. Da Zhuang, however, would tell you that a dead pig isn't afraid of boiling water. Boss Cai was fond of Two-Horses and had been teaching him to read. When I tried, Two-Horses was distracted and impatient, but with Boss Cai he behaved himself and learned a lot.

The driver shot him a glance.

Another truck came. Two-Horses turned to stick his thumb up at the driver, then said the line I had just taught him, "You're amazing!" His pronunciation was dreadful, but she suddenly cracked a smile and gave him the thumbs up back.

Two-Horses was elated. "Look, she understood!"

We had already encountered plenty of French women while labouring on the railway. They were all workers too, some of them quite young, digging out the route and laying sleepers just like us. They worked some distance away and there were always soldiers stationed between us, but they would sometimes stop to look in our direction then burst into laughter. Their voices made us forget our hunger and exhaustion, teased us, stirred our hearts until they were restless as thumping rabbits in our chests. We could only distract ourselves from our youthful impulses by putting our full strength into work.

I thought of Lin Yumei, her firm and delicate skin. Unlike my sisters, she never covered her mouth when she laughed but grinned openly to reveal large canine teeth. We met in a grove a few miles from school one day after class. I made an excuse to leave my friends, and she told her parents she was going out with hers. The grass was dotted with white wildflowers, a stream gurgled merrily beneath poplar and eucalyptus trees, a breeze blew through our hair. I asked her what she planned to do with her life. She said that she wanted to run a school for girls, where they could learn science, engineering and medicine just like the boys. She asked me the same question, and I told her that I wanted to run the school with her.

After an internal battle, I took her hand in mine. We were too shy to look at each other's faces but watched in silence as fallen leaves floated along the surface of the water. Our hearts were so happy that they yearned to drift with the birds above.

She changed her mind two weeks later. That day, a black sedan arrived at school to pick her up. She rolled down the rear car window and, seeing me staring dumbfounded in her direction, hurried to close it again. She returned the next day with a diamond ring on her finger and gold pendants in her ears, then she left for good. My classmates said that a warlord had taken a fancy to her and she had gone to be his concubine.

I also thought of Miss Lu, but her image was only a flash in my mind. Of course I felt guilty, but I would rather allow that memory to fade like the last of the snow melting away beneath spring sunlight.

"Ge, you ever 'ad a girl?" Two-Horses voice broke my reverie.

I shook my head. I think what he meant to ask was whether I had ever slept with a woman.

"Delun wouldn't go that kind o' place for fun," said Da Zhuang.

"What's up with that kind of place? Just the smell of 'em makes you go weak. You can't be tellin' me you've never been."

"And spend my hard-earn cash, my sweat and blood on that kind o' girl? I'm keepin' my money for a respectable woman."

"You haven't..." Two-Horses muttered, then stopped when he saw George coming over from the back of the line.

We were right by the armaments factory now, a huge rectangular building with people coming and going like ants. We could see rows of densely packed shells through the open doors, a small group of people appearing to inspect for quality control among the waist-height lines.

Old Shuan let out a sound of appreciation.

We entered a steel-framed artillery warehouse, five metres high and thirty long. It contained a variety of wooden crates and two ground rails for flatbeds. Our task was to pack ammunition from another factory building and load it onto trucks headed for the front lines.

Our supervisor was a short, stout Frenchman in his early fifties with a beer belly and an air of suspicion as he sized us up. George knew a little French and helped with the translation.

A group of French women would be loading cargo with us, our first close contact with locals. Every time we arrived at a new camp, our British supervisors would warn us repeatedly to stay away from them. They told us that violators would be harshly punished, even lashed.

Most of the women were middle-aged, wearing loose, dark grey overalls tied at the waist, an apron over their chests. There were also several younger women. They had their hair twisted into braids or hung loose. Though dressed in the same unflattering overalls, their steps were a light dance, their eyes clear and bright, wearing wildflowers behind their ears or in their braids. We were so close that we could smell their perfume!

A few of the women looked at us with pursed lips and frowns as if they couldn't bear the stench of our unwashed bodies. Others however were very kind, greeting us with smiles. They would sometimes suddenly look up at us and burst into laughter as they chatted. This made us bashful and a little uneasy. Was your hat crooked, your shirt back-to-front, your face stained with oil? If you looked down to check, their laughter would ring out even higher. Their voices carried us along with them and we would step up our pace. Our speed would show off how well we worked while also allowing them to rest a little, talk more, laugh more.

I strained to hear what they were saying, but they spoke too quickly. I only caught the odd inconsequential word like "tomorrow", "cream", "factory", "apple" or people's names – all with that throaty "r" sound. The flow of their voices, rippling as if they were reading poetry, was lovely to hear.

They were glad we were there to help. With us beside them, they didn't have to carry those heavy boxes. Their work was more pleasurable and, most important, much faster.

I remembered those Canadian women who had braved the bitter cold to welcome us at that train station. They must have had relatives on the battlefield. Perhaps we had even seen their fathers, brothers and sons on the field in Arras.

We had never before seen this many guns, this much ammunition, this many hand grenades and artillery shells. They were cold to the touch, imbued with the callous inhumanity of metal.

Old Shuan and I were pulling along a fully loaded flatbed when he sighed and said, "You can't compare this lot to the guns we 'ad when I was a soldier. These damned machine guns, how many people'll they mow down! A soldier survives one battle just to risk death the next. Bullets don't have eyes do they, life and death, it's all up to fate." He sighed again. "Seriously, all fate."

How many women, I wondered, were being made widows by this war? How many, right at this moment, were losing their brothers and sons?

19

Two-Horses was in a particularly good mood at dinner. As he drank his potato soup, his smile would have anyone believe he was sipping braised pork.

What really caused his smile, however, was that he had become friendly with a black-haired, grey-eyed French girl in the factory. He was good at talking to her, gesturing to her and making her giggle while managing to maintain his pace, working at an extraordinary speed as if he had suddenly grown three heads and six arms.

"What did you two talk about?" I asked.

"Lots!" His expression was triumphant, but of course he was bragging. He had not been with her for long before George found an excuse to send him somewhere else.

We gathered around him, joined by some men from the other teams as we squatted to listen. We were staying in an idle shoe factory, our blankets spread on the cement floor to serve as beds. It was mid-April, but the air was still cold through its many broken windows. We had collected all manner of ragged clothing and bits of cotton under our bodies to keep out the worst of it.

"Go on, tell us," I said.

"She was a teacher, teachin' little kids," Two-Horses said. "She 'as an older brother and an older sister. The brother's on the front lines and her sister's married with three kids. She says there's lots of trees outside her 'ouse, and lots of flowers too. One of them trees she says is big enough for four people to touch 'round the trunk. Summertime, they've all friends comin' over to eat under it. They's got a snow-white tablecloth and they puts flowers on top. They got warm bread, soft too, like our rice cakes what've just been steamed. All kinds of food, sweet, salty, spicy, you name it. The smell brings loads o' bees, she got stung by one, right on the corner of her mouth." He pointed to the right side of his mouth. "She got a big lump right there, and it 'urt to eat for a really long time."

Everyone knew he was making it up, but nobody stopped him. More gathered around.

"What else?" somebody urged him on.

"Also, she loves singing, and she goes to the fields by 'erself to sing. They're just like the ones we got in Shandong, with corn, sorghum, wheat, soy, cotton—"

"Rapeseed," someone added.

"Yeah, and sweet-smellin' rapeseed flowers," Two-Horses confirmed.

People continued to add their own.

"Rice!"

"Millet!"

"Mung beans and runner beans!"

"Y'all don't forget wild hemp!"

"Don't you worry," said Two-Horses. "These fields 'ave

got it all. Yantai apples, golden jujube, Cangshan garlic, Zhangqiu spring onions. Packed full with all kinds, with rich dense soil that'll grow anything, and all the crops and fruit trees don't even know what a locust looks like. Once the seeds is planted, you can just go strollin' down to the fields to see. Few days later, they're ready to harvest. Those Zhangqiu onions, green and tender and big–"

"I planted spring onions!" someone in the crowd called out. "Those onions couldn't even compare! Bit spicy, bit sweet, have 'em raw, cold, stir fried, seasoned, stuffed with meat, however you eat 'em they're gonna be delicious."

Everybody nodded.

"When she sings, the birds in the trees all joins in with 'er." Two-Horses began to whistle, imitating different kinds of birdsong. Those who could joined in, and suddenly we found ourselves in a world of birds.

That's how the whistling competition began.

But then a few British guards who had been standing outside the doors heard our noise and charged in with their guns, shattering the atmosphere. Everybody dispersed, returning to their own spaces.

The lights went out.

After Two-Horses and I lay down, he said to me softly, "Gonna see that girl again tomorrow. 'Er teeth are so white when she smiles. I've never seen such white teeth. No idea 'ow much tooth powder you'd 'ave to use every day to get teeth like 'ers. 'Er eyes are pretty, too. I said *bonjour*, and she laughed, then I says, *you're amazing*, and she laughed even more."

"You're really learning," I said.

"Teach me some more. 'Good morning', 'good afternoon', 'good evening', 'ow do you say all that?"

I laughed. "Sure you can use 'good morning' and 'good afternoon', but when are you ever going to say, 'good evening'?"

"Doesn't matter, just knowin' 'ow to say it shows I've got a good brain."

"You do have a good brain! You just need to be a little more patient."

"Who says I'm not patient? From tomorrow on, I'm gonna study French with you every day." After a while, he added, "Ge, how old do you reckon she is?"

"Eighteen or nineteen, maybe."

"Her 'ands look like she's done farm work, 'er arms are strong and she's got a tan on her face. There's a grey mole on the right corner of her mouth, 'bout the size of a sesame seed."

"Wow, you've looked at her really carefully."

He chuckled, embarrassed. "Ge, tell me how to say 'you're pretty' in French."

"I don't know how."

"Well then, what's the use of learning foreign languages?"

"I know how to say apple blossom. You can tell her she's like an apple blossom."

I repeated the line to him a few times. I could hear him practising as I fell asleep.

That night I dreamed of the vast wheat fields back in my hometown, stretching golden yellow all the way to the sky. I walked through them with my arms open, flowing through the ripe ears of wheat.

20

W᠎E WORKED IN THAT FACTORY FOR TWO WEEKS. Since we exceeded our quotas every day, our French supervisor began to smile, even patting us on the shoulder occasionally to praise us or tell us to take a break. The French were friendly compared with the Brits.

My French improved considerably in that short period, thanks mostly to Tom. He began those French classes for half an hour each day. At first only a few joined, including me and Two-Horses, but soon we were nearly a hundred. Because I was his assistant, he gave me an additional half-hour of class each day and even a few French novels, including Stendhal's *Le Rouge et le Noir*. I would ask him for help whenever I had time outside class, too.

The girl that Two-Horses liked did not reappear. Each morning he would walk into the factory full of expectation, looking for her in the crowd. His eyes would dim once he realised that she was not there, and he set to work with his head lowered.

He no longer squatted down with everybody else back at

the barracks to chat or play games. He didn't even want to chat with me. Instead, he would sit off in a corner by himself. When we were in the trenches, Boss Cai found a folding knife about half the size of a palm and had given it to Two-Horses. Two-Horses had considered this a treasure ever since, carrying it wherever he went. Now, it came in handy. He would carve things on pieces of wood and bullet casings, which were very easy to find.

Da Zhuang and Old Shuan teased him, saying that the black-haired beauty of France had got married and moved away. Two-Horses listened, then felled big Da Zhuang with one kick. Seeing that, Old Shuan added hurriedly that she was neither married nor moved, but they still made fun of him behind his back.

Two-Horses attended all of Tom's French lessons and pestered me to teach him before bed each night. He asked me sentences like, "Do you have livestock?", "What did you have for lunch?" and "What colour do you like?" I spelled out the French words phonetically with Chinese characters to help him learn faster. He couldn't read Chinese well either, so I had to create easy-to-remember sentences with the Chinese characters. Soon, he could speak dozens of French sentences with Chinese intonation, even forming new sentences by blending them together himself.

The French girl returned to work in the third week. Her eyelids were red and swollen, her face thinner, but Two-Horses still managed to make her smile. It wasn't only her; all the other women, even those older, stern-faced ones, were amused by his Chinese-style French.

George was sick and hadn't accompanied us to work that day. As for Edward, he wasn't concerned that we would get into trouble and seemed to enjoy the women's laughter. After leading us to the factory, he went outside to smoke.

That night, someone nudged me awake. I opened my eyes to see Two-Horses with a sparkle in his.

"Ge, her name's Ella." I could hear his excitement even through his whisper.

He began to gush with the words he'd been holding back. "I ran into her outside when I'd gone to the toilets. She said her dad had died. She said how he'd died, but I didn't understan'. She says she has loads of younger siblings." He turned to his side and used his hand against his waist, then moved it down incrementally to show all the respective heights of her young brothers and sisters. Ella must have used the same method to tell him about them. "They used to keep pigs, but they ate 'em. I gave 'er a bullet casing carved with birds and flowers on it, she loves it."

He paused as if listening for sounds of movement in the room. Hearing nothing but snores, he extracted a round object from beneath his quilt and handed it to me.

I almost cried out in delight, it was an apple! It was small, but its delicate aroma still wafted into my nose. I sniffed deeply at its skin. It had been more than six months since I had last eaten one.

"Ella gave it me," he said, proudly. "And she says tomorrow she'll gimme two. This one's ours, tomorrow I'll share with the others."

I gave the apple back to him. "You take the first bite."

He took a mouthful and handed it back. I took a bite, holding it in my mouth for a while before I chewed. The sweet, acidic flavour seemed to enter every cell of my body. If I could eat an apple every week, I thought, I'd be willing to spend every waking hour digging trenches.

"Ge, what do women like?"

"They like nice smelling, pretty stuff. Hairpins, scarves, perfume, jewellery, that kind of thing."

He sighed. "But I don't got any o' that."

Suddenly, a horrifying shriek came from outside. Before we could even react, there was another loud noise and then towering flames. The electric lights hanging from the ceiling swung back and forth, sending dust falling over us.

"It's a bomb!" Old Shuan jumped up. "Get out, now!"

The room fell into chaos, everyone surging to the only exit. Two-Horses held tight onto my arm, worried that we might get separated. Old Shuan, Da Zhuang and Boss Cai followed closely behind us. Outside, a plane roared as it swept through the sky overhead.

Many had never seen planes before, so they just stood there staring dumbly until others dragged them onwards.

But where could we hide? More bombs fell with deafening noise. Ahead was a sea of fire, the grove erupting into flames. Everywhere was sound, smoke, people killed or wounded by the explosions.

Some fell to their knees and kowtowed, as if they were begging for the Heavens to spare them. Some tried to scale the barbed wire fences, but in terror their bodies would not heed their instructions and so they fell halfway. More ran around like headless insects, including the British and the foremen. There was no sign of Woody.

A bomb struck the corner of our barracks, sending stone and earth flying. As I looked back at the flaming building, another bomb exploded seven or eight metres from where we stood. Without thinking, I leapt onto Two-Horses and covered him. A hail of rock and dirt hit me, stunning me.

After a while, we stood, our faces covered in mud, our heads spinning, ears ringing.

He felt his arms and legs, and I mine.

He laughed. "We're alive!"

I broke into nervous laughter.

"Oh, son of a bitch!" he exclaimed. "Where's the apple?"

My hands were empty.

"What a waste, we only had two bites."

"Where are Old Shuan, Da Zhuang and Boss Cai?" I asked.

We looked around but couldn't see them.

"They definitely got out." Two-Horses pointed to a hole in the barbed-wire fence.

We started to run over to it, but I fell the moment we began. Only then did I notice the blood flowing from a spot five or six centimetres below my right hip.

"Ge, you're wounded!" Two-Horses cried.

He pulled me onto his back and staggered forward. Many people fled with us, passing together through the barbed wire fence and into a wasteland of waist-height shrubbery and a few trees.

Planes still flitted overhead, dropping several more bombs, missing their mark and harming no one, but setting alight a tree and the surrounding grass.

We ran for a while until we reached a scarcely planted field. We could still hear the sound of explosions, but there was no longer any sign of the planes. My trousers were soaked in blood. I had not felt the pain of it as we fled, but now it pounded unbearably through me.

Two-Horses lay me down carefully, then took off his shirt to wrap my wound. It soaked red in moments.

A dozen or so labourers all came to help. One suggested

that we pack mud into the wound to stem the bleeding, another that we could make a salve by chewing grass, another that the best thing we could do was pray.

We waited there as the explosions began to fade. Finally it went quiet, indicating that the Germans must have withdrawn. But we couldn't go back. We didn't know whether the hospital had withstood the bombing. Even if it had, it would be packed with wounded already.

"I 'ave to take my brother to the 'ospital! It's all my fault." Two-Horses wept.

I wanted to comfort him, tell him not to cry. It was a ridiculous idea to find a hospital so far from the city, what hospital? And even if there was one, would they treat the wounds of a Chinese labourer? At this hour?

Before I could react, Two-Horses had slung me onto his back again. This time, his strength was suddenly much greater, his steps sturdier. He ran along the ridges of the field, wind whistling past my ears. He used French to shout, "Help, help!" The others ran along with him, calling out, hoping that someone in the surrounding farmhouses might hear their cries.

Their voices seemed so insignificant beneath the empty night sky. Like insects that could be crushed to death beneath your fingertips.

I fainted from the pain.

21

When I came to, I found myself lying in front of a white stone farmhouse, its roof slanting above lit windows. An old man with long sideburns stood in the doorway, aiming a shotgun at the kneeling figure of Two-Horses beside me. The others were gone.

A tall, slender young woman came outside, wearing a white nightdress with a black shawl, her hair coiled into a bun. She placed her hand on the man's shoulder. "Grandpa, don't worry. They're not bad people. If André was here, he would help them. I'll get things ready."

The old man nodded in unhappy silence. After the woman had gone back inside, he came to inspect my wound with the gun still raised, then pointed at the open door for Two-Horses to carry me inside.

Perhaps it was the light, or perhaps it was the new hope, but I felt remarkably clear-headed. My injured leg seemed paralysed, lessening the pain. The living room was warm, with several pieces of heavy wooden furniture including a large, packed bookshelf and an antique reading lamp, softly aglow. A fresh scent, like peppermint grass, filled the room. The walls were covered with art and photographs.

It had been a long time since I had been anywhere that could be called a home. Everything was so neat and clean that it seemed like a paradise on Earth. If I could have walked around, I would have liked to pull a few books off that shelf to look through.

The old man gestured for Two-Horses to place me on a long wooden table in the next room, covered with a blue tablecloth. Beside the table there were two wooden basins, the larger one filled with water.

"Hold him down," she said to the two of them and, fearing that Two-Horses would not understand, motioned with her hands. One held my upper body and one my lower, preventing sudden movement. The young woman untied the shirt that Two-Horses had wrapped around my leg and used scissors to cut away my bloody trouser leg, throwing the rags into the basin. Blood splashed onto her nightclothes, but she did not react. She must have had experience treating the wounded.

I lost consciousness again.

Pain awakened me once more as she cleaned my wound with a wet towel. I cried out before remembering where I was. I lowered my head, one hand grasping Two-Horses' hand, the other reaching beneath the table to grip one of its legs.

The young woman sterilised a pair of metal tweezers, then turned to me kindly and said, "This is going to hurt a little."

"I won't move." I closed my eyes.

My heart pounded when the tweezers entered the wound, my grip tightened on Two-Horses' hand. I could have crushed his fingers with just a little more pressure. I gasped, sweat dripping from my face. The old man pressed hard against my feet.

A century never lasted so long. I opened my eyes to see several thumb-sized shards of black in the basin alongside smaller pieces. The woman spoke briefly to the old man and he nodded.

She began to stitch the wound together. My teeth gnashed in agony.

After she had finished with the needle, she leaned over me and smiled, saying nothing. She rinsed the wound's surrounding area once more, then wrapped it in gauze.

I wanted to thank her but lacked the strength to speak. I quickly fell back to sleep.

When I woke, I found that I was sleeping in an extremely comfortable bed, with fresh sheets and a fluffy pillow under my head.

Two-Horses was sleeping by my feet, his back against the wall. He opened his eyes when I moved.

"Ge, you're finally awake!" he said excitedly. "You've slept a whole day." He was wearing a check shirt and black Western trousers that must have been given to him by our rescuers. The outfit quite suited him.

"You 'ad a fever earlier," he said, "but that French girl fed you some soup. She came in the afternoon and a bit later to change your bandages, too."

I did not remember waking, nor drinking the soup.

There was a tray of mashed potato, jam and sliced bread on the table. Two-Horses said he had already eaten, and that this was for me. I hadn't been hungry when I woke, but my stomach grumbled when I saw the food. Two-Horses helped me up and breathed a sigh of relief when he saw me eat. As far as he was concerned, if you could eat then you were going to be OK. He spoke with me a little, then lay on the rug where he quickly fell asleep.

The window beside me was covered with thick brown curtains. I wanted to open it and look out at the moonlight. An ancient poem came to me: "The moon shines bright for everyone to see. Oh, autumn longing, which homes are you visiting?"

It'd be autumn in a few months. Where would I be then? Would I even still be alive? Was my study back home covered in dust? Had the bamboo forest in the garden grown thicker? My younger siblings must have grown much taller. My brother might already be helping Father manage the shop. Mother would naturally be missing me most. What was she doing right now? Two-Horses was sleeping fitfully, making low whimpering sounds from time to time. Was he having a nightmare?

I thought of what that young woman had said to her grandfather the day before. André... who was André? Her husband?

Where was he? Why was she living with her grandfather? What about her parents?

I had seen her wedding photo on the wall. She was wearing a white gown, leaning beside a man in a military uniform. Her face was fuller than it was now, and she had a smile in her eyes.

Was that man André?

We left after she changed my bandages the next morning. She had already used the last of her gauze on me, so cut strips of cloth from her sheets that she could use instead. She gave us a sack of potatoes, five hard-boiled eggs and some clothes. She and her grandfather stood together at the door as we left, watching us all the way out of sight.

I realised then that I had forgotten to ask them their names.

22

For those who wanted to escape, the bombing had been a heaven-sent opportunity. But where could we have fled to?

Back at the barracks we saw that the hospital, residential area and prison were still emitting black smoke. The drill grounds had become a temporary hospital and morgue, where more than two dozen corpses lay on the ground covered in black sheets. Dr Hill treated the injured nearby with the help of some newly trained assistants. Tom moved all over the place asking after the wounded, while Woody and some of the foremen were directing uninjured labourers to clear the rubble.

George spotted us and came to greet us. "I thought you'd run off. Come on, get to work!" He noticed my leg injury and said, "Are you really hurt or are you just trying to get out of work?"

I glared at him. I had borne my pain in silence all the way, but now my whole body was trembling and my arm was slung limply over Two-Horses' shoulder. I would have collapsed were it not for his support.

Dr Hill could not help me; he was performing surgery on a wounded man's arm. Either the anaesthetic wasn't strong enough or there was none at all – the man's howls were mortifying.

A few labourers with only minor injuries were resting on the ground. Two-Horses set me down among them and found me some water. After I drank, he went to ask after Da Zhuang, Old Shuan and Boss Cai.

George told him, "Da Zhuang was struck by shrapnel, it's bad." He pointed to a place behind Dr Hill where the wounded were being tended to. Two-Horses told me to wait where I was while he sped away in that direction.

"You get to work!" George shouted after him, exasperated, but Two-Horses paid him no attention.

I struggled to my feet, asking the people beside me to help me over to him.

That stumble consumed all my energy. When the two people who had supported me set me down, I lay next to Da Zhuang gasping for breath.

"Brother, ah... you... you're... bleedin' too." Da Zhuang turned to look at me. The movement was feeble and his face ashen, resting in Old Shuan's lap. His forehead and stomach were wrapped in strips of clothing.

Boss Cai sat silently by, his eyes full of grief and resignation. Two-Horses sobbed.

"Two-Horses, am fine. Old Shuan's bin crackin' jokes for me." Da Zhuang tried to console him.

I forced a smile. "Of course you're going to be fine." I wanted to cry.

"Boss Cai ses 'e'll write me mum and dad a letter," Da

Zhuang said to me. "I 'aven't written 'em in a while. Half-Immortal Wu, the village fortune teller, can read it to 'em."

He turned to Boss Cai, who asked, "What do you want the letter to say?"

"Say I've been livin' the sweet life, meals and meat every day. Say I've made some good friends, learned to write a bit and speak a bit o' foreign. Ask 'em 'bout the harvest. Ask 'em if they's 'aving trouble with drought and locusts."

The same letter he had asked me to write two months earlier.

"I'll write it this evening," said Boss Cai.

Da Zhuang turned to look at me. "I don't wanna die. Still 'aven't found me wife."

"What kind of woman do you want?" I asked.

"She's got black 'air, long and shiny, all the way to her hips. Her arse is bigger than mine." He paused a moment for a few breaths. Light flashed in his eyes and his expression turned a little embarrassed. "I like fat girls," he added. "Her tits is like watermelons, soft." He coughed and went on, "At night, I... I've planted the fields... then I go home... an..." He began coughing again.

"Tell us more when you're better. When you get back to the village, you're gonna find your fat girl right away," Old Shuan said. "We'll all be at the weddin'. Two-Horses, Delun, Boss Cai and me, all us together."

"And how about that type of Dezhou braised chicken you always want?" I said. "I'll bring you a few. The skin is all crisp and shiny, smells so good."

"Don' mess with me." A thin smile appeared on Da Zhuang's face.

Two-Horses had stopped crying and came over to say, "Brother, do you want to buy a new ox? War might be over in a few months and we can all go home. You won't even have to settle for just one, you can afford three. And we'll send you even more."

"That... many ox, then aye'll... be 'appy." Da Zhuang gazed blankly at the sky. "I never seen such beautiful clouds." He turned to Old Shuan. "Tell me... that....joke..."

Old Shuan began to speak. Halfway through, he stopped and sobbed.

The corner of Da Zhuang's mouth lifted into a smile.

He died around noon.

That night, Two-Horses and Old Shuan made a sailboat out of woodchips. They used strips cut from Da Zhuang's clothing for its sails.

Early the next morning, our section buried Da Zhuang and twenty-five other labourers around a mile from camp. A foreman came to supervise us. The grave was near a large, sprawling oak tree, dense with leaves. The oak's thick branches extended in all directions as if reaching out to comfort the souls of the dead.

With Two-Horses' help, I placed the sailboat into the pit. I made sure that its prow was facing east.

23

"A ticket to Saire, please." David stood up straight to make himself look younger. He took a note from his wallet and handed it to the middle-aged woman in a silk scarf behind the counter.

He had set out from Arras the previous morning, arriving in Dunkirk by bus about two hours later. The small hotel where he had stayed the night before was simple yet comfortable. He took a hot shower and slept well despite waking up a few times in the night.

She took his money and asked, "Are you going horse riding?" There was doubt in her voice.

"Horse riding?"

"Yeah, the riding field is pretty good over there. My son goes every week for lessons."

"Is there still a village there?"

"Nearby, yeah."

David sighed with relief. "That's where I'm going."

He boarded the bus with a group of twittering high school students. They laughed and joked on the way. He tried to concentrate on the scenery: trees, flat fields, rolling hills, ambling livestock, scattered farmhouses and harvested farmland... Could this gleaming tarmac have been that narrow dirt road?

...A column of trucks sways down the road, raising a cloud of dust, turning the leaves grey. The trucks are stuffed with people, faces dimmed with dirt, malnutrition and motion sickness. Some vomit until their strength gives out, then sit on the floor, their heads resting against the cold metal.

...He reels with dizziness, presses to the edge of the crowd, panting heavily. Someone beside him curses in a dialect he does not understand, whether at him or at the journey's torment he does not know. He is on the last truck. He looks around, feeling a little better, shocked to see green fields spread before him – so vibrant, so inviting – making him want to touch them. He thinks of the farmland around Wuping, luscious from the spring rains. A memory surfaces: he and his younger siblings flying kites on the ridges, running from one patch of green to another. Father stands nearby, holding a pipe and smiling to Mother. "The harvest will be great this year!"

...He leans forward and reaches out to the greenery. The truck rocks as it hits a pothole and he almost flies out. Luckily, someone behind him grabs him by the back of his clothes.

"We'll be at the riding school soon!" called the driver loudly.

David collected himself.

Ahead on the right, there was an oak tree on a hillside. Its thick branches extended in every direction. Some of them were so large that they touched the ground before reaching even further like the tentacles of a great wooden octopus.

He recognised it at a glance. Seventy years is a lifetime for a human being, but for an oak it may just be a blink. He asked the driver to let him out by the tree.

The driver laughed and said that he hadn't expected someone of his age would want to climb trees. He also told him that the riding school was ten more minutes on foot down the road, and how to get to the village.

David followed the gentle slope up the hill. He stroked the vast branches that reached the ground. Had the souls of Da Zhuang and his companions made it home? Was this oak so sturdy because it had been nourished by the flesh and blood of those foreign labourers buried beneath it?

He knelt before the tree and poured water on the ground as if it were wine, offering it to the souls of the dead.

He walked to the riding school after resting for a while at the oak.

Beneath a cloudless sky, low white railings split the course into five different areas of varying size. There were several riders on horseback. A slight rider leaned forward on a brown horse, his hips raised, focused on the path ahead. The horse lifted its front hooves and leapt over the X-shaped obstacle before them with ease.

The students from the bus were there, watching the exercise while an instructor beside them explained. The training area was surrounded by stables.

David closed his eyes and the camp's bustle appeared in his mind: playing the *erhu*, singing, storytelling, gambling, the air vibrant with voices. How could it not be so? More than five hundred youths trapped there like prisoners, with nowhere to go after work.

And the craters from artillery shells? They must have

been filled in long ago. The traces of war had been erased from this place like cobwebs under a broom.

He followed the directions the driver had given him towards the village.

It had felt like a lifetime on the night that Two-Horses had carried him, but today he walked for less than fifteen minutes before he came to an area of farmland with cottages scattered across it. There was a wide-open view of rolling pastures and woods. Flowers adorned the roadsides, making him feel as if he had stepped into a postcard.

He and Marguerite had hoped to buy a little cottage in the countryside beyond Paris, where they would grow fruit and vegetables and raise chickens and ducks. Her breast cancer diagnosis had changed that; they needed to stay in the city for treatment.

"Strolling around the vegetable garden and orchards every day, painting a few pictures... oh, I can't talk about it." David remembered her sigh.

He had often driven her to the countryside during her illness. "Do you like that cottage?" he would ask her. "Or would the place with the apple orchard we saw earlier be better?"

The doctors said she would live for two years at most. Not believing them, he found a practitioner of Chinese medicine in Paris. He stewed herbal soup for her to drink every day and taught her *qigong*. In his opinion, curing cancer couldn't be left to just doctors, but also required a peaceful mind and nourishment of the heart. Marguerite laughed, but she drank her herbal soup graciously and practised *qigong* daily. Sometimes, when she saw him carefully measuring out the different herbs with his little scales before brewing them, she would tease him that he should become a pharmacist.

Two years, three, four, then five whole years had passed, but in the end she could not survive her cancer. "Delun, it's all thanks to your medicine and *qigong*," she had smiled just a few days before she died.

But David cursed that old Chinese doctor. Hadn't he vowed that she would be cured?

The hospital had stopped her treatment a month earlier at her request. The doctors believed it was having no effect. Nurses injected morphine to relieve her pain every so often. She was tired, lethargic all the time. David and Anne watched over her in turns, sleeping fitfully by her bedside.

The day she died, it was as if she had known. With strength from who knows where, she had clasped their hands, gazing into their faces for a long time. After she let go, exhausted yet smiling faintly, she looked at David expectantly. She closed her eyes, her breathing became shallow and weak. David knew that the time had finally come. He embraced her, resting his face against hers as he whispered a poem in tearful Mandarin:

Our oath is greater than death.
To have and to hold, for all my life.
How painful to be so far from you.
Fate will not let me fulfil my vow.

As he finished his recitation, Marguerite released her last breath.

Like a sleepwalker, David stopped at the hedge of a white stone cottage. What a marvellous thing memory was. Sometimes you forget what happened just a few minutes ago, sometimes you recognise a place you visited half a century before.

Both sides of the house were full of flowers and plants. On the right, a rope swing hung from a large tree and an adorable pink treehouse was nestled in the branches.

The front garden had changed, but he knew it was the right house.

It was only then that he realised how brash he was being. So much time had passed, the woman who saved his life must have moved long ago. He remembered the concentration and composure on her face as she removed the shrapnel. When he had thanked her for the precious food and clothing that she gave them, she had responded by gently saying, "I hope we all live to see a day without war". Those words had inspired him in the days to come, making him remember the goodness of the human spirit even as he lived a prisoner's life.

He bowed deeply to the house. As he turned to leave, the door opened and out came a young woman in blue denim shorts and a ponytail. With curiosity in her voice, she asked, "Hey, who are you looking for?"

She looked so much like that woman! David's heart leapt in amazement. Tentatively, he asked, "Did your family live here in 1917?"

"1917?" She frowned as if this were the remotest of antiquities. "Sixty-eight years ago... yeah, Grandma and Grandpa lived here."

"Was your grandpa's name Andre?"

"How d'you know my grandpa's name?"

"Please, what was your grandmother's name?"

"Eileen."

"Eileen. Your grandma, is she... is she well?"

"She's in good health, she still reads books and the newspaper every day. She likes to do the crossword and the gardening. She's out for a walk with my grandpa right now."

David almost cried with joy. "Your grandfather's still alive!"

"Of course. They've lived here forever. My parents try to make them move to the city but they won't budge. I come to see them every month. My sister, brother and their kids come a lot too." She looked at her watch. "They'll be back in about half an hour. You're welcome to come in and wait for them."

"Oh, that won't be necessary. I have to take the bus back." Perhaps he should wait for them to come back, he thought, but he felt that he would not know what to say. He knew that they were well, that they had grandchildren, and that was enough. He added one last thing. "Please tell your grandmother that the Chinese she helped back in 1917 came to thank her."

"Can I ask what she did?"

David smiled. "I think you should ask her."

The girl huffed, regretting the lost opportunity for a good story. "Fine. Are you sure that you don't want to wait?"

David said he was sure. He bid farewell with light in his heart and a spring in his step.

24

It took two weeks to construct a new dormitory and prison. The prison had doubled in size, half of it now housing people who had become mentally unstable. More British soldiers had also arrived to set up anti-aircraft guns to shoot German bombers out of the sky.

We could hear the prison inmates' voices despite its high brick walls. They wailed, sang and laughed. A few mimicked the sound of the planes that had attacked us.

For a while, the camp's atmosphere was downbeat. Mealtimes had always been animated with chatting, joking, people showing off their skills. Now we ate in silence, even those who liked telling dirty jokes kept quiet. If we had time after meals, we just sat in the sun or caught lice. The sun wasn't always shining, but there was never any shortage of lice. They were as omnipresent as the air.

Sometimes, I thought I saw Da Zhuang. I would blurt out his name, only for whoever I had mistaken for him to turn around and send my heart sinking.

Old Shuan became as quiet as a man of stone in the

weeks following Da Zhuang's death. He never played the *kuaiban* or told stories. He avoided my gaze at work, simply grunting to show that he had heard whenever I spoke to him. He avoided me and Two-Horses. Perhaps he feared that we might mention Da Zhuang, who he'd always been closest with.

But it was difficult to mourn in a place like that. Grief requires energy, and after thirteen or fourteen hours of physical labour every day – repairing the camp in addition to factory work – we were so exhausted that we could barely move.

Grief also requires space, and that was a luxury so rare that we didn't even have it in the bathroom. Our lavatories were separated from the British soldiers. Theirs comprised a log cabin with low interior walls, while ours was a long, narrow ditch behind some trees. One day, a labourer from Hebei used the British lavatory. For that, he was tied to a rock and whipped.

We became numb. Depression spread among us like disease, catalysed by constant hunger and exhaustion from being worked like cattle. We no longer united in the defence of our companions when the British took to them with violence, slapping or whipping people in unjust punishments. We simply bowed our heads and shrank away. Some even stayed to watch, the spectacle of pain feeding the hatred and gloom in their hearts.

The camp renovations were extensive: we built a new hospital and kitchens in addition to the prison and barracks. When they were finally complete, we were left only with our factory labour each day. We had free time again, and soon the sound of the *erhu*, the flute and singing returned to camp. The men began to crack jokes and tell stories. Even then, we would still glance at the sky from time to time in fear.

Rumours about the ferocity of the German forces began to fly around camp. Some said that they had captured a great deal of French and British weapons and that they were forcing them into retreat on the Western Front. Others said that the Germans had developed a weapon that infected its targets with plague, making you spit blood and die soon after. Yet another added that German soldiers were fed supplements that enabled them to fight like tigers even after several nights without sleep.

Tom told me that China's Duan Qirui government had declared war on Germany and Austria on 14 August, but instead of sending troops, they had opted to dispatch more labourers to Europe and Russia.

One day after dinner, Boss Cai and I were sitting together on a boulder away from the crowd. Two-Horses was gambling, which was unusual, but he wanted money to buy a gift for Ella. He seemed to be doing well, I could hear his excited shouts from all the way over at the rock.

"Tom says that China joined the war," I said.

"So I hear." He was calm. "It shows that China believes the Allies will win, and that we will be able to reclaim Shandong from Germany and gain some international recognition. But China is too weak, the Western countries will not necessarily be interested even if we were to send troops. To them, our country is a fat piece of meat to be sliced however they choose. Plus, the Japanese have already defeated the Germans in Shandong. They're ambitious. Next it will be the three eastern provinces, then the north, then all of China."

"China has joined the war as an ally of Britain and

France, won't they help us deal with the Japanese?" My classmates and I had participated in many boycotts of Japanese goods when I was a student. I abhorred the corruption and weakness of the Duan Qirui government, but I was excited to hear that China had joined the war. I felt that the Chinese government had finally found its backbone.

"Help the Chinese?" He sighed. "Why would they do that? Their considerations do not extend beyond their own interests. The British defeated the Qing government half a century ago when they burned down the Summer Palace and gardens in Beijing. Was that not a demonstration of how they would treat us in the future? As if to say, look, we've burned your emperor's favourite gardens, we have taken all the treasures that were inside. What are you going to do about it? You're a defeated opponent, you must heed our instructions. The West is neither friendly nor sympathetic towards us, they only want to exploit and rob us. Japan's national strength surged after the Meiji restoration, and they eye China and many Southeast Asian countries like tigers stalking prey. The West are suffering heavy causalities in this war and are unable to protect even themselves. Of course they won't assist us against Japan."

"Who do you think will win, the Germans or the Allies?"

"It doesn't matter, it will be a tragedy either way. People dying like flies, historical architecture reduced to ruins. And for what? Nothing more than the selfish greed and lust for power of a few. When I was your age, I yearned for a civilisation like the West. I believed that Europe was not only materially developed and scientifically advanced, but had an immortal culture. I have not seen it that way for a long time. When the Western powers broke down our borders with guns and cannon fire, they shattered my longing for

European civilisation. When the Chinese government signed that humiliating treaty with Japan, any hopes I had for China were also extinguished."

I looked at him wide-eyed. "Then why did you come here?"

He smiled. "Please ignore the pessimistic things I'm saying. I'll be forty-seven this year, by no means elderly, but I've been through enough to turn anyone into a curio. You're still young and should live well. Perhaps by the time you're my age, the world will be at peace, the rulers wise and the commoners rich. But I don't expect to live to see it."

"I still don't understand, why did you come here?" I decided to tell him my own reasons. He was the same age as my father, and though my father lacked Boss Cai's physical strength, they were still somewhat alike. Being with him gave me a sense of familial affection, and I felt that if I explained my situation to him and he gave me some words of comfort, then perhaps my father would one day do the same.

The words I had been suppressing burst forth. I even told him about how I had crashed my bike, how I had watched the roaring train, how I had sold my pocket watch to buy clothes and food. After I finished, I breathed a long sigh of relief. "I let my parents down, I let Miss Lu down. But I had no choice."

He nodded. "If you had stayed in that marriage, your suffering would have lasted a lifetime. It is not a bad thing for you to do this hard labour in France for a few years. Most of China's educated youth are bored of their continuous study, ignorant of the outside world. They only know how to recite poetry, paint and play word games. They completely lack strength and wisdom. When these people open their mouths it's all Confucius, but they have not learned the importance of travelling around the world to experience and study different systems of governance like he did. It's China's sorrow that such people govern the country and manage the people's livelihood."

"I heard that you taught at a university and opened a martial art's school," I said. "Regardless of the state of the world's affairs, you'd be able to make a living and have no need for concern. Why would you come to suffer here in Europe?"

He stared into the distance for a while in silence. "I came for revenge."

I remembered the strange spark in his eyes when he spoke of the Germans. I waited for him to say more.

"I used to be content, the kind of scholar I just described. I married a woman I loved. We had a daughter. I named her Baozhu, 'Treasured Pearl'. The name is a little cheesy, but I loved her so much that I felt that no other name encapsulated how much I cherished her. I started teaching her how to read and draw when she was two years old. I set up a little play space in my study with all her toys so that I could watch over her while I read. She was clever and empathetic. When I was tired, she would give me a massage, drumming on my shoulder with her little fist. She'd ask, 'Daddy, are you feeling better?'"

His voice trembled and his eyes were damp, but he continued. "I rushed home after teaching every day. She was always waiting for me at the gate. She would run over when she spotted me, her two braids swinging. I'd put down my teaching materials and scoop her up in my arms. I'd lift her into the air and she'd giggle and tell me to go in circles. 'Daddy, go faster, I want to fly!' she said. So I'd spin and spin..." He laughed through his tears. "I'd spin her until we were dizzy, then we'd both sit on the ground, laughing. My wife would watch us with delight, saying that we were a pair of lunatics, one big and one small.

"Baozhu loved to read ancient poetry with me, but she always found faults with it. Once I taught her Li Bai's poem *Quiet Night Thought*: 'Moonlight falls before my bed; / I wonder if I'm seeing frost upon the ground.' She said, 'Daddy, this ancient person has got it all wrong. Look, moonlight on the courtyard clearly looks like white sand, not frost.' Another time, I taught her the *Book of Songs*. After hearing me recite *Guan Ju*, she shook her head. 'Daddy, this man is no gentleman. He likes only pretty girls. A true gentleman values virtue, not appearance.' She was five when she said that!" Boss Cai laughed. "You tell me, was she not a little prodigy?

"When Western forces entered Beijing, I took my family and fled to Baoding. Beijing was hell. Many houses had burned, families still inside. Some German soldiers treated it like a game whenever they ran into Chinese, cornering them in cul-de-sacs and opening fire, leaving none alive. Dead were everywhere as we ran, left to the dogs with no one to bury them. Poor Baozhu..." Tears streamed from his eyes.

I lowered my head. I could not bear to look at him.

After a while he continued, "Baozhu, my playful and fun-loving Baozhu, she cried all the way, refusing to say a word. She quietened down when we arrived in Baoding. Her first words were: 'Daddy, if they come, throw me into the river, please.' Seeing me cry, she wiped my tears with her hand and said, 'Don't worry, the Water Dragon King will save me.'

"We believed that we were safe then. But before long the

Germans invaded Baoding. One day my mother fell ill. I took her to the doctor, and when we came home..."

He stopped. I lifted my head to look at him, his eyes lifeless, like a wandering ghost. He said, "If I hadn't needed to care for Mother, I would have already followed my wife and child. My mother died late last year, so here I came."

He gave me a look of gratitude, as if to thank me for letting him share his happiness with his daughter. He wiped his tears, stood and strode back to the barracks.

I remained, watching the sun change from orange to blood red on the horizon. I stayed there until Two-Horses came to find me, happy with his winnings. I went along with him to watch someone perform opera.

25

Two-Horses also had a hard time following Da Zhuang's death, but he quickly recovered his old self. Not only was he a born optimist, but he got to see Ella.

We had thought we would be staying for just a few weeks, but after three months there was still no sign of us leaving. Other than our work in the factory, we sometimes mined coal, repaired bridges and roads, and loaded goods in train stations or docks. Noticing that we were interested in their machines, several friendly French workers taught us how to use them. Two-Horses and I learned to operate some of the mechanical tools.

Ella started coming to the camp to see Two-Horses. She couldn't come in, of course, but she could catch a glimpse of him through the fence and talk with him briefly before the guards drove her away. Two-Horses pulled me over to interpret whenever she came. We all had to yell to be able to hear each other, but her voice was loud and slow, and she used short sentences with simple vocabulary, so I could translate without a problem.

One day, Two-Horses started pacing around the fence as soon as we returned to the barracks. Ella had told him at work that she would visit that evening. Looking out from behind the barbed wire, you could see her figure approach and the colour of her clothes, but you couldn't make out her expression.

Ella said, "I made potato cakes last night. We've run out of sugar at home."

"I can get you some sugar," Two-Horses told me to say.

"Where can you get sugar from?" I translated her question.

He smiled strangely. "I have my ways."

"I've knitted you two pairs of socks," Ella continued. "They're red. I used my old sweater."

The socks the British provided us had long since worn out. George said we would get new socks and shoes, but nothing had happened since. I patted Two-Horses' shoulder. "Lucky you!"

Two-Horses grinned. "Ge, I'll give you a pair."

"I liked the bird you engraved," Ella said.

"I'm making something else for you."

"What is it?"

"I'm not telling."

That Two-Horses, he was good at getting women to like him.

"How long will you stay here?" she asked.

"I don't know. But no matter where we go, I'll come back to see you."

"Really?" Ella's voice was full of hope.

Then, two soldiers with rifles on their shoulders slouched over from the sentry post and told her to leave. I don't know whether they could speak French, but they could guess what was going on either way. The reason they didn't stop her right away was probably just because they were so bored in their guard post and wanted to see the fun.

In a unison of French and Chinese, we shouted, "The guards are coming!"

Everyone around us also called out, hoping the hurricane of our voices could sweep her to safety. Everybody liked Ella, envied Two-Horses' good luck and wondered how they had fallen in love. But everybody also knew they would never make it. Someone mumbled that a Chinese rickshaw puller together with a white woman was like a fish from the lake with a beast of the land: impossible. They couldn't even communicate! However, she brought hope. Not only to Two-Horses, but to everyone. Even if you did hard labour every day and were treated like a prisoner behind barbed wire, life could still bring happiness.

Hearing our cries, Ella turned and ran. I heard one of the guards saying in English, "This girl's mad!"

Two-Horses rushed through dinner and set to work. He had found a beautiful feather when we were loading supplies at the docks and had brought it back to the camp as a precious treasure. He was using it to make Ella a pair of earrings.

When we were working at the factory a few days later, Two-Horses gave Ella a little sack of sugar. I don't know what he could have traded for it with the foremen.

26

At the end of September, a letter finally arrived from my father. It had been sent in a cloth package of about half an arm's length.

George handed it to me haughtily, as if he were doing me a great favour. I was delighted. I stuttered my gratitude, thanking him repeatedly. With half an hour before dinner, I flew to a private place and sat against a tree trunk, my heart thumping.

I opened the bundle with a sharp stone. Other than the letter, there were also two sets of neatly folded grey underwear, a black cashmere scarf, a mink hat, a pair of thick-soled cloth shoes and a pair of white socks. I put them back into the package and opened the letter.

The first line read, "Unfilial Delun."

I stopped, my head spinning, then continued.

"For many years I have funded your education, laboured to find you a fitting wife. How could you not consider your parents' kindness over all these years, that you could leave for

Europe on your wedding night without a single word, abandoning your wife and home, rendering your siblings lost and helpless? This is detestable, hateful."

There were only three sheets of paper, but the time I spent reading them felt like hours.

After denouncing me, my father wrote that my mother had sunk into a deep and tearful depression after I left. His cough had worsened considerably and he had lost his appetite. My brother and sisters barely laughed any more and were behind in their studies. Miss Lu was taking care of the whole household: overseeing the business, managing expenses and dealing with the servants. He also wrote that since I had brought so much shame on our family, I deserved no pity. He had been unwilling to send me clothing, but my mother and Miss Lu had insisted, so he had to comply. Those cloth shoes had been sewn by my mother, and the socks were knitted by Miss Lu.

He said that he had known of my arrogance and ambition, and would forgive my sudden absence for the time being. To repent, I should spend every day in introspection and reform myself through suffering in the labour camp, thus erasing the frivolity and impetuosity of my spirit. When I returned to China, he said, I would be a good husband to Miss Lu, redouble my filial piety and assume the responsibilities of the Zhang household's eldest son.

The letter left my body ice cold. I folded it away slowly. As I saw it, the package contained not warm clothing but the Zhang family mansion, my father's stern reprimand, my mother's tears, my siblings' helplessness and the bustling figure of Miss Lu.

There are still two years left on my contract, I said to myself. We'll see what happens.

Early one morning a week later, the foreman woke our section and told us to assemble on the training ground with all our belongings. The rest of the camp did not stir. An hour later, we were lining up to go to the train station. Two-Horses was restless, looking back constantly as if Ella might miraculously appear. "Ge, where are we going? Will we come back?"

I wished I had a satisfying answer.

We arrived back in Arras at around two in the afternoon. It was still in ruins but had improved over the last three months. The debris had been removed from the main road, a few trams and transport trucks moved through the streets. On the balconies above, clothes and bedsheets hung out to dry. There were even pedestrians, some of them well-dressed. I saw one lady wearing a red, wide-brimmed hat decorated with elegant velvet flowers. A queue spilled out of a small food store, most of the people in it either elderly or women with children. The store's windows were broken, but they had been nailed over with wooden planks on which someone had painted a mural of bread and sausages in bright colours.

Perhaps the war is ending, I thought.

A strange procession came in our direction, two young women wearing overalls and banana-shaped hats leading more than twenty children of varying ages behind them. We were on the left, they the right. The oldest was around twelve, the youngest probably no more than four. Though clean and tidy, the children's outfits did not seem to fit. Many of them carried suitcases and sacks. The youngest, with a neat but short fringe cut into her blonde hair and a knee-length blue woollen sweater, was hugging a furry brown puppy. She was struggling but did not want to part with it.

Beside her, an eight- or nine-year-old boy carried a hen, its clucking head peering over the brim of a sack.

They looked at us and we them. As we passed by, the puppy in the girl's arms broke free and ran towards us. The children cried out. I stepped out of the formation and leaned down to pick it up, feeling its warmth and heartbeat. It wagged its tail and licked my face.

The little girl ran over and stood nervously in front of me. I gave the puppy back to her and said in French, "It's very cute."

She hesitated before taking the dog, staring at me with big round eyes as if fearing I might snatch it away.

"Oh God, Emily," the taller of the pair leading the group called out, "come back here now!" The panic in the voice suggested we were regarded as monsters.

Beside me, Two-Horses fished a wooden cat figurine out of his pocket. It had a movable head and legs. He held it out in his palm, offering it to the child.

"Oh," the little girl whispered. "For me?"

Her voice was so sweet to hear!

Two-Horses nodded.

The girl grabbed the little cat and turned to run. After a few paces she stopped, turned her head and fixed us with a smile befitting a lady before saying, "*Merci*."

Once she had returned to the line, the other children crowded around her to see the toy in her hand. The women leading them looked at us with disgust as they kept the children in order.

After they had gone, Two-Horses said, "They're goin' to the train station, right?"

I said that they probably were, and wondered whether or not they were orphans.

After a while he said, "I made that cat for Ella."

27

We returned to the same camp that we had stayed in before. It had expanded considerably and now also housed labourers from Africa. The different races were segregated entirely, doing their drills and eating in different areas. Tom said that they were from Algeria, Egypt, Madagascar and South Africa, pulling out a map to show us where those countries were.

Early the next morning, we set off in open-top trucks. The foremen made us bring trench-digging tools, along with bundles of tarpaulin. It was a fine day with the sun shining, so I couldn't guess what the tarpaulin was for.

After three hours of driving, we passed an abandoned village where houses devastated by gunfire stood among overgrown weeds. Some were demolished completely, reduced to piles of brick, stone and broken household objects. Others had holes so huge a man could walk through without stooping. One wall had been essentially destroyed; nothing remained but a stone pillar as thick as my arm, wreathed in red and green ivy. A black frying pan hung from its peak, swaying in the wind. Nearby lay the remains of an aircraft, the fuselage burned out but the wings more or less unscathed. Something was printed on one wing, too faint to discern. Green weeds stretched half a man's height from its underside, as if they had been nourished by the surrounding death.

If not for the war, I thought, the village would have been beautiful. I could picture fresh flowers blooming around the little houses with their red and grey rooftops. I could imagine villagers walking or cycling along the old, cobbled streets. I was glad we hadn't encountered dead bodies. Maybe they'd already been removed by soldiers or villagers.

We arrived at a near-annihilated trench around noon.

The sun shone in a cloudless sky, throwing stark light on the horrific scene beneath. Everywhere we looked were discarded firearms, tanks... and corpses. Some were in the trenches, some drooped from the barbed wire, some were even in the trees. Their blood stained the soil.

A few of us turned instinctively away, while others vomited. The warm breeze spared us nothing, bearing the foul stench of death into our noses and lungs.

We were no strangers to disaster, but nobody had seen anything like this before. The British soldiers and officers fell silent, removing their hats and helmets in mourning for their fallen.

A young man among us suddenly let out a heartrending cry, followed by deranged laughter. White foam accumulated around his mouth, twisted into a smile. He picked up a stone and began to strike it against his head. Blood streamed down his face as he babbled. Someone sprang forward and tried to snatch the rock from his hand, but the young man knocked him to the ground. Others intervened and managed to subdue him, restraining him with rope.

We ate before getting to work, surprised and disgusted that we still had our appetites – our stomachs had learned to overcome our minds over the past year. Who knew where the next meal would come from?

After being split into groups, we were told that some would be assigned to collect weapons, others bodies. I prayed for the former, but when does reality kowtow to desire? My group was tasked with retrieving the bodies of British troops for burial.

George said that the Germans had been fighting them here for most of the year. In the last standoff just four days ago, more than five hundred British and six hundred German troops had been killed. Defeated, the Germans had abandoned their trenches and withdrew to a stronghold in the north. The British had advanced to a small town previously occupied by the Germans.

Shouldering our shovels and carrying the tarpaulin, we passed through a hole in the defensive barbed wire and continued towards the German trench. Two-Horses nudged me, nodding at a nearby tank next to a shell crater. The treads were split, a huge hole ripped through its front. A mangled body in a khaki uniform was draped across the gun. We approached. Old Shuan nudged the body with his shovel. The body fell, face up, onto the outstretched tarpaulin: a young man with an ashen face, hair matted to his forehead with blood. His stomach, swollen like a balloon, rumbled.

"He ain't dead," Two-Horses said.

"It's just the gases in his belly playing tricks," replied Old

Shuan. "In a few days, it'll get all red and infested with maggots."

There were five corpses in the crater. A pair lay tangled in their final battle, a Brit and a German whose stomach he had pierced with his bayonet. The Brit's own uniform was stained red from a head wound, looking as though he had been shot just as he killed his enemy. Another German's head was split down the middle, a paste of blood and brains pooling beneath him. The final pair were Brits who had been blown apart, their limbs severed from their torsos.

"Just a kid," said Old Shuan, pointing at one of the soldiers.

I felt a sudden pain in my stomach, then vomited until I could hardly breathe. My eyes filled with tears. Two-Horses helped me to the ground, pounding gently at my back. I kept spewing bile even after my stomach emptied.

I struggled to my feet. Standing, I spotted a mud-stained hand reaching up out of the soil where I had vomited.

George ordered us to place only the British bodies onto the tarpaulin. Germans were to be piled into heaps for burial in a mass grave, but only after we had finished carrying the British to the trucks.

Our path was lined with corpses. They showed every imaginable expression. Some twisted in agony while others rested at peace, probably killed by an unseen bullet. Some seemed to smile, as if pleased to depart this ugly world.

One soldier had an unfinished cigarette between his fingers. Wounded, he must have decided to enjoy one last snout before the end. Perhaps artillery fire still raged around him as he smoked, his comrades falling one by one.

We found another with one arm severed from his shoulder, the other reaching forward with its fingers outstretched. Just beyond his final grasp, a cluster of unremarkable yellow flowers grew shining in the sun. His green helmet leaned to one side, half stuck in the mud. The half protruding from the soil had a message in small letters: "Mum, I love you".

Some bodies were already rotting. We could hear the rustling sound of maggots devouring their flesh.

Rats scurried boldly between us. They were everywhere, so bold that they just stared blankly even if you raised your shovel to strike. It dawned on me then why the rats in the trenches had been so fat.

Those who had died more recently still had elasticity in their faces. It appeared possible that a nudge might be able to rouse them from their dream.

We lifted them in pairs, one of us taking whatever remained of their heads, the other of their feet. When we had filled a tarpaulin with four or five bodies, we left it in place and went in search of more. Exhausted and covered in blood, we became numb. Staggering with effort, we would trip over the bodies if we weren't careful.

A sudden dizziness overwhelmed me as I came to a crater's edge, the basin filled with water. My feet failed me and I fell, half-submerged in putrid liquid. I thought I would suffocate with the stench. Two rotting corpses floated over the muddy surface, their eye sockets empty in bloated, white faces. I lashed out in panic, my hand coming into contact with one of their cheeks. It was as soft as jellied tofu. I screamed and scrambled over a body at the edge of the pool, grabbing for Two-Horses' helping hand.

All tarpaulins filled, we carried them back to the trucks with one man to each corner. Some were so heavy that our backs ached and our knees throbbed.

"My God, if only they were dwarves!" Two-Horses said, exhaling deeply. No one laughed.

The trucks waited for us on the other side of the trenches, which had been covered with makeshift bridges for us to pass over.

We filled them quickly. More replaced them. We worked until sundown.

The second day was the same.

The third day...

The fourth...

28

We didn't learn of Boss Cai's death until three days after it happened.

Since he told me about his past, he had become even more uncommunicative. He no longer spent time with our group of friends, nor spoke while he worked or ate. One day, he asked George to transfer him to the other side of camp to train the new Chinese recruits. George, always a little afraid of him, was happy to let him go. On the day he left, I offered to walk with him, but he declined. He told me to take care of myself before striding away.

It was late autumn. Rain had been pouring on and off for just over a week. The camp was consumed with mud and the scent of mildew. It seemed that even the bricks would leak if you wrung them out.

While we were collecting dead bodies on the battlefield, Boss Cai's thirty-ninth section were digging trenches with British soldiers barely a hundred kilometres from camp. As they were readying to leave, German troops launched a surprise attack. The British were outnumbered and began to withdraw after dozens of casualties. The labourers followed, except for Boss Cai – who joined the soldiers covering the retreat. Inspired, some other labourers came to join the fray. Having served in the army in China, they knew how to use weapons. Eventually, British reinforcements arrived and drove the Germans back – but Boss Cai was already dead. His body was one of forty-six Brits and thirteen Chinese.

At dinner that evening when we heard the news, a lightly wounded man with bandages around his head who had been there in the trench told Boss Cai's story vividly.

"We were all wonderin' how to escape, but not him, he grabbed a gun from a dead Brit and opened fire on the Germans. When that gun was out, he found another and started shooting again. The way he was going at it, it was like he had a deep, deep hatred of them. Who knew he was such a good shot? He must have practised plenty."

Old Shuan asked, "How many did he kill?"

"At least seven or eight."

"How did he die?" I asked.

"The Germans rushed the trenches, eyes blood-red. He went hand-to-hand with them, with just a shovel. I didn't dare watch! If I hadn't pretended to be dead, they'd have killed me too."

"Where's his body?" I asked again.

"How should I know? A bomb fell, everything shook and I passed out. When I woke up, I was on a stretcher surrounded by the dead."

He continued his account of the battle while I quietly left.

I went to ask George if we could hold a memorial service for the Chinese who died in the battle. He said they weren't in our section, so it would be best not to get involved.

That night, the people in our section lit candles before bed and burned paper money we had made, giving tribute to Boss Cai and the other spirits. In the flickering light, I recited Shen Yue's mourning poem in farewell:

> *Last autumn's moon shines again over the house.*
> *Come spring, the blooms and grasses will all return, flowering with their sweet scent.*
> *Alas, once human life begins to wither, it can only be lost forever.*
> *Inside, all is left in disarray.*
> *Dust settles over the chairs, a canopy hangs above an empty bed.*
> *The living go on, left with their pain.*

Two weeks later, Edward died too. He hanged himself.

It seemed like he could no longer bear the humiliation of being called a deserter, and so he had taken the path of no return.

29

WE SPENT ALL OUR DAYS PAVING ROADS, digging tunnels and trenches, repairing railways and bridges, transporting ammunition or clearing bodies from the battlefields. Though we often travelled quite far by train or truck to get to wherever we were needed, we still spent most nights at the camp.

Winter passed, then spring. When summer came, we finally received new clothing and shoes without the stink of sweat and blood. On the first day we wore them, we also got haircuts and asked Tom to take pictures. We held our heads high and our chests raised, looking full of vigour with shiny copper buttons reaching all the way to our chins.

The day afterwards, we found out why we had been given new clothing: an envoy had arrived from China to inspect our living conditions, making sure that the Allies were fulfilling their part of the bargain. George said we would not have to work, the envoy would be arriving that afternoon. For lunch we ate noodles, pork and even egg-drop soup – all foods that we had thought long lost to us.

We cheered. Our motherland had not forgotten us. Some

wanted to ask how the situation was in China, some to accuse the British soldiers of rudeness and other misdeeds, others how to terminate the contract early. They would not hesitate to miss a few months of wages in exchange for reuniting with their families.

After lunch, we rehearsed a performance to welcome the envoy: singing, martial arts performances, a double pantomime act and stilt walking. Someone found a few pieces of red cloth and wrapped them around their waists to perform a folk dance, using a washbasin as a drum. For a time, the camp rang with laughter.

As we rehearsed, some British officers, soldiers and foremen came to watch and applaud. Halfway through the stilt walking, the performers invited the British to join in – they had clearly been itching for a turn. They showed the Brits how to get on the stilts, how to walk. They all fell of course, which drew loud laughs. But after a little practice, they managed to walk pretty well behind our performers.

We forgot our grudges towards the British and the foremen and tried hard to impress them with our best skills. They, in turn, forgot temporarily the strict discipline they imposed on us, and laughed along with us. Everyone was lively, everyone was happy.

We waited until dark, but the envoy never came. Later, George said that the envoy had met with a few senior British officers at a hotel, but he did not know where they were now.

Everyone felt let down by our homeland. Old Shuan said, "We've been workin' body and soul here, he should have come to offer his respects. China joined the war last year as an ally of Britain and France. They didn't send troops, they sent us." His eyes were alight with rage. "Though we never touch a gun and don't go on the battlefield, without us to dig the trenches and fix their railways and all the other hard work in the rear, could the French and British soldiers concentrate on fighting?"

"That's right," someone added. "This crappy envoy is just putting it on. Maybe he'll make up some nonsense that we're over here eating fish and meat every day, having a great life."

"A great life? All I do is want to go home and I can't," someone in our section said. "My son's turned one and I haven't even seen him yet!"

"Nobody forced you to come, you signed your own name," another reminded him.

"And did I ever think we might die here when I signed up? When they read the contract to me, they said we weren't goin' anywhere near the fighting, didn't say nothin' about digging trenches on the front line, burying the dead, getting shot at."

Everyone agreed.

Someone said, "The contract also said we would be provided with full board. Liars! Food is deducted, clothes are deducted, only half the money we were promised ends up in our pockets!"

Another suggested that the envoy had not come because he feared the foreigners.

"If the Germans defeat the Allies," one man said, changing the subject, "what're we gonna do?"

"That won't happen, will it?" someone cautiously asked.

"I dunno, tough to say. Look at them German tanks! And them machine guns, firing round after round. One man can take down a whole platoon wi' those."

"If the Germans win, then we'll be prisoners of war."

"But we ain't soldiers. How can we be prisoners of war?"

"They don't care about that, they just know we've come to help the Brits and the French. Look, imagine you're in a fight with your neighbour. Then his family sends him a big stick to whack you with. Once you're finished with him, you're gonna go after them, aren't you? Ain't that right?"

"So if the Germans win, we won't be able to go home."

"I heard that when Germans take prisoners, they kill them on the spot."

"I heard they have bonfires to roast and eat children."

"And you believe that?" Old Shuan interjected. "You've seen dead Germans yourselves, they're beardless kids."

But his words were immediately drowned out by everyone cursing the Germans. As far as many were concerned, all our suffering after leaving China was the doing of Germany.

Someone raised his voice to declare, "If the Germans are going to win, we should fight! Just like Boss Cai."

"Y'all ready to die? We don't even have guns. The moment one of those tanks comes over, we're meat paste."

"Nothing's guaranteed to us even if the Allies do win. That envoy came all the way from China to our gates and then didn't come in to greet us. It doesn't matter whether it's because he doesn't respect us or that he's afraid of foreign devils. In the end, our lives are one thing in his eyes: cheap. You tell me, when the war's over and we go back to China, will the officials be there with warm welcomes? Maybe they think we'll have the smell of foreigners about us after these years in France and take out all their anger against them on us."

"You thinks they'll lock us up?"

"Can't say for sure."

Someone sighed and said, "Would've been better never to've come at all."

"Even if your arms and legs are broken and you're on your last breath, you must still go home to die."

"If you don't die there, your soul'll be lost!"

The sound of the guards' footsteps came from outside. We climbed under our blankets, a gloom settling over us all.

30

As soon as Tom gave Two-Horses the picture he had taken of us, Two-Horses asked me to write Ella a letter to send along with the photo. He signed it "Philippe", the French name he had given himself. He had seen a portrait of Louis Philippe I in the newspaper and thought the name sounded imposing. When I meet Ella's family, he said, how am I s'posed to say my name is 'a pair of horses'?

She wrote to him every month, describing all the trifles of her home life.

After I read her letters to him, he seized them and read them repeatedly, stroking each word as if it were alive. He sewed a pocket on his shirt for the letters and lined it with a piece of tarpaulin he had found, afraid that his sweat would dampen them.

Tom also gave me a photograph. I had wanted to send it to my parents but abandoned the idea. If they saw me wearing that coarse cloth, they would think I was bringing shame to the Zhang family ancestors. I didn't respond to my father's rebuke or offer any defence in my reply, just asked after my parents' health, my siblings' studies and described my life in France. Of course, I only said that I was working in different factories, mentioning nothing about digging trenches or clearing corpses from the battlefield.

I also wrote Miss Lu a brief letter, in which I thanked her for her dedication to the Zhang family and apologised once more for leaving without saying goodbye.

Around then, rumours in the camp told of an armistice between the Allies and Bulgaria, and civil war in Austria-Hungary. Tom said the British had broken through the Germans' Hindenburg Line.

One morning in early October, I was awakened by the sound of agonised coughing. Sitting up, I saw that it came from Wang Wubao. He was in another section and relatively old among the labourers at almost thirty. He was deathly pale, his body trembling. The person beside him was patting him on the back to ease his congestion. He saw me get up and said, "He has a fever, a headache and is coughing blood."

I ran outside to tell the sentries that someone was sick, asking them to get George to find a doctor.

Half an hour later, George stormed into the room and said furiously, "You want to laze about and skip work, right?" His litany ended the moment he saw Wang Wubao.

Soon, two soldiers arrived in white facemasks to put Wang Wubao onto a stretcher. They stuffed all his belongings and bedding into a sack that they also placed beside him. We stood at the door as they left and saw Dr Hill hurrying over in his own facemask, instructing them to take Wang Wubao to a canvas tent, one of several erected beside the hospital a few days earlier. They were surrounded by barbed wire, leaving a passageway for an armed patrol within. We had thought that those tents were for new labourers.

Wang Wubao died that afternoon. We heard that his body and personal belongings were taken into the open country for immediate cremation.

The following day, the foremen directed us to clean the doors, windows, walls, floors, tools and kitchens with warm soapy water. We had to strip, just like at the medical examination in Qingdao, while they took our temperatures. If anybody showed signs of a fever, they were sent to those canvas tents straight away. They told the rest of us to soak our clothes in salt water and dry them in the sun.

After a few days, the man who had been patting Wang Wubao's back fell ill and died. We also heard that one of the soldiers who had carried his stretcher on that night had succumbed too. Rumour had it that the soldier's symptoms had been particularly fearful – that blood was seeping from his nose, ears and mouth and his skin had turned purple by the time he died.

All kinds of information, true or false, spread through the camp. Some claimed that the Americans had brought the disease, some that it was from Spain and some that tens of thousands of Allied soldiers were sick. Others said it had spread to China, or that in some parts of the American continent entire villages had been wiped out. A few suggested that German gas bombs were responsible for transmitting the plague through Europe.

More and more labourers and British soldiers fell ill. One day, the British officer in charge of the twenty-second section became sick. He was transferred to a city hospital. After that, two new doctors arrived at camp with a Christian minister in their retinue, all British. Some members of the sixteenth section were assigned to nurse the sick, carry stretchers and burn corpses.

Sick people were stretchered into those tents every day. The labourers were taken into some, the rest into others. We were kept separate even in hospital.

Some of the sick died, but many made brief and miraculous recoveries. A man from Hebei had been taken to the tents with fever and vomiting, then slept for several days. Dr Hill and his assistants were so busy that he received no treatment. When he woke, he was well enough to get up and eat. After Dr Hill examined him, he announced with astonishment that the man was cured.

When he returned to the barracks, we asked him about the conditions in the tents.

"People lying all over the floor, everywhere you look it's like they are possessed, no strength at all," he said, looking fearful. "The sound of coughing is everywhere, some of them sound like they're going to cough their lungs out."

When we asked him about his secret cure, he told us that he only slept. He didn't want to say much lest Yama King of Hell overhears him and drags him straight back to death.

Those of us who remained healthy continued to work, but shifts were shortened – sometimes we returned to the barracks after a mere eight hours. Some said that the best cure was to eat and sleep well. We could only eat what we were given, but at least we had plenty of time for sleep.

Some in the camp claimed that one could defend against the disease by massaging acupuncture points on the feet, others by practising tai chi. Many did so each day.

Two-Horses carved an image of the Bodhisattva Guanyin holding a willow branch. He worshipped it daily, praying for Ella's safety and health and that he would see her again. Many in the camp asked for Guanyin's blessing along with him.

I wasn't a believer, but I asked for her blessing just the same.

Fate is like a cobweb in a storm. It will hold fast if the winds are light but break under the force of a gale. Come breeze or gale, that wasn't up to me.

31

THE AFTERNOON SUN hung obliquely in the sky, and we were already off work. It had not rained for several days, each footstep raised dust from the ground. Someone was playing the *erhu*, another the flute. While lacking harmony, their music still brought life to that camp in the wilderness.

Elsewhere, men sat outside playing poker, backgammon or mah-jong, squabbling and laughing together over their homemade tiles. A pair had stripped off their shirts to practise a tai chi exercise. They pushed at each other's hands, one forward then back, until they were drenched in sweat.

Another circle of men kicked a shuttlecock to one another. The shuttlecock was made out of lost feathers along with scraps of leather from the discarded shoes of British soldiers. They practised so often that their game was a spectacle, they could play special tricks with the shuttlecock flitting between them.

Old Shuan's voice rang into the mix, cracking his *kuaiban* as he narrated the tale of *Romance of the Three Kingdoms*. A crowd had gathered around him. Of all our camp's storytellers, he was the best, using straightforward vocabulary and even some Shandong dialect. His voice would rise and fall, bringing heroes and villains to life with its rhythm. At a narrative climax, everything would fall silent, his audience straining not to miss a single word. Sometimes he would draw out a long, dramatic pause that he filled with *kuaiban* clapping until his listeners urged him to continue.

Two-Horses sat surrounded by apprentices, teaching them to weave baskets out of straw. One student planned to make a living selling them when he returned to China, but Two-Horses' own love of crafting was like an enchantment. Pining for Ella, he had stopped using vulgar language and instead turned his longing into art. A few days earlier, he had asked Tom to send her a package that contained paper figures of Mandarin ducks in water, an animal woodcut, earrings made from tin cans and a handkerchief upon which he had embroidered her name. His thick fingers were incredibly dexterous with the needle.

A few armed British soldiers were standing nearby, looking over at us from their conversation. They weren't worried; they were just curious about what we were doing. We couldn't go anywhere other than work, but all they could do was look at us. They had no freedom at all, their lives perhaps even duller than ours.

I was reading a French novel that Tom had given me, my back against a tree trunk. I could read quite large volumes now with the help of my dictionary.

My head started to ache after a dozen or so pages, so I went to lie down in the barracks. But when Two-Horses came to find me for dinner, I found that I had no appetite. I touched my forehead – it was scalding hot. I asked Two-Horses to tell George that I might have the fever.

"It can't be!" he cried, coming to my side. "You were jus' fine!"

Struggling through a violent fit of coughing, I held up my arms, gesturing at him to stay away.

The coughs stopped him in his tracks, and a group of men who had been playing cards went rushing out in a panic. More than a dozen people had died over the previous fortnight, while many others were still fighting for their lives in the tents.

"Go!" I called out, shooing Two-Horses away.

"Ge, wait here. I'll be right back." He ran like the wind.

The *erhu* stopped outside, then its creaking music began again. People weren't callous, just accustomed to seeing the sick. Even if they wanted to help, what could they do? Many labourers saw life and death as preordained. When your time comes, you can't escape it; if it's not your time yet, Yama wants nothing to do with you.

Two-Horses returned with two masked labourers holding a stretcher. As they placed me onto it, I felt a pain spreading through my whole body, then my nose and mouth let out a smell of decay.

Exhausted, I closed my eyes. My strength failed me, but I could just about hear the conversation above me:

"That's the thirteenth today."

"The Brits say thirteen's an unlucky number."

"Looks like he's done for."

I could also hear Two-Horses, Old Shuan and the others: "Delun, you're going to be fine!", "You'll be OK!", "Ge, I'll come see you!" ...Sounds became waves that cracked against my aching head, then the waves receded, and I felt light as cotton, like I might float away.

...I flew up, my hands holding the sky, my feet touching the clouds. I saw the red, grey and thatched roofs of Wuping. Sunlight warmed the stone pavement, letting off steam just like mother's Spring Festival rice cakes. I could hear footsteps all around me, and children's voices. They were singing:

Red flowers blossom,
White flowers blossom,
Red flowers, white flowers, all flowers blossom.

It was my siblings and I who were singing!

I saw the great stone lions on either side of our door. A servant was sweeping the courtyard with a long-handled broom, dried leaves whirling into the air as he brushed rhythmically along.

Bowing piously, my mother placed incense into the copper burner in the front courtyard. Smoke curled into the air. My sisters followed her, suppressing their laughter, not daring to run away and play.

My father's stern expression did nothing to conceal his love as he read in his study. He read with pride, pacing around with his eyes half-closed, intoxicated by the ancient poetry. Only pretending to listen, my brother held a book while gazing at a flock of birds that were foraging outside.

I wore a grey silk robe, standing atop the stone bridge as I watched the koi beneath...

"Your soul has left you," I heard a voice say. It was my own.

"No, it's not time!" The answering voice was mine as well.

A cold hand pushed against me. I opened my eyes, gasping for breath. My lungs seemed suddenly perforated, suffocating me no matter how hard I struggled to snatch oxygen from the air.

I finally managed to inhale just as we entered the white tent, assaulting me with the stench of rot and human waste. The camp beds were crammed, the air wracked with coughs, cries and sobs.

I saw one of the new doctors in his white coat, behind him a cluster of soldiers and labourers who had undergone training to be his assistants. They didn't stop at patients' bedsides or give them medicine; they just wandered around as if they were checking to see whether the sick were still alive.

I was placed onto a straw mat in a quiet corner that I later learned was where the stretcher-bearers would place the people they believed would soon die. Both the doctor and his hastily trained nurses avoided it; we were corpses already.

My breathing settled. I closed my eyes, trying to summon fond memories, to ward off pain and fear. My body's thirst for oxygen made it impossible, the images flashed incoherently in my mind. Cool streams, dewdrops on petals, my parents chatting gently, an ant carrying a leaf, the heavens full of stars, Lin Yumei raising her head to laugh, sparks rising from my father's ivory pipe...

And then my eyes were filled with red. A red lantern, a pair of red shoes, a red veil, red silk...

If I had never left Wuping, what would I be doing right now? The thought made me feel pathetic. Wuping was already a distant dream; I could never go back. But I didn't want to die like this, not in this filthy, wretched place.

I remembered something I had read in the Bible recently: "Jesus said, 'Come to me, all of you who labour and carry heavy burdens, and I will give you rest.'"

Rest, rest, I mumbled to myself.

32

WHEN I WOKE, I found myself in a bed on the other side of the tent. Two-Horses was sitting on the ground beside me, his eyes lighting up over the brim of a white mask when he saw that I was awake.

"I moved you," he said. "I went to find George and told him I wanna be a nurse. He was thrilled."

My throat was too painful for me to say anything, but I managed a faint nod. Of course George was thrilled, everyone wanted to be as far from the sick as possible. Even some members of the section who had been assigned to nursing had refused to enter the tents.

I wanted Two-Horses to leave. Each moment he spent beside me was another person inhaling that deadly air. Straining, I lifted my arm to point at the exit.

He understood. "Ge, don't worry. I'm strong aren't I, plague will look at me and not dare. Plus, I made us both crosses like the one Tom wears round his neck." He showed me a coin-sized wooden cross with a red string, then from another pocket a similarly small Guanyin. He placed the pair in front of me. "Look, our god and the foreigners' god are all 'ere to look after us. From now on, other than when I'm eating and drinking and going to the toilet, I'll spend all my time in the tents. I'll even sleep 'ere." He pointed to a mat beside my bed. "Anything happens, all you need to do is call me. You're awake, I'm with you. You're asleep, I'll look after the others."

The sound of drumbeats came thumping from the camp outside.

"They're drumming and dancing to ask the gods to keep the disease away," Two-Horses said. "Everybody says that if the foreigners are scared of it too, then we have to rely on our own methods. George said the Brits didn't like it, but we asked 'em and they agreed to it in the end. Looks like the Brits don't know what to do."

He fetched a basin of water, then placed the wrung-out cloth on my forehead. Soon after, he found a sack full of rags for me to use as a pillow.

Suddenly, a cry of pain burst from a patient just a few beds away. Twisting, he tried to sit up, spat mouthfuls of blood and tumbled to the ground. Two labourers rushed over to help him, but the doctor gestured them away. After crouching to inspect the fallen patient, he announced, in shoddy Chinese, "Him die."

Two-Horses blocked my view. "Ge, I'm here, you're not gonna die."

If I do die, I wanted to say, please take my ashes to Wuping. But I had never been so exhausted, I could only whimper. I felt that if I listened carefully, I would hear death's footsteps. Two-Horses held my hand in silence.

Someone called him to stretcher another sick person

from the camp. "Ge," he said before leaving, "you wait for me. Old Shuan is making you some porridge!"

There were a few patients with only mild symptoms who could sit up unsupported and even walk around. They begged the doctor to let them leave. The man to my right, so tall that his feet stuck over the edge of his bed, was one such case. When the nurse told him that he needed to stay, his expression became a grimace of neither laughter nor tears. He sat, held his face in his hands and shook.

After he had stopped shaking, he looked at me, stood up and said, "I'm goin' home."

He strode towards the exit, ignoring the doctor's orders to stop.

Another nurse barred his way.

Calmly the man said, "My home is that way." He moved the nurse to his side. "I'm not sick. I am goin' home to tend my fields. The crops need watering."

The nurse grabbed onto his clothes, and he responded by pushing him onto the floor.

Two more nurses ran over, trying together to hold him while the other scrambled to his feet to help. The large man punched and kicked, breaking out of their grasp and running to the exit. From nowhere, a soldier flashed into the tent and slammed the butt of his rifle against the man's head, knocking him to the ground and stomping twice on his body.

The man stopped moving.

I spent the following days fluctuating between life and death. Sometimes my condition improved enough for me to eat a little soup or porridge with Two-Horses' help, sometimes I coughed so much that I felt my lungs might explode and I hadn't the strength even to lift my head. Time collapsed. The distinction between minutes, hours and days was unclear. The only thing I desired was to see Two-Horses.

Every day people left the tent, and every day others were carried in.

Finally, when Two-Horses was feeding me some porridge, I sat up by myself. Three days later, the doctor allowed me to return to the barracks.

I knew that it was Two-Horses who had dragged me back from the brink of death.

33

STEADILY, the residents of the nearby villages started to return. Some came alone, others with their families, but all of them at a hurried pace uninterested in the world around them, thinking only of home. They brought along furniture, sacks, boxes and cookware on wheelbarrows and wagons, and sometimes even children sitting perilously on top. The children were dirty and exhausted, drained from their long travels.

We often came across them on our way to or from work. One day, we passed through a village that had been bombed into ruins. Its residents had just returned. Travel-worn and silent, the men took off their hats as they stood before the home they no longer recognised. We could see the women already picking among the ruins, searching for anything they could still repair. Broken chairs, smashed pans, toy cars with missing wheels…

We would have jumped off the truck to help them if only the British would let us.

Almost a month later, we passed through the same

village again. The villagers had cleared a space in the debris and built five wooden shacks, around which men and women worked together on more permanent homes. Even the children were helping as they sawed wood, shaved planks and moved rocks.

One Friday, we were busy repairing a railway when we saw British troops escorting about three hundred German prisoners, walking along in rows of five. They wore ash-green military uniforms without helmets, hats or belts. Some had calf-length boots, others cloth shoes. Several were wounded and bandaged. Their varied expressions were gloomy, preoccupied, silent, even cheerful. A few of the younger ones, perhaps only fourteen or fifteen years old, waved at us pleasantly as they passed.

I heard someone mutter that they didn't look like baby-roasting demons at all.

Within a few days, Tom told us that there had been an uprising in Germany. The Germans were done for.

We were not yet finally rid of the plague, but the camp was full of joy. There were far fewer sick than in the previous month, and the number of patients recovering was higher than ever. Besides, everyone was so used to seeing the temporary hospital tents that we had gradually forgotten their existence.

Most of our assignments since October had been to collect discarded bullets and shells from the battlefield, or to bury the dead.

Standing beside the mountain of shells that we had created, we looked pitifully small. Once so terrifying, the bullets now lay quietly beneath the bright and beautiful sunlight, oblivious to the world as the trees' shadows danced over them. Villages, homes and families had been destroyed amid the sound of their roar. The young and the strong had disappeared.

Given the choice, we would have opted to fight rather than collect rotting, maggot-infested bodies, but to our surprise we grew used to that terrible job. But when I saw some of us laughing as they tossed bodies onto the trucks with pitchforks, my heart still felt tight – as if I were a corpse on the tip of those long spikes. These once-living people now had only dirt and weeds as their companions. If their bodies were never found, they would dissolve into nature's embrace.

With victory in sight, the mood of the soldiers and foremen also improved. They relaxed their supervision, allowing us some free time to leave the camp on Sundays. We believed we would soon return to China, so we began to raise money to buy gifts to take home.

There were three villages within an hour's walk of the camp, and a small town half an hour further. One was an ancient castle hamlet that had escaped the war largely unscathed, while the others had suffered varying degrees of damage. By the end of October, almost all the village residents had returned and rebuilding work started.

When we visited the castle village one day, the residents weren't overtly hostile to us; they hadn't put up signs in Chinese to say we were unwelcome. But they stopped what they were doing and stared at us in silence when we approached. Even the children stopped playing to look at us in fear.

When we saw that, we decided to turn around and go to the town instead.

Two-Horses said angrily, "Ella says that the people in her village aren't like this, they welcome the foreign workers who've helped them."

Someone responded, "She just said that to comfort you."

"Ella wouldn't do that. She says her family all wanna meet me."

"Are you really going to stay in France and get married?"

"What's it to do with you? God's watching over what we do!"

He said the same thing every time anyone asked.

He had become superstitious, inventing all sorts of methods via which he could divine his fate. He would pick dandelions, blow at their seeds, and if the flower became bare in one breath he would marry Ella. If the seeds had other ideas, he would pick up a branch and count its leaves. An even number meant yes, an odd number meant no. His other methods included counting how many houseflies he saw in a day, whether he tripped on a rock, whether he choked when he drank water, whether he dropped his chopsticks, and whether or not someone bumped into him while he was walking.

Still indignant at the villagers' attitudes, Old Shuan said, "It's that last week that caused it all. One rat's droppings ruin the pot."

He was referring to the fact that a farmer from the village with the castle had come to complain that Chinese had stolen his silverware and chickens.

"That was the eighteenth section, nothing to do with us. Didn't they lose some wages and get whipped?"

Old Shuan said, "These French don't distinguish between us, we're all the same to them." He continued, "Did you hear about the camp in La Seyne-sur-Mer getting into a fight with locals when they were transporting cargo at a pier a few days ago? There were just a few of them to begin with, but then the whole camp came to help, a hundred people."

George had mentioned this to our section, warning us never to get into a conflict with the locals. If we did, then it would be us who were punished for it.

Everybody discussed this at once.

A yell came from behind us. We turned and there stood a group of children. The one who had yelled at us looked to be six or seven with brown hair and a floral yellow dress. They ran noisily back to the village together after her shout.

Old Shuan asked me, "What did she say? Seemed like she wasn't happy."

Boundless fields and meadows stretched out beneath the azure sky. How beautiful the scent was! It livened all the senses, allowing you to enjoy it to the fullest. A grey hare appeared from nowhere, hopping along the path before disappearing once more into the wild grass.

I didn't want to ruin our brief, precious moments of freedom. I said, "She told us not to trample the crops."

Two-Horses shot me a look, then lowered his head and quickened his pace to walk alone. I knew that he'd understood the girl. She had called us criminals, thieves.

We arrived at the town. It had a few shops supported by soldiers from a British-American military camp nearby.

We knew about the shops because we had been there before doing roadworks about four months ago. Since then, they had removed all the unsightly planks that had been sealing their broken windows, and flowers bloomed in pots by the doors.

As usual, there were very few young men not in military uniform. The civilians we saw were mostly women, the elderly, children or middle-aged men.

They were more used to seeing Chinese people in the town, so they weren't interested in our presence and were even friendly compared with the more rural folk. They welcomed us, knowing that we had money and were out to spend it.

"*Jinlai, jinlai.*" To our surprise, some shopkeepers greeted us with the Chinese words for 'come in'. The francs in our pockets disappeared one by one. Old Shuan got himself a black tweed hat, Two-Horses a set of tools for wood carving and some small ornaments for Ella. I bought a razor for my father, and for my mother a fine shawl with a village scene embroidered upon it. I also bought things for my younger siblings and the servants, then found a set of crochet coasters shaped like flowers: a perfect gift for Miss Lu.

Many of the men bought sweets, biscuits and toys. One found a half-metre-long clockwork train that ran on tracks, saying that even the richest people in his town may not have seen such a marvellous thing.

We were in a bakery, eating a lunch of bread and sausage, when we suddenly heard the raucous sound of trumpets and drums coming cheerfully from the street. Before we even had the chance to see what was happening, a boy of twelve or thirteen in blue overalls rushed through the door. He was sweating profusely, his face shining with delight and he was missing one shoe. He brandished a newspaper and, with a voice already hoarse from yelling, shouted, "War is over! The Germans have surrendered! The war is over!"

The only response was the sound of the plate in the hands of the proprietress crashing to the floor. There was an instant in which everyone in the bakery seemed frozen in time, unable to move.

The boy swallowed, and in a lower voice said, "The

newspaper... says the war," he gasped for breath, "says the war's really over."

People seemed to return to reality, rushing to his side at once to see the newspaper in his hands. Some started weeping, while others danced with their arms around those next to them, and some leapt onto tables to sing the national anthem. Standing right next to me, the proprietress grabbed my face and kissed me firmly on the cheeks, then my companions one by one.

Everyone shouted and jumped for joy, running outside to join the revelry that had started in the streets. It was crammed with people. Soldiers, commoners, white, black, Asian all mixed together, everybody holding hands, hugging and kissing each other. Flowers and confetti flew ahead, with all kinds of musical instruments playing. Violins, accordions, horns, trumpets, trombones and flutes all came together without rhythm or melody to form an ecstatic musical cacophony. Even the church bells and factory whistle joined in the fun. Some people were crying, some were laughing, some were doing both, and many cheeks were covered with lipstick.

"If only Ella were here!" Two-Horses waved a French flag that an older woman had just given to him.

I smiled, but dark clouds were gathering in my heart.

34

One drizzly Saturday, the old stone streets of Montbrison were empty but for the patrons of one elegant cafe. They chatted quietly around the tables, as if afraid to disturb the day's tranquillity. David had arrived on the train from Dunkirk the previous day and had come to the cafe early in the morning after spending the night at a hotel.

Watching the rain-spattered windows, David gave free rein to his imagination. A series of unrelated images flashed before his eyes: trenches full of mud and scurrying rats, endless sorghum fields, yellow *lamei* blossoms, severed arms hanging from barbed wire, streams flowing through the mountains, Marguerite dancing around the living room with the baby in her arms, a wall covered in black-and-white photographs, Anne running on the beach with two pigtails, Anne on a swing in a pink dress...

He thought about the last time he had seen Two-Horses. He and Marguerite had already moved to Paris, where they had been living in the Latin Quarter for a year and a half.

David had started work at La Grange machinery factory as a lathe worker but would soon be promoted to senior technician. Marguerite was teaching at a secondary school near the Panthéon while studying art. Their new jobs and new surroundings were keeping them busy every day.

One day after work, he saw Two-Horses waiting for him by the factory gates. He wore an ill-fitting suit and a formal hat, looking rushed and uneasy with an old-fashioned black suitcase at his feet. David wanted to run over to embrace him but then realised that his enthusiasm would only complicate things further. So he walked up to him slowly, following the flow of the people leaving. Two-Horses looked ready to either laugh or cry, and he held his breath before saying, "Ge, you didn't tell me your address. I went everywhere in Lyon asking around, it was so hard!"

He guessed that Two-Horses had visited L'Usine de Machines Faustin. He pretended to be indifferent. "Didn't I write to you when I left Lyon to tell you not to look for me?"

They walked around to find a secluded corner. "Ge, why? Why?" Two-Horses said. "What did I do wrong? What happened? You didn't say anything in your letter!"

No, he said to himself, I won't ever tell Two-Horses what happened in Lyon.

He had predicted that Two-Horses would come to find him, so had already planned in advance what he was going to say to him. But at that moment, he knew his prepared lines about how he liked Paris were not only unconvincing, but would suggest that he was happy for Two-Horses to keep visiting.

"I don't want people to know that I was a labourer," he said. "I can have a fresh start here."

Two-Horses looked stunned. "We helped them to win the war. Even if they look down on us, we can't look down on ourselves." Two-Horses continued when David did not answer, "Da Zhuang and Boss Cai both died in the war. What difference is there between them and the French soldiers who died? Is Chinese life so cheap?"

David was silent a while before saying, "Just act like I don't exist, don't come to find me."

"You're saying you look down on me, you don't want to be friends with me?"

"Go back."

"I won't tell people about your past."

"Don't come here again."

Two-Horses looked at him, the earlier excitement vanishing from his face. "You're not the Delun I knew before. He was kind and faithful."

"The Delun you knew before already died."

Two-Horses took a few steps back, shaking his head. "I've made a mistake. You're not my *ge*." He took a package out of his suitcase. "Ella wanted me to give you and Marguerite this sausage." He threw it into the bin. "May as well give it to the rats."

David watched Two-Horses stride away. He stood there until it was dark, then walked home slowly.

Remembering that scene, David let out a long sigh. His life was coming to an end, but he still felt like he had only just appeared in this world. All his memories were so fresh and alive, like a bunch of freshly cut flowers still covered in dew.

But had all those things actually happened? Anne's pink dress, for example. In his memory she had adored it, but

Marguerite said that she never had such a dress. Sure enough, he had rummaged through all her childhood things and photos and never found it.

Without a doubt, particularly at his age, memory was untrustworthy. But life is composed of fragments of memory, big and small. There were lost, unimportant fragments, but he remembered the things that really defined his life. How strange it was. A trivial matter, a careless word, a stranger who flashes by, these tiny coincidences might determine your fate.

If he had not encountered that smoke-filled train on the night he left Wuping, he might have returned home and entombed his fantasies of true love in that marriage bed with Miss Lu. If he had not heard those students' conversations in Qingdao, he might never have boarded the *Manchester*. If he had not worked as a mechanic in Lyon after the war, he never would have met Marguerite. If he had never met Marguerite, he would have returned to China with Old Shuan.

If he had returned to China, what would his life be like now? Would he have been caught up in the evils of war like his family? Or would he have followed in the steps of Old Shuan and ended up falling prey to a political movement?

At ten o'clock, David stood at the blue wooden door of the Green Garden Retirement Home.

He rapped on the brass knocker and was greeted by a middle-aged woman in a lilac uniform. She seemed sharp and capable, her hair combed into a ponytail, not a single strand out of place. She introduced herself as Louise, the woman he had spoken to on the call to make this appointment the day before.

He introduced himself and followed her into a courtyard full of flowers. A few oak trees grew there, decorated with ornaments made by the residents' families and the children at the nearby school. Multicoloured windmills spun in the branches.

"How is Philippe today?" David asked.

"He slept all day yesterday, then woke up in the middle of the night yelling that he wanted to see an atlas. He's been well overall in recent weeks, unlike two months ago when he was always losing his temper and hitting people." Her voice became apologetic. "Perhaps I shouldn't have told you that, but I should warn you."

"Do his children come to see him often?"

"His second son died a few years ago, and his daughter has been gone for more than a decade. His youngest son passed away most recently, he was my pa's best friend. His eldest son died in North Africa in the Second World War, in his early twenties. He was a handsome lad, he had his father's big stature and his mother's grey eyes. The youngest son went to war, too. He was lucky enough to survive, he only lost a couple of fingers. His grandchildren sometimes come to see him, but he doesn't recognise them. Oh, and he doesn't like to speak French these days, mainly Chinese. He gets really talkative sometimes, chirping away. I don't know what he's saying, but he seems happy. One of his grandsons spent some time in China and can speak to him in Chinese. He taught me a few words!"

"You haven't seen each other in a long time, have you?" she asked him.

"That's right," David said. "Does he have hobbies?"

"He loves looking at maps. He also does origami when he's in a good mood. He could do it quickly before, but now it takes him half a day to make one little boat." She sighed. "My pa said he used to live near Dunkirk, but when they moved here, he and his youngest son opened a successful woodwork shop together. Philippe was so skilled with his hands, made a real name for himself. We still have the cabinets and chairs they made, they're really sturdy."

They passed through another blue door at the far end of the courtyard. David signed his name and time of arrival at the check-in desk.

Louise continued to describe Philippe's condition, saying he could no longer walk because of a stroke eight years ago and had lived in the care home ever since. "Wait here, I'll bring him."

The room was warm and comfortable, the sound of Beethoven's *Moonlight Sonata* soothing through the air. On a long red bench beside the door sat a well-dressed, silver-haired old woman. She didn't even glance at David, just concentrated on patting the back of a plastic doll in the crook of her arm while mumbling to herself. An old man sat in a wheelchair nearby, bald but for a few white hairs above his ears. He stared blankly at the children's crayon drawings on the wall, his head tilted to one side, his mouth slightly open.

David touched his own hair subconsciously. It was thinner than in previous years, but there were no bald spots yet. He had always been pleased with his thick hair.

He did some addition in his head and believed all the answers to be correct.

He used a full-length mirror in the hall to straighten his chest and tie, holding the knot purposefully. His hands were steady, his eyes bright. He checked his coat and nodded with satisfaction when he found no stains or crumbs.

Louise pushed over a wheelchair in which sat an old

man. His eyes were closed, his body hunched, his face dotted with dark age spots. His legs shook slightly on the footrest.

More than half a century later, they met again.

On the verge of tears, David walked over and bent down to speak. "Two-Horses, it's me. Delun!"

After a while, the old man opened his cloudy eyes and said, in Shandong-accented Chinese, "You bastard!" He clapped his hands and began to sing, swaying his head with satisfaction.

Louise laughed and said to David, "We all understand that word. No matter who he sees, that's the first thing he says. Sometimes he yells at me and the other nurses '*gun dan*', we know he's telling us to scram."

"Can I take him out for a walk?" David asked.

She hesitated. "Usually not, but you've come all the way from Paris. You must be careful, though. Don't mind how weak he looks now, when he's in high spirits two of us are no match for him."

David promised they would not run into mishap.

"I wanna go! I wanna go!" Two-Horses shouted at Louise.

"Just for a little while," David entreated.

"Go on then. You must be back by half past eleven for his medication."

David pushed Two-Horses outside. The rain had stopped, the sun was out.

"Look, a rainbow!" David pointed.

Two-Horses did not look, but sang instead:

Ah! Flash, flash, it leaps to the sky,
Just like that, in the twinkling of an eye.
A man-eating beast,
And it's mine to defeat.
Show me your power,
And I'll show you who's strong.
Tiger, tiger, meet Wu Song!

He slapped his leg as he sang, out of rhythm but seeming proud of himself. David smiled. "Two-Horses, I remember you singing and dancing with those sandbags on your back all those years ago!"

"Who are you?"

"Your brother, Delun! We were in the same section, together every day."

Two-Horses furrowed his brow and thought for a moment, but quickly gave up. "Do I have other brothers too?"

"Three of them. Da Zhuang, Old Shuan and Boss Cai."

"Why haven't they come to see me?"

"They're far away!" David pointed to the sky. "They live up there."

Two-Horses understood. "It's good there, no need to worry about when you're getting food or drink. Have you come to take me home? Ella's made a delicious meal, she's waiting for me." Louise had told David that Ella had been dead for nearly twenty years. A cold had become pneumonia, and she was gone.

They turned onto a path leading to a riverbank. It was thick with flowers, with white butterflies flitting about between them. There was no one else around.

Two-Horses suddenly cried out, "Ella! Ella!"

David tapped on the trunk of a cypress tree with his knuckles, pretended to listen carefully, then said, "Nobody's home. Ella must have gone out to buy groceries."

"Oh, she's gone to buy groceries," Two-Horses muttered, then struggled to stand, as if he wanted to look for Ella. He lost his balance and tumbled forward, but David was fast. He caught him mid-air, then they fell to the ground together.

David gasped and climbed out from under Two-Horses, who was wiggling like a beetle caught in a spider's web. David sat up and turned Two-Horses over, dusted the dirt from his mouth with his sleeve and then let him rest his head on his leg. He had to take a break before he could attempt to get Two-Horses back into the chair.

Two-Horses looked comfortable, as if he had forgotten David's existence. When David touched his forehead, he looked surprised. "Who are you?"

"I'm Delun! We came to France together on the *Manchester* almost seventy years ago. Remember the giant waves on the Pacific?" He imitated the waves with his hand, crashing one after the other. "Waves higher than the boat. So bad we both threw up. We threw our guts up."

Two-Horses nodded. "Those were some big waves. I told Ella but she didn't believe me."

"I told Marguerite, she didn't believe me either. Said I was exaggerating."

"Who's Marguerite?"

"My wife."

"Where's she?"

"She's with Ella."

Two-Horses thought for a moment. "It's been ages since I've eaten cake."

David remembered that he still had a madeleine in his pocket from the cafe that morning. He used all his strength to lift Two-Horses, whose eyes lit up when he saw the madeleine. He had already snatched it, shoved it into his mouth, chewed it and started to swallow before David could remind him to take it slowly.

Afraid he would choke, David begged him to spit it out. Two-Horses didn't listen, so David tried to force his mouth open. Still resisting, his eyes round and his throat moving, he kicked David before finally swallowing the food in his mouth.

"Do you know what those witches give me to eat?" Two-Horses panted angrily. "Thin, watery slime! They lie, say it's for my own good! If it was for my good, then it'd be cake. Maybe they think I haven't paid them enough, or they think I'm ugly and want me to starve to death. I tell them to *gun dan*, and they just laugh! Ella doesn't know what's happening, she hasn't brought me any cake in ages."

"Ella's busy, she has to look after the children," David said.

Two-Horses looked embarrassed and lowered his voice. "Are the kids still sleeping?"

"Yes, they're all sleeping."

"We should talk quietly then." He put his finger to his lips and made a shushing sound.

A cool breeze blew ripples over the surface of the river, out of which leapt a black carp. It flipped over elegantly before diving back into the water, leaving a small splash behind it.

"Let's play skipping stones!" Two-Horses said, his voice raised in excitement. He tried and failed to grab a small oval stone. David picked it up for him and placed it into his hand.

213

Two-Horses threw it towards the river where it sank with a plop. He looked at the river unhappily. "I used to be able to skip it seven or eight times. You try."

David wanted to stand but his leg was already numb. The rock he tossed sank just the same.

Two-Horses picked a white flower and threw it towards the river. The flower landed at his feet. "Those roses are beautiful," he said. "The smell fills your nose."

There were no roses.

"Where?" asked David.

Two-Horses turned to look at him with an expression which called David the world's most preeminent idiot. "The ones in the wire! And there was a stone wall. And it was black with smoke."

David knew where he meant. Beyond that wire and fire-blackened walls had been piles of bodies, the corpses of French soldiers. They had been killed by mortars, their clothes blasted into strips. Some of them were missing hands and feet.

He was glad that Two-Horses only remembered the roses.

He shifted his body carefully, rested Two-Horses' head on the ground, then pulled himself up using both hands and the tree trunk. He feared they would get stuck if they sat there any longer. He lifted Two-Horses and tried to help him back into his wheelchair.

"I can do it myself!" Two-Horses tried, but finally had to let David help him. He sat back in the chair reluctantly.

After a while, he asked, "What's your name?"

"I'm your brother, Zhang Delun."

"Where do you live?"

"Paris."

"I've been there. Loads of apple trees. The blossom's like a woman's lips. Chickens and ducks everywhere." He did an excellent imitation of a duck. "It was so hot in summer, I took off my clothes and was still sweatin' so much that I had to get into the river to cool off. An' winter's so cold, the wind drills straight into your bones, almost turned me into an ice lolly. When I get a customer, I find all my strength. Rickshaw is an art – feet steady, head down, waist bent, legs swishing, neatly does it! Eyes sharp as a hawk, spotting all the potholes and stones on the ground, turning the handle, dodging them all. If you're hot you can't drink cold water, else your lungs will explode and you won't have the strength to pull again. Booze too, though it smells good you must jus' sip – no gulps or you'll burp and it'll slow you down. If you're goin' far, you can't show off how fast you are. You gotta keep it steady. Then the guest will be comfortable, maybe sleep a little, then they don't know how slow you go. If you think you're tough or one of your customers is a pretty girl, you want to show off and run like lightning, but if you do it too much you'll spit blood. If you spit blood you're like a balloon with a hole, and you can't use your strength. Have you pulled a rickshaw?"

"I have not."

Two-Horses was smug. "I knew you hadn't from the moment I saw you."

"Nobody can compete with you. You're Two-Horses! You pull faster than a pair of horses." David pushed the wheelchair slowly onward.

Two-Horses' laugh showed his few remaining teeth. "What do you do?"

"Lots of different stuff. I was a welder, I operated cranes,

I repaired tanks, I built houses and designed heavy machinery."

"What's a tank?"

"It's just a car with tracks instead of wheels, so it can climb slopes."

"What's a track?"

"It's a..." David did not know how to explain, so he stopped and found a stick to draw a tank on the ground in front of Two-Horses.

"So it's that thing!" Two-Horses said. "What's it called?"

"A tank. We repaired them together."

"I repaired a tank?" A gleam appeared in Two-Horses' clouded eyes.

"Not only repaired it, you drove it!"

"Oh, I'm amazing!"

"You are! You also lifted a boulder."

"Who are you?"

"I'm your brother, Delun."

"You're not a bad bastard. Better'n those witches. Let's go for a walk tomorrow, too."

"I will come to see you tomorrow and the day after that. We brothers have so much to talk about."

"Go fast!"

"You mean when you were in the tank?"

"No, I mean you, you bastard! Now! Don't loaf about, faster! You're slower than a snail. Think you'll get customers at this speed?"

"Where shall we go?"

"Just forward! To the mountains, to the clouds!"

"OK! Sit tight." David began to run behind the chair, resenting that his legs were like sticks with no spring. The dirt road was full of potholes and bumps, and the wheelchair obstructed his view. If not for his grip on the handles, he would certainly have fallen.

With each jolt of the chair, Two-Horses clapped and shouted excitedly, "You bastard, good job!"

David gathered his strength, ready to give it his all. It had been a long time since he had been so happy.

35

We thought the Brits might terminate our contracts early now the war had ended, but it turned out that we were even busier than before.

We filled the trenches, brought more corpses back from the front lines for burial, repaired railways, airports and train stations. We rebuilt cities and villages, excavated mines and worked in factories of all kinds. Though many soldiers had returned from the front lines, they couldn't meet the demand for labour – they also avoided certain jobs.

In camp, complaints about overwork and poor food increased. The milieu of homesickness was denser than ever.

Around the time of the Spring Festival, the Chinese workers launched two large strikes. We won the first, our reward being that we would actually receive the overtime pay owed to us. The second was fruitless, however, ending after only a week of confrontation with the British.

In early February, after a brief assessment and training, I was assigned to work as a skilled mechanic at a heavy-machinery plant in Lyon. More than three hundred Chinese were chosen, with Two-Horses and Old Shuan also making the cut. In the end, though, Two-Horses couldn't come because of a foot injury he sustained while repairing the railway and Old Shuan stayed behind because he'd been promoted to foreman of our section after George's contract came to an end.

I was sad to leave Two-Horses and the section behind, but I was still looking forward to Lyon. I finally had my chance to explore, to broaden my horizons just like I had imagined when I first came to France.

My schoolteacher who had been to Europe once told us that the world's first film had been shot in Lyon. He showed us photographs of the ochre-roofed old town, the art museum's winding floral gardens, the four metal horses pulling the chariot of a goddess into war at the centre of the Place des Terreaux.

Two-Horses helped me pack my bags, stuffing in a few hot cakes that he had wrapped in cloth. I don't know what he traded to get the flour. He was still limping, but Dr Hill said that the bone had healed and that the inflammation was under control, so he could work again in a few days. "Ge, you'll be back in two months, right?"

I said of course.

"Ella's comin' back this week, it's a shame you won't see her."

"You need to keep up with your French, otherwise when you see her you'll be a mute with a thousand words to say."

"Don't you worry, Ge, I can do it!"

"I know you can. You've made great progress. Look how well you speak and write."

I took out my French-Chinese dictionary, full of pages with their corners folded over, and handed it to him. He knew a lot of Chinese characters now, so would be able to use it. Dumbfounded, he pushed it away. "I can't accept somethin' so precious. You're gonna need it every day in Lyon!"

"There will be plenty of bookshops in Lyon, I can buy myself another."

He took the book and placed it under his pillow. It joined Ella's most recent letters, the crucifix and Guanyin. Those were the things he always carried with him, fearing that someone might steal them. "The war's over," he said. "I don't know why I'm always so hectic, even when I'm asleep. My dreams are crazy. They wake me up and then I can't even remember what it was about." He paused, looking suddenly awkward. "Someone told me that if white people and yellow people have babies together then the kid'll be a freak, and it won't even live long." It seemed like this had been troubling him for a while. He looked at me with anticipation.

"Don't listen to them," I said. "People are people. We've all got the same organs, our skin looks different and that's it. When I was at school in Qingdao, one of the teachers had a white American wife, their kids were beautiful and they could speak Chinese and English!"

He erupted with pleasure. "Ge, I should have said something earlier. That question's been driving me mad."

Ella had written to say that she planned to marry Two-Horses, and that she had already made the proper arrangements with the local French government. All their marriage needed now was British ratification.

The bugle sounded. Two-Horses said, "I won't see you out."

I patted his shoulder, took my bags and walked towards

the door. I turned back in the doorway and saw him lying on his bed with his back to me, his head under a blanket.

After spending most of the day on the train, our troop of newly trained mechanics arrived in Lyon. Thousands of French-recruited Chinese labourers had already been stationed in Lyon for some time, so we lived and ate with them. Their camp was just to the west of the city, and you could see the Basilique Notre-Dame de Fourvière standing on top of the hill. As soon as we arrived at the camp, we were told that we would have one half-day off per week, that our shifts were ten hours long and that our time was at our disposal otherwise. If you subtracted the time it would take to get to and from work and to eat, we only had the half day off – but we were still thrilled to hear the foreman's announcement! The camp didn't even have barbed wire around it.

We went to walk around the city centre the moment we dropped off our bags. We rode a taxi, caught a bus and went up in a lift in a high-rise luxury hotel. Everyone praised the city. When we passed a cafe, several of us dashed in to buy a cup of coffee. We took turns tasting it, but everyone agreed that it was too bitter to swallow. I bought a map so I could start planning how I was going to see every scenic spot.

Early the next morning, we started work at L'Usine de Machines Faustin, where I had been assigned to work as a welder. The French welders already employed there were mostly middle-aged men, but there were also some younger men who had returned from war, and around a dozen women of all ages.

The person responsible for training the new Chinese arrivals was a reserved, taciturn young woman named Marguerite. She had a round face, blue eyes and long brown hair that she wore in two braids coiled into a crown on top of her head. She was short in stature, not even to my shoulder in height, but powerful, her arms swinging determinedly as she walked. She always wore loose bib overalls, and sometimes a kerchief around her head that waved like a little banner to the rhythm of her footsteps. Her welding skills and her deft hand when operating the cranes had stirred a little jealousy among the French men, but they were mostly quite respectful to her.

"Marguerite," one of the men said, half in jest, "now the war's over, you and the other lasses should get back to the kitchen."

"Back to the kitchen? You men know how to cook don't you?" Marguerite answered. "I'm going to university!"

"You're what! Men don't want a university girl."

She glared at him. "And I don't want them back."

Sometimes, Chinese labourers would try to sneak liquor into the factory, fishing out a bottle from their chests to take a few sips as they worked. But Marguerite's sharp nose could locate the perpetrators quickly, even if there was just a whiff of alcohol in the air. She would hold her hand out in front of the offender without saying a word, a cold look in her eyes. He would hand it over to her obediently before she strode away to pour every drop down the sink, following it with a burst of water from the tap.

We tried to guess how old she was.

I said early twenties, but someone else said eighteen and another twenty-five or twenty-six. One man said she might be almost thirty, otherwise how could the line between her eyebrows be so deep?

Despite her stern appearance, she was very patient with us when she gave directions, reminding us repeatedly to wear our protective gear and to make sure the welding surfaces were clean. The factory sent a translator, but after she discovered that I could speak French, she would sometimes come to me for translation instead.

She came over to me once while I was welding machine parts and pointed out where my seams needed to be smoother or tighter. She showed me how to avoid causing cracks, standing so close to me that I could hear her breathing and see the tiny, fine hairs on her arms shining silver in the light.

I tried again under her instruction; the result was perfect.

She nodded in satisfaction, smiled at me, then moved on to teach somebody else. I spent the rest of that day in a sort of daze, always thinking about her smile.

My welding skills improved so dramatically over the course of the week that I was able to help her train the other Chinese labourers. To them she said, "If everyone can work with the same quality and efficiency as Mr Zhang, we will be able to complete our task here at least two weeks ahead of schedule." Then she added, "He also never drinks at work." When the translator finished the last sentence, everybody looked at me and winked.

Soon, my Chinese colleagues began to tease me.

"I think Marguerite's taken a fancy to you, always walkin' over to you."

"She teaches you all too!" I retorted.

"Ah, but it's not the same. When she's teachin' you, she's all soft and doe-eyed–"

"Softer than the softest willow catkin," another interjected, "softer than the softest braised meat."

Everyone burst into laughter, and someone called out

cheerfully, "Look, look, Delun's gone all red! He must be thinking about Marguerite day and night!"

Another imitated Marguerite's serious look and said, "You should all be more like Mr Zhang. He doesn't drink, he doesn't gamble, he doesn't smoke opium, he doesn't swear, he doesn't chase after women..."

The subject changed when he mentioned women. Somebody had found a brothel near the camp, and so many of them had been running off to it after work. Since then, detailed discussions about the women who worked there had become a nightly fixture. In a place without women, talking about them becomes life's greatest pleasure.

I crept out of the door when they started chatting. Their teasing embarrassed me, but at the same time, my heart was full of joy. The sky was scattered with stars beside a pale moon that shone a dim light across the trees, and a chill breeze passed through the air. I wrapped my clothes tighter around my body and pressed my hat down over my ears. Thinking of Marguerite, I couldn't help but smile, then scolded myself for getting carried away. But even as I reprimanded my imagination, I remembered her hand holding mine, showing me how to hold the welding torch. Her touch had been an instant, but the instant was infinity in my mind. I didn't return to my room until it was unbearably cold outside.

36

Days passed by, and soon we had been in Lyon for a whole month. I learned to repair machine tools and operate cranes. Sometimes I would be sent to other divisions to help, but of course I was never happy to leave the welding department because it meant that I wouldn't see Marguerite that day.

Two-Horses wrote to me during that time. Though many characters were written wrong and he had used circles to replace those he could not attempt, I felt gratified by his progress. He said that Ella had arrived three days after I left. With Tom's help, the Brits had even made an exception to allow her into the camp – they were increasingly relaxed now that their own return home was imminent. What's more, Old Shuan was now a foreman and could help Two-Horses sneak out to see her after work. She had found somewhere to stay in town, helping a family cook and clean in exchange for room and board.

Our relationship with the French in the machinery factory was still like that between well water and river water: we did not mix. We took our meals and our breaks apart, but

Marguerite paid no attention to what the other French said behind her back and, after we became acquainted, would sometimes come to hang out with us during breaks. She wanted us to teach her Chinese, and asked all sorts of questions about China.

The line between her eyebrows faded as her smiles increased. Our friendship grew, and I realised she was as talkative as a morning bird.

We were still in Lyon at the end of May, and the foreman said that we might stay until summer. I had redoubled my efforts to learn French in that period. Marguerite told me that I was improving rapidly.

One Friday just as we were about to leave work, Marguerite stuffed a note into my hand. I waited until I was alone before opening it. Her handwriting was beautiful. "Meet me at the entrance of Basilique Notre Dame de Fourvière on Sunday, three o'clock." It felt like my heart stopped for at least five minutes before resuming its beat.

Instead of returning to the barracks or wandering around the city after work, I went to a barbershop and asked for whatever haircut was fashionable among young French men. Then I went to a clothes store where I finally settled on a V-necked grey sweater with a checked shirt that cost me two weeks' wages. I had to ask the clerk to reserve it for me while I ran back to camp for the money.

That Sunday afternoon was our time off. After lunch, my colleagues all went out for a walk while I found an excuse to stay behind. Once they had gone, I changed into my new outfit and left.

The Basilique Notre-Dame de Fourvière, built during the Franco-Prussian War, is on the hillside by the west bank of the Saône. I had been there several times, and on each occasion I was awed by its carvings and frescos. It was approaching half past two when I arrived. I had wanted to bring flowers, but I was afraid to be too conspicuous and so I opted for a little box of chocolates with a red ribbon instead.

I looked absentmindedly at the colourful stained-glass windows and carved walls, each of them narrating stories in the Bible. They were as solemn and beautiful as ever, but I was out of my mind with nerves.

There she was. She had exchanged her work boots for black mid-heels and let her hair loose to her shoulders. A long green dress flowed as she walked, its floral pattern like butterfly wings in her wake.

She walked over to me, and I noticed how lovely her perfume smelled. I forced a smile and cursed my muscles for being so uncooperative. My voice quivered as I said, "Your hair looks lovely short. Your dress looks lovely too. You look lovely everywhere."

Her smile showed her white teeth and made that dimple on her right cheek more obvious than ever.

Her long, curled eyelashes flashed a few times as she said, "I like your new hairstyle, too. And the sweater."

I gave her the chocolates. She untied the ribbon, opened the box and said brightly, "Oh, how did you know that almond flavour's my favourite?"

I hadn't, I'd just picked the prettiest.

She put one in her mouth and gave me another. In my nervousness, I ate it too quickly and almost choked, coughing for a while before I could breathe again. She laughed. I would happily choke every day if it meant that I could hear that laugh.

There were only around a dozen other visitors to the church. We walked inside and quietly looked around at the frescoes and the vaulted ceiling. When we came to the front, Marguerite took a pew and indicated for me to sit beside her. I sat around a metre away from her, watching as her eyes closed and her hands folded in prayer. After she finished her prayer, we left to the rear terrace, overlooking the city centre and the Saône. The afternoon sun shone over the river's calm flow and the red-tiled renaissance architecture on either bank, conveying a sense of nostalgia.

Marguerite said, "My papa was a sailor. He says that wherever there is water, there is a soul. I loved to come up this hill with him when I was a child. We would sit here chatting and sometimes sharing our favourite poems. He said that of Lyon's two rivers, the Saône was feminine and the Rhône masculine. They gave birth to the city of Lyon when they met. We would always sit for a while in the church to still our spirits before we went back down."

"You're Christian?" I asked.

She shrugged. "No. Well, when I was a child I would sometimes go to mass with my mother, she's a devout Catholic. But I'm like my papa, I believe in myself, and in the power of nature."

"It seems like your father had quite a big influence on you."

"You could say that."

"But you were praying just now."

"Prayer isn't only for Christians. Papa said that he prayed every day at sea, once in the morning and once at night."

"What do you pray for?"

She gave a mischievous laugh and said, "I'll tell you one day. Do you know how I got out today? I told Maman that I was going dancing with some girlfriends and she didn't suspect a thing. She always says to me, Marguerite, you are almost twenty years old and if you don't have a young man by twenty-one, then you'll never get married. She also says that I can't afford to be picky seeing as so many French lads have been killed. I asked her what's so bad about not getting married, anyway? I can spend more time with you, help you with the chores, chat with you. She just sighed. She had to work a job cleaning trains during the war, but she's the type that thinks women should stay at home. You know, she was actually born a de La Salle – a really wealthy family. I don't know how, but she fell in love with my sailor father. They had to elope."

"Does she want you to stop working?" I asked.

"Certainly, she talks about it every day, but Papa's subsidy for injured servicemen doesn't cover all our expenses. What's more, I like working with the machines. My first day felt like the first time in my life that it had a purpose, and I had the opportunity to meet all kinds of fascinating people."

"You said your father was injured in the war?"

"Yeah, in Verdun." She sighed. "And now he's always drunk, acts like the whole world owes him something. I told him that the bullet had destroyed his face, not his heart. He said I was a naive and stupid girl." She reached out and touched a leaf to her side. "I wish my brave and happy papa would come back to me."

"It must wound people's souls, the front lines." I told her what we had seen when we were digging the trenches, but I didn't mention that we had been there collecting bodies.

She smiled. "You're a good man, but do you really think those of us in the rear were living well? Every day we lived in fear for our loved ones at the front, and we had little food or clothing. I was sixteen when I started work. I worked hard, from dawn 'til dusk, just to send supplies to the front, hoping that the war would end. Now we're at peace, and Papa has come home, but the happiness I longed for has not. Papa gets angry quickly, shouting and breaking things. He scares Maman so much, she even hides behind me. He came at her with a kitchen knife once when he was drunk. I got in the way and managed to hit it out of his hand with a chair. He just stood there, stunned, like a ghost. Then he turned around and left. I was paralysed. Last year, my sister got married to an older man who she doesn't love, now she lives in Marseille. She did that just to escape him, to escape home."

Didn't I, I thought to myself, didn't I come to France to escape?

"Papa was great when I was a child. He would take my sister and me to the riverbank, we'd make art in the sand, we built a treehouse and he would tell stories every night before bed. He had so many stories – when he was a sailor he went to Africa, the Middle East, South America and Asia, even the Cape of Good Hope. He always said that if anyone ever bullied you, you had to fight back hard. Maman always wanted my sister and me to stay home, but not him. He wanted us to explore." She turned to look at me. "Like you, coming all the way from China to help us win this dreadful war."

I lowered my head in shame. I wasn't some brave adventurer, but a coward who had fled reality.

Her words had moved me. Stammering, I said, "But... most French and Brits don't consider us Chinese their allies. They... they look down on us, they think we're just coolies. In their eyes we don't even have names, we're, we're just numbers. They watched over us with whips while we worked... whips and sticks." I began to sweat as I sought through the words in my head, looking impatiently for the right ones. "Always watching, always ready to use corporal punishment... or imprison us. It didn't matter whether it was hot or cold, we still had to work for more than ten hours... not enough to eat. The places we stayed... were often... with barbed wire... except for them... sometimes... they let us out, but we, we have no freedom. If we die, they just throw us into a pit like dogs."

She seemed to understand. She grabbed my hand and looked at me in amazement. "Mr Zhang, is this true?"

Her hand was calloused, rough and knotted from years of hard labour. As far as I was concerned it was the most beautiful hand in all the world. I wanted to lower my head and kiss it, but there was an old couple nearby watching us. I brushed away her fingers subconsciously and took a few steps, putting some distance between us.

We walked together in silence for a while until we came to a stone bench near a flower trellis blooming with white and purple morning glories. We looked around and, seeing no one, sat down with room enough for another between us.

"May I call you Delun?" she asked.

"Of course."

"Delun, I'm not one of those people. I believe that we are all equal, we all have souls, we all have feelings."

I wanted to express my gratitude but didn't know how. I just looked at her and said, softly, "Marguerite."

She smiled. "Delun, tell me about where you're from, your family."

I told her about my parents and my siblings, the stone

lions guarding our door, the apple trees, the bamboo forest, the koi pond, even the street vendors outside.

She listened intently, waiting for me to finish before saying, "I would love to visit one day. Would you be my guide?"

I hesitated, then said, "I would be honoured."

"You're educated, I saw you reading Stendahl's *Le Rouge et le Noir* during break." She began to recite: "'*Mon bonheur sera digne de moi. Chacune de mes journées ne ressemblera pas froidement à celle de la veille.*'"

I began to recite another line. "'Julien saw hawks launch themselves from the rocks over his head, and watched their silent circling. His eyes mechanically followed the birds of prey. The hawks' quiet, powerful movements impressed him; he envied their strength; he envied their isolation.'"

"Delun," she whispered, a gentle glow in her eyes. "Oh, Delun."

I grabbed her hand, brought it to my lips and kissed it. She moved to sit close to me, resting her head on my shoulder. My heart was beating so hard it made me dizzy. I kissed her hair and she lifted her face. Our lips touched. We kissed for a while before separating.

"Stay in France, or I'll go with you to China," she said, as if in a dream.

My head was suddenly filled with the red-veiled figure of Miss Lu. I stood up.

"What's wrong?" She sat upright, shocked.

"I... I... I have something... something I need to tell you." My voice quivered. When I finished talking, the colour was gone from her cheeks. She lowered her head and covered her face with her hands. We were silent like that for a long time.

That's it, it's finished, it's over, I thought. Fate has

dragged me to the pinnacle of happiness, just to push me right back down. She finally raised her head, her expression solemn, the crease like a dagger between her eyebrows. "What are you going to do?" she asked.

"I can't be with Miss Lu," I said. "If my parents refuse to annul our marriage, it will be a marriage in name only."

"What about her? What does she think? Did her father or yours ask her opinion on all this?"

"I don't know," I said, despondently. "I truly don't know."

37

Marguerite and I avoided each other at work for the next two weeks. During shifts, I worked hard and spoke little. In my free time I took solitary walks, avoiding my colleagues and their questions. The bustling streets, the blooming flowers, the scents wafting from the cafes and the beauty of the rivers all became as nothing to me.

One evening, as I lingered on Bonaparte Bridge to watch lamplight shimmer on the river's surface, someone came to stand beside me. It was Marguerite, still in her work overalls. She pressed her hand softly in mine. "If you're a sinner behind bars," she said, "I'm willing to be there with you."

From that day on, we met often after work in one of the less crowded parks. She taught me French and asked me questions about China: education, food, culture, religion, my friends and family. We knew a day would come when we had to talk about Miss Lu, but we didn't want to cast that shadow over these first stirrings of love.

Her affection made my life vibrant, my work light and joyful. We tried to hide our relationship at the factory, but our sharp-eyed co-workers could see it anyway. It was just a few of the older women asking her malicious questions at first, but gradually rumours spread throughout the entire workshop. The Frenchmen warned me that if I had anything more to do with her, they would break my neck.

After that, I was one of a dozen or so Chinese who were transferred to the crane department, which needed urgent help. Though Marguerite and I were in different units, she would still slip out to see me. Whenever I saw her waving at me in the distance, my eyes would mist with joy.

I couldn't take her back with me to China, so I began to consider the possibility of marrying her in France. There was a legal precedent already for doing so, and if I married Marguerite then my father could no longer force me to be with Miss Lu. Each night I agonised over how to tell them, both my parents and Miss Lu. I wrote letter after letter but found them all unsatisfactory.

After I kissed her one day, Marguerite looked up at me with concern. "Do Chinese men still take concubines?"

I knew why she had asked. I had seen the French newspaper with a report warning French women against marrying Chinese men. It said that not only were our two cultures poles apart, but that the Chinese were tyrannical with their wives, even taking concubines after marriage.

I held her hand to my chest and, looking directly into those enchanting eyes, said in Chinese:

Our oath is greater than death.
To have and to hold, for all my life.
How painful to be so far from you.
Fate will not let me fulfil my vow.

I translated it into French for her, telling her that it was a poem more than three thousand years old from the *Book of Songs*. It meant that I had vowed to be with her all my life.

On that night, I finally wrote the letters to my parents and Miss Lu. To my parents, I said that I could not leave Marguerite, that if they could not accept her then I could never return. To Miss Lu, I apologised again and said that I would do anything to satisfy her if she demanded financial compensation. That was all I could say. I knew I could never atone for what I had done to her.

I sent the letters early the next morning. That same day, Marguerite and I got engaged under the flowered trellis in the garden of Basilique Notre-Dame de Fourvière.

38

I went to meet Marguerite's parents a month later. Their apartment was on the third of four floors of an umber-hued building near the Saône. It had mottled walls and black balconies full of flowers and vines climbing up to the roof. The old cobblestone street outside slanted slightly towards its centre, and at the street level there was a cafe, a clothes shop, a barber and a toy shop selling marionettes.

Marguerite led me up the dark and narrow staircase. Almost at the door, she glanced at me. I nodded, to show her that I was prepared. We had rehearsed this meeting several times.

"Under absolutely no circumstances are you to mention Miss Lu," she warned me once again.

The door was unlocked. She breathed deeply, readying herself to enter. It was just then that her mother opened the door from inside, as if she had been waiting there a while. She was a slight woman with large eyes and deep brown hair the same shade as Marguerite's, combed meticulously into a bun. She had on a lace-trimmed lilac dress with a high neck, around which she wore a pearl necklace. The contrast between her pallor and the excessive rouge made her look a little ill.

She wrung her hands uneasily together. "Ah, you're David?"

I had given myself that name on the day of our engagement, to make it easier for her family to accept me.

"Madame Lamberton, it is my pleasure to make your acquaintance." I presented a bouquet of white lilies, her favourite according to Marguerite, then kissed the back of her proffered hand after removing my hat.

I was wearing a dark grey suit, polished leather Oxfords and a blue twill tie. Marguerite had laughed when she first saw me, saying that I looked like a banker with pockets full of gold. I had borrowed money from three different labourers to afford the outfit.

Madame Lamberton's expression relaxed as she studied me, seeming satisfied. She led me into the living room where she pointed me to the couch by the window, then went to the kitchen to fill a vase.

It was a dark room, despite the lights. The windows were closed and framed with faded red velvet curtains. The low ceiling had yellowed in some places. Their furnishings were sparse but high quality. Marguerite had once told me that when her parents married, Madame Lamberton's father had given them furniture and gold and silver jewellery as gifts before breaking off all relations with them.

Madame Lamberton returned, arranging the lilies in the vase before sitting down in a chair opposite, her posture perfectly straight with her hands clasped together. She began to ask about my work, so I told her that the crane department's supervisor had already applied for permission to employ me after my contract ended and that he would help me apply for French citizenship.

Finally, I added, "I received a medal and bonus this month for hard work."

She nodded. "And your family in China? Will they bless your marriage to Marguerite?"

"I have written to them already, they won't oppose it."

"Are you sure?"

"Even if they did, I would not leave Marguerite."

"I cannot, and will never, allow Marguerite to move to China."

"Maman!" Marguerite cried out. "You didn't say that yesterday."

"Madame Lamberton, you don't need to worry. I have no intention of asking her to do that."

"After you are married, will Marguerite still have to work?"

"Maman," Marguerite protested, "that's my business. I want to work! I like my job!"

Madame Lamberton gazed lovingly at her daughter. "You can't stay working with a bunch of men if you want to become a teacher. You need to go back to school. Look at your hands, they're like a washerwoman's."

"What's wrong with that?" Marguerite protested again. "There's nothing better than being able to rely on yourself!"

"I support Marguerite's decision to go back to school, even if she wanted to go back tomorrow," I said. "I would never let her suffer." Marguerite glared at me unhappily. I added, "I intend to study mechanical design and engineering myself. My supervisor says he will create opportunities for me."

"Where will you live once you're married?"

"Marguerite and I have talked this over. There's an apartment available near the factory. I will still have plenty of money left over after rent."

"You promise me that you won't take her away from Lyon while I'm still alive. I already lost one daughter, I cannot bear to lose Marguerite as well."

"I swear it, Madame Lamberton."

She unclasped her hands and relaxed her posture. Her gaze wandered to the flowers on the table. "That bouquet is truly lovely."

Marguerite winked at me to show that I had passed her mother's test. I breathed a sigh of relief, feeling sweat on my palms.

Then the sound of slow and heavy footsteps came from outside. Marguerite and her mother stood at the same time.

"Papa's home." Marguerite seemed a little panicked.

The door crashed open. Monsieur Nicholas Lamberton staggered through it, head lowered. He was of medium build, with dishevelled hair and an unfastened waistcoat that revealed a shirt drooping over his belt. He smelled of alcohol.

Madame Lamberton stepped over to support him. "Nicholas, you said you wouldn't drink today. David is here!"

Lamberton pushed her away and lifted his ghastly head, fixing his bloodshot eyes upon me in a face ruined by a thick, twisting scar that ran from his forehead to his chin.

I tried to appear calm. "Monsieur Lamberton, I'm so pleased to meet you."

He snorted, then steadied himself on the edge of a

chair before approaching me with a defiant look in his eyes. My arms tensed and my heart throbbed as I looked back at him. What will I do if he hits me? I could take him in a fight, but you can't go around beating your future father-in-law.

I forced a smile and offered my hand, but he did not take it. Instead, he sat in the chair recently vacated by his wife. "So, you're the Chink."

Madame Lamberton came over to stand behind him, as if ready to mediate a dispute.

I sat, trying to sound cheerful. "Not Chink, Chinese."

Marguerite sat beside me and held my hand.

He laughed, the scar on his face writhing like a worm. He addressed the ceiling to say, "The Lamberton girl who fears nothing under heaven has fallen for a coolie of the Heavenly Kingdom. Fascinating, just fascinating."

"Pa," Marguerite said quietly, "do you want to rest a little, first?"

His wife lowered her voice to say, "Nicholas, David has a very good job, and he's well educated."

"Education is bullshit! Just look at our friends. Iago was a fucking college professor. Could his fucking education stop a bullet?"

Madame Lamberton flushed redder beneath her rouge. She mumbled that she was going to fetch the pie she had baked before going into the kitchen.

Marguerite had warned me that when her father was drunk, swearing was often a sign that he was about to start breaking things.

His hand gripped the armrest like a talon. There was a white porcelain ballet dancer to his side.

Marguerite moved the figure to the cabinet beside the

sofa. "Papa, the war is over. Everything can have a fresh start."

"What did you say, my dear? A fresh start?" He laughed coldly. "You think Iago, Jean, Barry, you think they're in fucking heaven drinking Bordeaux to their heart's con-fuck-ing-tent? Soaking in hot fucking springs? You think this showy fucking Chinese opium junkie beside you can–,"

"Monsieur Lamberton," I cut him off. "I am sorry... I am sorry about your friends. They... they're corpses rotting in the earth. Their meat fattens rats and..." I didn't know how to say maggots, but that didn't stop me, I continued with my faltering, poor grammar, "maybe they died at the edge of stinking ditches, maybe they were alone... maybe they called for their loved ones as they died. Monsieur Lamberton, I'm not like you... not a soldier on the battlefield, but I... I dug those trenches, carried, carried the shells and sandbags, I... took hundreds of bodies, loaded them onto the truck. I saw my friends die. Their bodies... a mass grave without tombstones. Death... called me, but... let me go. We are not the same, our skin... not the same, but... but... blood is red. I've never, I've never smoked opium. You speak...when you speak of opium, thank your allies, the British. They used opium to ruin us in China...many died, countless families in poverty."

Marguerite looked from me to her father anxiously.

Lamberton looked straight at me. It took all my strength to face his bloodshot eyes.

I continued, "Monsieur Lamberton, I have no money. These clothes ... these clothes I bought with borrowed money. Because I love Marguerite, and because I respect you and your wife, I wanted to leave a... a good impression. So that you could allow... allow us to be together. If you do not bless my proposal..."

Suddenly, I realised that Marguerite and I had not discussed what we would do if her parents did not consent to our marriage. I turned to look at her, and she looked back with determination.

"Papa," she said to him, "if you don't give us your blessing, I will leave with him anyway. You know how much I love you, how many tears I shed when you were at war for those three years. But if you continue to insult David – his Chinese name is Delun, by the way – I will leave you. My things are packed, my suitcase is under my bed. I did not sleep last night, just planned everything. You and Maman have already lost Alice, and if you don't hear me now then you'll lose me, too. Didn't Maman abandon her family for you? She lost so much for you, and look at how you treat her now, Papa. Where did my papa go? He used to dance around the room with Maman, he used to laugh and tell jokes, and he loved to show us magic tricks. I hate drunks, I hate the way it makes men act, I will never live with one."

Lamberton jumped up. I stepped between him and Marguerite, my heart pounding.

Madame Lamberton appeared in the doorway, holding a tray of desserts. She cried out, "Nicholas!" Then she lowered her voice and went on, taking painstaking care over every word. "If you touch her, I will leave you, too. Marguerite has been working like a man since she was sixteen. You look at your own daughter's hands. Look!"

The room was still. Nobody spoke.

Lamberton sat back in his chair slowly, his eyes on the floor. Like a sculpture. His wife put the tray on the coffee table. Marguerite and I sat, too.

Still, nobody spoke.

Madame Lamberton sliced the pie and handed a piece to

her husband. "Nicholas, it's your favourite, *chausson aux pommes*."

He took the plate, cut into the pie, and lifted the fork to his mouth like an obedient little boy.

Madame Lamberton turned to me and Marguerite. "Let's discuss the wedding arrangements," she said. "We need to settle the date and send a telegram to invite Alice."

39

A FEW DAYS LATER, Marguerite and I walked arm in arm along the main streets of Lyon for the first time. We were wearing our best clothes, hers the green dress and mine the outfit I had worn to meet her parents. She had done her make-up with particular care and fixed a brooch I had given her to her chest.

"Are you sure you want to do this?" I asked just before we left.

She took my arm and said calmly, "If they don't respect our union now, they will never respect our children in the future."

I nodded, shame creeping into my heart as I realised that I wanted to retreat, to pray to a god I didn't believe in.

Before long an eight- or nine-year-old boy in checked shorts ran up to us and sang, "Yellow skin, tiny eyes, shorty, saying ching-chong-ching-chong and crying his eyes out if he has no rice." He stuck out his tongue, stretching back his eyes with his fingers.

His mother, a haggard-looking woman with a sharp face

and an empty basket in her hands, glared at us icily from the side of the road. Beside her were an elderly couple, three young girls, a man with his hands in his pockets and two women basking in the sun. They all watched silently as we approached, their faces showing astonishment, disgust, ridicule, confusion or a mixture of all these emotions.

The women's expressions were the most exaggerated, their eyes wide and their mouths hanging half open as if we were some alien menace. I felt Marguerite's hand shake a little, then she squeezed harder on my arm, as if she were trying to communicate in code.

I felt short of breath. No matter, I thought, straightening my back and steadying my stride. But I didn't dare to look at Marguerite. I worried that if I saw even a trace of hesitation or anxiety on her face, then I would drag her away to hide and in doing so lose her forever.

Our oath is greater than death.
To have and to hold, for all my life.
How painful to be so far from you.
Fate will not let me fulfil my vow.

I repeated those lines to myself in my head.

Another child ran over to sing with the first. By the time we reached Place Bellecour, an entourage of teasing children skipped around us, the older ones throwing rocks, one shouting "whore" at Marguerite. Their parents smiled in approval.

I wanted to grab the child who had insulted Marguerite, but another squeeze from her hand told me to ignore him.

We'd been walking arm in arm for less than twenty

minutes, yet when we returned to her parents' apartment, we were so exhausted that we couldn't even speak.

Three months later, I received a divorce agreement signed by Miss Lu's father. There were a few lines from my father, too. They were his declaration that I was no longer a member of the Zhang family.

40

David had lost track of how many miles he had walked that day, head lowered like a bison on its stubborn quest for water in the arid wastes. The sticks in his hands had become crutches rapping against the hard concrete floor. Blood pooled around the blisters at his heels, the wound in his leg ached dully. He endured the pain, continuing his path.

He had intended to take the train to Lyon but changed his mind on his final evening in Montbrison. His mind was too crowded, only walking would ease it. It was irrelevant to him whether it would take a day or a week. He had time. Before departing, he bought himself a lightweight tent, a torch, a compass and a first-aid kit.

If only his memory were as light as his tent. The longer the life, the greater the burden.

Memories seep into your blood, change you. Some brighten you with joy, some drag you down like mud. When the latter cram themselves into your veins you have two choices: you can either allow yourself to wither away in silence, or you can exorcise them in whatever frenzied ritual you need to cast them out.

David believed that Monsieur Dreyfus' suicide had been an extreme example of that kind of ritual. Dreyfus had busied himself in his cafe day after day, year after year, never taking a moment's rest. Yet his brother's grief-stricken gaze followed him wherever he went. Death had relieved him of memory's burden, had been his only way to repent.

"Zerah was clutching the bread in his hand. It was only the size of a grapefruit and hard as rock." Dreyfus and his brother had been prisoners of Bergen-Belsen. Now he was talking to David, suddenly mentioning his past after a few games of chess in the park. "I was ten, he was eight. We were starving. I don't know where he found the bread, I only had one thought the moment I saw it and that was to take it for myself. He wouldn't give it up. I forced it from him. Oh, he was gripping it so tightly, like he was going to crush it into dust. I kicked him, I punched him and when he finally let it go I snatched it and wolfed it down like an animal. I finished it and I... I looked up at him... I wish I had never looked up at him... He died that night. Oh, merciful God, what have I done?"

Now, David envied Monsieur Dreyfus' courage. He could not divulge his past, he could only punish himself with the memories that had tormented him for half a century.

He had been walking for two days, leaving his footprints on cement, gravel and soil. Sometimes, a passing car stopped to offer him a ride. He had straightened his back, exerting himself to appear younger as he smiled and told them that he wanted the exercise. Those well-meaning people would pull away with a wave, unaware that they left behind an eighty-five-year-old man.

He just wanted to reach Lyon alone.

He had been walking on the main road for a while before he decided to rest in the nearby woods. The trees were gorgeous with the patchwork colours of autumn: yellow poplars, red maples, orange beeches and all varieties of evergreens. There was a smell of soil and of fallen leaves becoming mulch in the air.

David put down his rucksack to find somewhere to sit. There were no boulders around, but he did find the trunk of a large, fallen tree. When he came to sit down, however, he found that his legs were hard as steel, that his joints were locked from movement. He began to rub them carefully, working from thigh to calf. Slowly, his legs awakened, regained their connection to his nervous system. The pain in the small of his back, which he could usually ignore, became suddenly unbearable. He began to massage his waist and perform a few stretches. Finally, he managed to sit down and let out a long sigh of relief.

He thought of the Chinese word *"laoxiu"*, which is often used to describe people as old and rotting. He knew his advanced age meant that he would meet Yama before long, but he was not yet rotting – he could still draw out the strength of youth if he fought for it.

He took off his shoes to stretch his feet and examine his blisters. He gritted his teeth in pain as he removed his bloody socks. Skin hung loose where the blisters had ruptured, exposing the blood and white flesh beneath. He cleaned the wounds with a cloth from the first-aid kit in his rucksack, then applied ointment, a plaster and clean socks. As he did so, he thought of himself and his companions in the labour corps, the blisters and bleeding they had suffered when they dug trenches or went on long journeys. If they had first-aid kits back then, their days would have been much happier.

He ate, drank and relieved himself. Having pitched his tent in a sun-filled clearing, he opened the skylight and lay beneath it, squinting up at the colourful leaves against a backdrop of pure blue sky. He was pleased with himself, having walked at least ten miles that day.

As he withdrew his gaze, it fell upon an orange ladybird on the skylight's brim.

"Marguerite, is that you?" He smiled. "Very well, come take a rest with me."

He would not be able to walk any more that evening; it felt as if his bones were in pieces. He wanted to sleep, but his mind was still too full.

Marguerite had always taken care of his blisters when they had gone hiking together through mountains and streams. "Raise your foot, tilt your heel." It was as if he could hear her voice. She would be so careful, but she simply was never a very good nurse and would inadvertently touch his wounds, rushing to apologise when she made him cry out. It did not matter; he liked it when she looked after him anyway. She would frown as she examined him, her mouth slightly open as if pondering some matter of incredible gravitas.

Once, they had danced together in a meadow after a walk through the wilderness. He was clumsy, while she dragged him around in circles until they collapsed together with laughter. "I'm pregnant!" She looked at him with the depth of love in her eyes.

Every day, they talked about what they would name their child. They would need to choose a short name, with a corresponding Chinese pronunciation. If it were a girl, she would be Sophie, Anne or Emma, while a boy could be Paul or

Jean. Otherwise, it would be too difficult for their family in China to pronounce. He believed that if he were to take a child back home then he would earn the forgiveness of his parents and siblings, even their approval of Marguerite. Not having children was the greatest sin one could commit against one's parents, so if he brought descendants to the Zhang family, how could they cast him and Marguerite aside? He wanted his father to choose the child's Chinese name. Thinking of his father meticulously combing through all the classics and books of poetry, he could not help but laugh aloud.

At that time, he had already been working at L'Usine de Machines Faustin for eight years. In the third year of his employment, the supervisor who had helped him so much fell ill and had to retire. The man who replaced him was hostile towards David. He had him working twelve-hour shifts each day, enduring the mockery of his French colleagues all the while. They would ask him how many months it had been since he bathed, whether he would grow back his braid and whether he had smoked opium. He ignored them, but they enjoyed asking nonetheless. Sometimes, they would wink at him and say that there was a raft full of coolies waiting for him at the docks, that he should go and pack for China.

One day, a drunken co-worker intentionally vomited on him and then, holding his nose, declared that the Chinese stank because they grew up eating rotten fish and rotten shrimp. Everyone, including the supervisor, burst into laughter. Silent, David removed his coat and went home to bathe before returning to work. He was grateful that Marguerite was out at class. She did not need to know about it, or any similar incidents. All he needed to do was work hard and make money to give their future children a decent home. It was for their sake that he would take root in Lyon.

The mere thought of Marguerite made him feel like the happiest person in the world. Her blue eyes, her thick hair, her curling eyelashes, her freckled nose, her smile, the dimple, her short, rough fingers and the way she strode as she walked... When he went to work, on his way home, any time that he was not with her, the image of her in his head made him blissful.

Two-Horses had also stayed in France to marry Ella. Their wedding, attended by a huge crowd of people including her many siblings, relatives and neighbours, was in her hometown. Two-Horses had mobilised all ranks of his connections in the labour camp, working day and night to make handicrafts that he would exchange for meat, bread, cigarettes, all the things they needed. Ella's family roasted one of their pigs for the wedding feast and everybody – including David and Marguerite – danced by the bonfire to the music of fiddles and accordions all night long.

David hummed one of the band's tunes. How strange that he could still remember it more than half a century later.

A sound came from the trees outside, as if something were stepping on the fallen branches. He peered out from the tent's opening and saw a red squirrel clinging to a tree trunk. It hopped and skipped over to the tent then sat upright, its paws curled in front of its chest and its black eyes full of curiosity as if it wanted to look around inside.

David peered up to the skylight and saw that the ladybird was gone. He smiled to the squirrel and said, "Marguerite, when did you acquire the power of the Monkey King to change into all these different animals?" He slowly stretched his hand out of the tent and placed it on the ground. Just like a little human being, the squirrel inclined its head to one side, looked at David's hand, then scampered back to the tree where it quickly disappeared into the canopies.

David watched it vanish with regret. Life was like a banquet, it had to end eventually. Some people leave early, others stay late, some leave of their own accord and others are forced out the door. Some go alone, others with friends. In the end, only loneliness truly exists.

41

MANY OF ANNE'S CHILDHOOD WEEKENDS had been spent reading at the library of Sainte-Geneviève. She and her parents would each choose a book before settling down in the reading room, sometimes for most of the day. How she loved the feeling of their hands in hers as they led her from the library to the reading room. At the end of the wooden staircase, she would be captivated by the sight of the huge, spacious room before her. It resembled a train station with a symmetrical vaulted ceiling framed in black steel, half-moon windows and long wooden tables lit by green-shaded lamps.

Standing at the library doorway, she spotted her father sitting with his back to her seven or eight tables away. She hurried towards him in delighted surprise, only to find that it was just another elderly Asian man who resembled David from behind.

She often came to the library when she missed her mother, but today she was there to research the history of Chinese emigration to France, hoping to learn something about her father. She had visited the senior activity centre that David sometimes went to with the same goal, but his acquaintances' answers had been all the same: he rarely mentions his past.

Half an hour later, she was thumbing impatiently through the pile of books a librarian had recommended on the subject. Three covered First World War history, including the political and economic situation in China. A smaller volume introduced leaders of the Chinese Communist Party who had studied in France in the 1920s. One section described how those international students – including China's contemporary leader, Deng Xiaoping – had worked alongside Chinese labourers in the steel plant at Le Creusot. Could Baba have been one of those labourers? Or had he come to France as a student? Had he worked in the factory to pay his tuition?

To find more information, she knew that she would have to visit university libraries and the national archives.

First, though, she would ask Clara, who was a First World War historian. The pair had met and become close friends while they were undergraduates at the Sorbonne. After graduation, Anne had become a cultural correspondent for *Nouvelles du Monde,* while Clara left to read history at Cambridge. Clara taught at a university in London after earning her PhD but had returned to a position at the Sorbonne three years earlier. They usually got together at least once a month.

She called Clara's office from a phone booth near the library. Luckily, she was in and could meet at their usual spot at the Café de Flore in an hour.

Anne caught sight of Clara's orange windbreaker through the cafe window, conspicuous in a sea of grey and black. Clara was a tall, red-haired woman who loved bright clothes. They sat together at a corner table and ordered coffee.

"The cultural spotlight in this issue of *Women's City Weekly* is really well written. News, fashion, culture, society... all covered!" Clara repeated the magazine's slogan as if she were announcing it on stage.

Anne laughed. "Never could have done it without your encouragement."

They chatted, then Anne told Clara about her father's solo expedition and what she had learned about Chinese students and labourers coming to France during the war.

"So, you think that your father coming to France had something to do with the First World War, and that this trip is him revisiting his past?"

"Maybe it's just my own fantasy. Baba barely mentions his life when he first came here, but he did say he had worked in the trenches and with munitions. When Maman was alive, they went to Compiegne regularly to celebrate Armistice Day."

"I've read about the Chinese labourers in the national archives, but I don't know much. I interviewed a veteran once who said that many of the people who were sent to collect and bury the dead were Chinese. Give me some time. I'll ask my colleagues and see if they turn up any clues."

"It's shameful," Anne said. "I'm half Chinese but I can't speak Mandarin, I haven't been to China, and I have no idea about my father's past life."

"When I interviewed veterans, I often found that their children didn't know about the things they were telling me," Clara mused. "Some veterans insisted that they were just ordinary people, that nothing they experienced was worth my writing about."

They sipped their coffee for a while, both lost in their own thoughts, content in the comfortable silence that comes from many years of friendship.

Clara broke the quiet. "Romain Rolland once said that history is written for the living. We rifle through the pockets of the deceased, then march forward over their bodies. But... I think that many of the living are unwilling to search the pockets of the dead. And sometimes we find that the dead have hidden their contents so deeply that we couldn't find anything even if we tried. Or perhaps we'll only find something irrelevant, even misleading."

"History is a game of hide and seek. Between hiders and seekers."

Clara laughed. "That's a great title for a book: Hiders and Seekers."

Anne sat alone for a while after Clara left. Sunlight shone through the window onto the deep brown table and its red leather chairs. Apparently, the cafe's décor had not changed since the Second World War. Anne preferred simple geometric lines and the modern feeling of glass and metal, but she still appreciated the Café de Flore's historical charm.

She sank deeply into thought, recalling lying on the floor with a puzzle at the age of four or five. Baba was in the kitchen wearing Maman's floral apron and making spring onion pancakes. She had given him two little pigtails that stood straight up on top of his head. "You must cook them slowly over a low heat or they don't get crispy." He turned to her with a smile. She had been mad for spring onion pancakes, clamouring for them every morning.

"You smell weird," her classmates said to her one day, pinching their noses as they walked by. When Baba got up early the next day to make her pancakes as usual, she declared unhappily that spring onion-oil pancakes were the world's foulest food and that she would never eat them again. Baba looked dumbstruck, but then he put down the dough and fetched her some bread and milk as if he had read her mind.

Thinking of that incident, Anne shifted uncomfortably in her chair. Why had she suddenly remembered it after forty years?

A scene from secondary school invaded her mind. It was her friend's birthday party, and she had met a boy named Simon. She was captivated by his blue eyes, athletic physique and blond, shoulder-length hair. What's more, he liked Sartre and Goethe, too!

"You're beautiful," he said to her softly. He drew her along to the balcony as they danced. She became dizzy as his lips touched her face. When he asked her surname, she gave her mother's without a second thought.

The following week, she met him in a park near her school. They were leaning by a tree, kissing, when Simon suddenly stopped, his eyes flooding with hatred. "Look at that yellow monkey!" She followed his gaze. It was her father, standing with one of his French co-workers on the other side of the lawn. That co-worker was one of David's few French friends, who would invite the family over for Christmas every year. The factory was not nearby, so they must have been there for a particular errand.

"These monkeys come over here stealing French jobs. They ought to fuck off back to China!" Simon raised his voice, looking as if he were ready to attack her father. He had told her that his own father had recently been laid off. At that instant, David turned to them, as if he had heard

Simon's words. She pulled Simon behind the tree, kissing him wildly, her heart pounding, trying to distract him. She was terrified that her father might have seen them, or that Simon would do something awful.

The memory caused a heavy weight in Anne's stomach. She was consumed by a sudden loneliness, overwhelming all around her. Why hadn't she criticised Simon? Why hadn't she broken up with him immediately, instead of waiting a month? Why had she been so cold to her father in the following weeks?

"Do you regret leaving *Nouvelles du Monde?*" Pierre had asked her the previous month, when she complained that her magazine had lost an important source of advertising revenue.

"I didn't before, and I don't now. I never will," was her reply.

Pierre smiled, saying that he didn't know what the newspaper had done to offend her so greatly.

Waldo's fat, greasy face jumped before her eyes. He had been her boss at *Nouvelles du Monde*. She wanted to slap him whenever he got too close, but could not. Her projects needed his approval, and sometimes she even forced herself to flirt with him. He referred to her as "my little Chinese canary" when they were alone. When he pronounced her surname in an affected, deliberate way in front of their colleagues, she feigned composure and laughed it away, reminding herself that she was the only person at the newspaper with a Chinese surname.

One day, Waldo called her into his office just before they finished work, asking her opinion on a colleague's story. As she was engrossed in the report, he circled behind her and cupped her breasts in his hands. She stood.

"If you do anything like that again, I'll castrate you with a knife." She spoke calmly, threw the manuscript in his face and walked out. She resigned the next day and spent six months picking up restaurant shifts until she could find another position.

She had never told Pierre or Clara about those episodes, nor said a word about them to her parents. Those incidents were buried in the soil of her memory, seeds that would never sprout. Yes, she had fought with fellow students as a child. Yes, she had resisted, held her head high against their ridicule. But she had also given in, remained silent, even resented her parents.

A little girl dropped a spoon at a nearby table and the clear sound of its fall brought Anne back to the present. She watched the pedestrians outside. History was a game of hide-and-seek, she recalled saying to Clara earlier. At that time, she had been referring to what was happening between her and her father. Now, she realised, it was also an apt portrayal of her own life: she was both a hider and a seeker of her own past.

She suddenly knew why her father had gone on his journey alone.

42

After four days of walking, he was now ten kilometres from Lyon. He had traversed towns, villages, wild spaces and woods. Several times he had been lost, once only realising that he was walking in the wrong direction after five hours.

He did not ask for directions since he wanted to avoid people as a whole. He had washed and shaved when he found a stream, keeping himself presentable.

Pain had become as constant as breathing. He endured it gladly, even enjoying it: if only every ache could compensate for the guilt buried deep in his heart.

There was one evening when he felt that there was no way on earth that he would be able to get back up from his tent. But he did; he had got back up and then went on to walk five kilometres.

Dusk became night. David stretched his long limbs and faced the sky. His expression was of longing, as if yearning for the moonlight to sink into the depths of his scars.

The sky was full of stars. The brightest among them, he thought, must be Marguerite.

He remembered the sight of Marguerite before him, her hair tied back against heat from the midsummer sun that poured in through the window, illuminating the room with bright, vivid light. There was sweat on her neck despite her effort, and in her hand she held a slender white envelope with Chinese script on the front. He remembered it well. It was 10 August 1928.

"It's from China!" She beamed and placed the letter solemnly on David's desk before caressing her belly as if to share the good news with their baby who would be born in two months' time.

David had been writing to his parents every month since he and Marguerite were married, telling them about their life together in France and including photographs of them together. Each year on the eve of the Spring Festival he had sent them seven hundred francs, asking them to forward two hundred of this amount to Miss Lu. He had not yet received any response, but he believed that if he persisted in this way, they would eventually forgive him. Moreover, now Marguerite was carrying their grandchild, their hearts would surely melt with a desire to see the next generation of the Zhang family.

He and Marguerite had even agreed to visit Wuping when the child was approaching his or her first birthday. He could not reckon how many nights he had lost sleep with the excitement of imagining that trip.

He put down the book on mechanical engineering which he had been reading and picked up the letter. His hands trembled. The script on the envelope belonged to neither his mother nor father – he would have recognised it. Could the lines have been written by one of his siblings?

Marguerite left David to read in peace.

He knew who had written the letter as soon as he opened it and saw that it was addressed to "First Young Master of the Zhang Family". It was the housekeeper, Changqing. There were only two pages, and he did not move after he had finished reading them. He did not even notice that the letter had slipped to the floor.

Changqing explained that as the fighting between warlords had worsened, the family's business prospects had grown increasingly bleak. His parents had become sick with missing him, and their health had deteriorated. His siblings were no help with the business, and Miss Lu had returned to her parents' home after the divorce. The family had gone to stay with some relatives in Jinan, but Japanese troops had invaded the city. Their bombs had razed the Zhang family's temporary home. "Nobody survived," wrote Changqing. Then he mentioned that Miss Lu had received her share of the money that David had sent, and the remainder had been used for family and business expenses. Finally, he said that the Zhang family still had shops and properties in Wuping, and he asked when he would return to manage them.

Sometime after, he could not tell how long, Marguerite was by his side. "Delun, Delun," she said softly.

He seemed to regain consciousness. Tears gushed from his eyes. He covered his face with his arm but tears still rolled heavily into his lap.

"Delun, what's happened? What's happened? Tell me!"

He could not open his mouth, he did not want to speak anyway. It would be real once he had said it. No, it could not be real.

He lived in near silence for the following month. He would go to work before dawn, taking on his colleagues' tasks after completing his own. It would be dark by the time he had finished with the extra labour given to him by those who wanted to slack off, but he still would not leave. Alone he would stay behind to scrub and oil the machines, only returning home at eight or nine in the evening. He would shower and go to bed immediately after eating whatever hot dinner Marguerite had prepared, avoiding conversation on the pretext that he was simply too tired. There were a few nights when he roamed the streets alone until midnight.

Marguerite still did not know what had happened. She had not asked him again, knowing that whatever it was, it was awful. She kept to herself, silently preparing clothes for the baby's arrival. Madame Lamberton had already given them a crib, while Marguerite had painted cute animal pictures on the walls of the baby's room. After the letter, Marguerite asked her mother not to visit lest she disturb David's mourning. Marguerite had lost her father, she knew what it was like to grieve.

David was rarely home. The apartment seemed empty, as did her heart. She painted and sang, telling the baby inside her all the stories about pirates and sailors that her father had once told her.

One evening, David returned home to find her sitting on the floor with her back to the wall, legs splayed, wide-eyed and panting for breath. She was drenched in sweat.

The ambulance arrived an hour later. Their baby boy emerged into the world with his whole body blue. The doctors did what they could. When he stopped breathing, they said that he had died due to complications following a premature birth.

"Oh, Paul. Oh, my little Paul." Marguerite held the infant to her chest in his cotton blanket, calling to him gently.

They both spent much of the following year in silence.

At first, Marguerite would rearrange the baby clothes that she had prepared every day. Unfolding each item, looking at it awhile, putting it back into the wardrobe. Then one day she gave the crib to their neighbour, whose second child had just been born. A few days later, she painted over the animals on the walls.

Marguerite did not blame David, but he was on the verge of collapse. He believed that it was his fault, that the child would have lived had he taken good care of Marguerite. At the same time, he also believed that fate was responsible for throwing him into this oblivion; fate had robbed him of his family in China, and now it had stolen his firstborn, too.

One evening, he went alone to the Cathédrale Saint-Jean-Baptiste and knelt before Christ wearing his crown of thorns, praying for the souls of the dead. Afterwards, he walked to the Saône. He and Marguerite had strolled along that riverbank countless times, admiring the ancient architecture of the nearby buildings. He stood by the bobbing waters of the Saône, watching his own reflection. Suddenly, he found that he detested it.

It's all his fault! His fault! His fault! If he had never left China, if he hadn't joined the labour corps, his family would not have died. If his family had not died, then he would never have neglected Marguerite in his despair. If he had not neglected Marguerite, then Paul would have lived. Then he realised the futility of his logic. If he had never come to France, how would he have met Marguerite in the first place? How would they have had Paul?

A throng of people crowded the brightly lit streets on the opposite bank. Nobody could know his pain. Even if they did, they would not care. He was an evil-ridden foreigner, to be spurned not comforted. He was a Chinese labourer at the very nadir of society.

As long as he lived in Lyon, his face would bear the brand of a "coolie". He would never be able to rid himself of his disgraceful past.

His children would be mocked, too.

Why shouldn't he just throw himself into Lyon's maternal river? All the suffering would drown with him.

The water's gentle ripples fluttered crystalline beneath the lamplight like the arms of a mother coaxing her child to sleep.

The sound of a seagull's shriek made him turn to look behind him, and there he saw Marguerite. She was watching him silently just a few steps away. He had not noticed that she had been following him.

"Let's move to Paris," he pleaded. "Nobody knows us there, nobody knows I came here in the Chinese labour corps. We can forget our troubles, start a new life."

Marguerite said nothing, just looked back at him in sorrow.

"They're all dead." He began to cry. "My parents, my little brother, my little sisters, they..." He lowered his head, grief shaking his body, "Now our child... our child..."

Marguerite embraced him. They stood together in each other's arms for a while before walking home together along the bank.

A few months later, the supervisor who had originally been so kind to David introduced him to a friend who had opened a factory in Paris. Madame Lamberton did not come to wish them goodbye.

The night deepened. A breeze rustled its way through the trees. As David lay in his tent watching the trees' swaying leaves, his memories emerged like smoke from their burial places in his heart. Time cannot heal these wounds, he concluded, nor can it make you forget them. Eventually the wounds would weep pus, and the hard shell of a scab would develop over them. You no longer cry, but that kind of congealed pain is the most torturous of all.

The month before Marguerite's death, she had asked to return home. There was nothing the doctors could do for her but stall. David took her out for a walk in her wheelchair every day, her head resting on a pillow at her side – she had not the strength even to look up. She always wanted to go to the banks of the Seine, which reminded her of Lyon. They would chat as they walked along, mostly David doing the talking. When she could not speak, she would move her fingers in her lap to show him that she was listening. Sometimes she would be asleep by the time they arrived at the river's edge. When she slept, her wrinkles smoothed over her face, making her appear much younger. David covered her with a blanket, kissed her forehead and sat beside her with her hand in his, quietly watching the river and passers-by.

David addressed the sky's brightest star as he said, "I saw Paul in my dream last night. The little fellow was holding my hand, all unsteady, trying to learn to walk! When you sang, he waved his hands like a conductor." He smiled at the image of sweet little Paul. Why had he never told her how much he thought about him? He had been afraid to hurt her, but perhaps his silence hurt her even more.

"I know you miss Lyon. I do too. If I had been a little stronger, we might never have left. I once swore to your mother that I wouldn't take you from her. But we left her in the end." He remembered the look on Madame Lamberton's face when they told her they were moving to Paris, the grief in her eyes.

"Do you think I was a good father? Sometimes when I was playing with Anne, I would think of Paul. Or I would think of my family back in China, and I'd be impatient with her. Once, we were in the park and she didn't want to go home. I got angry and pulled her off the slide. Her little wrists were red where I'd grabbed her. She didn't cry, but I did. She wiped my tears and told me not to worry. She said, 'Baba, don't cry, I won't tell Maman.'"

Tears slipped from the corners of his eyes.

He kept talking, pouring out the words that had accumulated in his heart like layers of fallen leaves on the forest floor.

The stars twinkled above. He knew that Marguerite was listening.

43

He heard a car horn, the sound of rushing water. Both came as if from far away. He wanted to move, but his whole body ached, his head murky and confused. He opened his eyes to find indistinct shapes swaying in front of his blurry vision.

"Ah, you're awake!" A woman's voice. He blinked to find a young woman in a white nurse's uniform leaning over him, smiling. He realised that he was lying in a hospital bed with tubes sticking out from his body.

"How did I get here?" he asked.

"You passed out on the street yesterday and lost consciousness. Someone called an ambulance, which brought you here." She checked the monitor beside his bed. "Your heart rate and blood pressure are normal. How do you feel?"

He struggled to sit. "My head hurts, I'm a little nauseous and my ears are ringing. But I'm OK. Where are we?"

"Hôtel-Dieu de Lyon."

"Lyon?"

"Yes, Lyon."

"Lyon..." David whispered. How could he be in Lyon? "What's the date?"

The nurse told him. It wasn't so long after his birthday! He suddenly remembered that Anne had said that she wanted to throw a party for him and would make dumplings. Had she made them already? His mind was a mess. He pictured dishes with meat filling, soy sauce and Anne working in the kitchen. It seemed as if it was yesterday. Impossible, he was in Lyon! Was it something that had happened before Marguerite died? No, he'd better not think further.

The nurse said she was going to fetch a doctor. She had barely left before hurried footsteps sounded in the hall. A young woman in a cream windbreaker rushed in.

"Anne!" David cried out.

"Ba!" Anne came to him like a whirlwind, hugging him tightly. "How... how are you?" Her eyes were moist. Baba's skin was a lot darker, his hair in disarray, his face unshaven.

"Love, why are you in Lyon? How did you know I was here? Why are you so thin? You look so tired. Is it work?"

"The hospital staff found my phone number in your wallet. Dr Martin called me from ER. She said that you have a slight concussion and bruises, otherwise you're OK. She said that you woke up yesterday but went straight back to sleep."

David did not remember waking.

Dr Martin arrived. She was a woman of around forty with her hair in a loose ponytail. She chatted with them briefly, then placed her stethoscope on David's chest and back, asking him to cough.

"No problems with your breathing," she said, and asked

David for his full name, date of birth and place of residence. David answered without hesitation.

"People who've suffered concussion often lose short-term memory," said the doctor. "But it should return soon. Considering your age, you'll need a thorough neurological examination as soon as you're back in Paris."

"Might there be complications?" asked Anne, worried.

"Hard to say. I'm not a specialist, but don't worry too much, just get that check-up."

David was offended. "Doctor, my memory is fine. Ask me what colour dress and what shoes my wife was wearing on our first date. I can tell you anything."

She gave a thumbs up. "In that case, your memory is very good indeed. You've been walking a lot lately, haven't you?"

"Really? Maybe."

"You had blisters on your feet when you arrived. The nurses have taken care of them."

"When can I leave?" he asked. He had only been hospitalised once before, for pneumonia a decade ago. He disliked going to hospital, and considered coughs and colds mere inconveniences to be cured with ginger in hot water and chrysanthemum tea. He knew that his recent memory was a little poor, but that was normal for a man over eighty. Machine parts rust with long use. His overall memory might even be better than the average youth's!

The doctor said that he needed to remain under observation. After she left, David frowned and said, "I'm fine, why won't they let me leave? Get the nurse to pull out these tubes." He moved his legs, trying to get out of bed. The movement sharpened the pain in his head, as if someone were jumping up and down inside his skull.

Anne pressed David's shoulders. "Ba, stop moving.

Come on, I'm sitting next to you." They sat with their heads together.

"Anne, forgive me," he said. "I've caused you so much trouble." Seeing what appeared to be tears in her eyes he asked, "Did the doctor tell you something else behind my back?"

"Ba, how far did you really walk?"

"I was exercising! Don't worry about me. Your mother always used to say, your father is—"

"She said Baba is made of iron."

"Ah, your mother. It's she who was made of iron. So strong. Much stronger than I am."

"Ba, after we return to Paris, why don't you come to stay with Pierre and me for a while?"

"I'm fine living in my own apartment. I'm used to it, and it has all of your mother's things."

"Where have you been all this time?"

David mumbled that he could not remember.

Anne did not want to make things difficult for him. Besides, he was still recovering. Now she had found him, she could take her time with the rest.

44

David was released from the hospital two days later. Dr Martin had written him a prescription for painkillers, but Anne knew that her father would not take them unless he was in dire pain. She had intended to drive David back to Paris immediately but delayed the trip by a few days once he told her that he wanted to see Lyon. She had already called Pierre and Clara to update them and organised her work at the magazine.

They set out of the hotel together early the next morning. Anne had not planned to stray far out of concern for David's energy, but he insisted on seeing the old town district.

"When we first got married, your mother and I lived on the Rue de Boeuf," he told her as they walked. "You could see Fourvière Hill from our kitchen window. Sometimes we got up early and climbed it just to watch the sunrise from the top. We were so young and energetic, we didn't want to take the funicular." As the memory filled him with warmth, he thought that Marguerite had been right when she said that avoiding his past would only bring him pain and regret. "We often walked on Rue Saint-Jean – we loved all the winding alleys. Beyond number twenty-seven on Rue de Boeuf were four stunning mansions, then the alley off 54 Rue Saint-Jean. The houses were all so luxurious. As we walked, we'd say how it would be nice to have potted flowers here or repaint a wall there, as if we were about to move in."

Anne listened quietly. It was the first time Baba had mentioned his married life in Lyon.

David talked nonstop along their route.

"Ba, you're sweating," Anne said. "There are benches here. Let's rest a little."

"These shoes don't fit," David replied. "Otherwise I'd be able to go all day."

Anne smiled. "You've only just been discharged. Still, I almost can't keep up with you."

Directly opposite were the Gothic archways of Lyon Cathedral. David looked at it as if he had been transported into a dream.

"Ba, didn't you and Maman get married in the cathedral?"

The question woke David from his reverie. He seemed surprised to see Anne by his side and spoke as if just waking up. "Well, not actually inside the church, outside. Your grandmother wanted us to convert to Catholicism so we could have our wedding at Saint-Jean's, but your mother didn't want to. We compromised, and took our wedding photos at the doorway."

"Tell me about your wedding."

"We didn't have many guests. Your Aunt Alice's family,

your grandparents, some of their friends, a few of our co-workers and their families – just fifteen people. The minister who conducted the service was a friend of your grandmother's. If not for her, he wouldn't have broken the rule."

"Maman told me that she wore Grandma's wedding dress. She said it was tight around the waist even after being let out. She could barely catch her breath."

"She looked like a goddess that day. I didn't dare look at her. I was afraid that if I looked at her too much she might fly away."

"She was always a goddess in your eyes," she teased. "Even in her oily work clothes."

David chuckled. "Your dad was handsome that day, too. I wore a tie, and put a rose in my buttonhole. Your grandpa always hated formal attire. But your grandma forced him to wear leather shoes and a tie. You should have seen how he walked, like a steel scarecrow."

"It's such a pity I never met my grandfather. Maman said he told the best stories, and that he was a good dancer and poet. No wonder Grandma fell in love with him. She said you and he didn't get along at first, but later he liked chatting with you."

A shadow crossed David's face. The scene from half a century earlier appeared before his eyes: Nicholas' stiff body lying in his own vomit by the tavern, eyes wide open, the scarred half of his face inclined towards the sun. He and Marguerite had never told Anne about that. Madame Lamberton always told people that he had died of a sudden heart attack.

"I liked your grandfather. His only problem was drinking."

"I remember Grandma really clearly. She was always

dressed nicely, with lace dresses and hats, just like a great lady from the Middle Ages, like she had just stepped out of a fairy tale. She sang to me on her lap when I was little, telling me Grandpa's stories. Her voice was beautiful, like wind chimes."

"She left us too soon."

"If you weren't an orphan, your family in China would have come to the wedding, too. Maybe you would have had another Chinese wedding after the French one. I've been to a Chinese wedding, it was one of my colleagues getting married. It was all incredible, there was a dragon and lion dance."

David suddenly stood up. "I've rested enough. Come on, let's go."

"Don't you want to look inside the church? There's an astronomical clock inside. I've been fascinated by it since I was small. When it strikes, little people come out from inside."

"No, there are too many people there."

Anne looked at the church, puzzled. It wasn't yet nine o'clock, and there were only a few tourists outside taking pictures. But David had already walked away, so she followed along behind him. Around eleven, they arrived at a cafe. Anne ordered a latte and a tea for her father. The square buzzed with visitors. Nearby, a tour guide with a flag was addressing a group of Japanese tourists in white hats.

"Baba," Anne said, sipping her coffee. "You and Maman travelled to many different countries, but never China. Why is that?"

He did not want to discuss China, but he could not avoid her question. "Warlords were fighting when I left, the wars went on for decades. After the founding of the New China, political movements came endlessly. The country stabilised only recently. You probably know about all that. It's all in the papers and books." He paused. "Do you remember Uncle Liu?"

"Vaguely. I wasn't even five when he visited. I remember his scratchy beard stabbing me in the face. He had a loud voice, and he brought me Chinese snacks and toys. He taught me how to work the Monkey King *piying* shadow puppets."

"I first came to China with Uncle Liu. Everybody called him Old Shuan back then. I stayed behind when I married your mother, and he returned to China, joined the Red Army and became a big official. He returned in forty-four for work and found my address somehow. He came to see your mother and me in Paris and wrote us several letters in the following years. Five years later, the Communists won the civil war and founded the New China. Afterwards, he never wrote again. I wrote to him, but he didn't reply."

"Have you still not had any contact with him?"

David was silent briefly before saying, "Five or six years ago, I met a Chinese man when I was teaching tai chi at the elders' activity centre. He had a government position in Shanghai, so I asked him if he knew Uncle Liu, who worked there too. He said that they had worked together once. I was happy to hear it, but when I asked him how Uncle Liu was doing I found out that he had died. In the late sixties. He was exiled to some remote area in the northwest and had died there."

"Oh, how sad..."

David sighed and changed the subject. "Do you know that your mother and I have actually been married three times?"

"Really? No, neither of you mentioned it!"

"The first time was at the Chinese embassy. The French government had said that any French citizen who married a foreigner would automatically lose their citizenship. We went to the registry office, but the staff shooed us away like stray dogs. When we applied for a marriage certificate at the Chinese embassy, the staff held a ceremony for us. The machinery factory where I worked had renewed my contract so I could stay legally. We bought a newspaper as a wedding memento after we left the embassy. A government proclamation on one of the inside pages said that French women should marry triumphant French soldiers, not form families with the yellow-skinned coolies. They called on French women to 'awaken'!"

"No way!" Anne exclaimed. "What about the other two marriages?"

"We re-registered a few years later when the French government changed the law to let French keep their citizenship after marrying foreigners. The third time was outside Lyon Cathedral. There were plenty of people to watch the spectacle."

"So many twists and turns." Anne sighed. "What would you have done had Maman lost her citizenship?"

"She was willing to move to China, but it would have broken your grandmother's heart. We didn't dare tell her."

Anne wanted to ask about his life when he first came to France but felt that she should wait until they were back in Paris.

"Your father has been through a lot in this life," David said. "There was luck and tragedy, even luck within the tragedies and tragedies within the luck. Meeting your mother and having you were the greatest fortunes of my life."

"And the tragedies?" She recalled the box at her father's bedside, the letters and the bracelet within.

David gazed at a large tree across the street. Its leaves were almost entirely shed and its branches crossed into a beautiful web under the clear blue sky. He thought of his childhood in Wuping, which had two rows of similar trees on the main road. Their leaves grew to the size of a hand in summer, swaying like a green wave in the wind. He had relaxed and played in their shade with his friends and siblings. When autumn turned the leaves golden-yellow, he would run beneath them in shoes sewn by his mother, laughing and catching them as they fell. Some were flat as paper, some missed corners or were chewed by caterpillars and others were marvels of perfection. Despite his youth, a feeling of melancholic sentimentality sometimes washed over him as he studied those leaves. But then a gust would blow, whipping them into the air and flashing gold all over the sky. He smiled again and resumed the chase.

He would soon become a fallen leaf himself now, but where was his home? He never told Marguerite about his homesickness, fearing it would worry her, make her think that he wanted to return. But the feeling was difficult to conceal entirely, especially on important dates like the anniversary of his parents' death, his siblings' birthdays and traditional Chinese holidays. Sometimes, while chatting and laughing with Marguerite, he suddenly thought of his relatives or his hometown, then quietened or stopped talking. He did not notice his own absentmindedness until he saw the concern on Marguerite's face, when he would smile apologetically. If she asked him what had happened, he found some excuse to brush it off.

He should not think about such things, he told himself

now. From the day he decided to be with Marguerite, he knew he might never return to Wuping. But really, he'd had a good life in France. He should be content with that.

"My girl," he said, smiling, "when you get to my age, you will see."

45

David fell ill not long after they returned to Paris, running a high fever for several days.

Anne persuaded him to go to the hospital, where a doctor prescribed him with antibiotics for chronic pneumonia. His condition improved a few days later, but he developed a cough that kept him up at night. Before, he had laughed sickness away and recovered quickly. This time, he was ill for more than a month. Anne took him back to the doctor, but they could not give him a clear diagnosis, suggesting only that the cough was a complication from the pneumonia.

David eventually recovered, but the process had aged him significantly. His back became more hunched, his movements faltering and he trembled slightly as he walked. Sometimes he had to rest against a wall on the journey from his bedroom to the kitchen. He was increasingly uncommunicative and unwilling to leave the apartment, spending most of his time either in bed or in his rattan chair on the balcony.

Early the following year, David was diagnosed with

Alzheimer's. He could still care for his own basic needs and spoke reasonably well, but his cognitive abilities and short-term memory fell into rapid decline. Anne and Pierre asked him to move in with them. David was opposed to the idea initially but finally succumbed to their repeated persuasion. He asked only that they bring his rattan chair, the flowers and the photographs from the wall.

Every few weeks, Anne took David to the hospital for a consultation, but the doctor could only track his deterioration. They told Anne to talk to him often, get him to use his brain and his hands, and let him do whatever housework he could. For now, there was no cure for his disease.

David returned to himself somewhat in the early summer, but his face was haggard and he had gained weight from inactivity. He avoided people, and if Anne did not force him to go to the park then he simply stayed in his room, reading newspapers and magazines, even the advertisements. Sometimes he took a broom and swept the floor, but he would toss the broom aside halfway through to do something else. He refused to let Anne throw away his reading materials when he had finished with them, but arranged them like folded clothes on his desk, looking through them again the next day. When the mood took him, he repeated the news to Anne.

Mr and Mrs Wang came to see him, but he showed little interest. He was absent-minded, even standing suddenly to return to his room without saying goodbye.

Anne knew that her father's health was failing, but she could do nothing but care for him and worry. After consulting with her colleagues at the magazine, she decided to spend most days working from home. They could stay in touch by phone and fax, sometimes meeting at her house.

Work was going well. The magazine's advertising revenue had been increasing steadily since the publication of some popular articles on workplace discrimination against ethnic minorities, and interviews with divorcées.

She tried a few times to delve into her father's past, but he shook his head, either telling her that there was nothing to say or ignoring her completely.

"Ba, do you have any family back in China?" she asked casually over dinner one evening.

He was about to place a meatball onto Sophie's plate, but the question made his hand tremble, and the meatball fell to the floor. He lowered his head, pushed aside the plate in front of him and went to his room without saying a word.

"Maman, why's Grandpa angry?" Sophie asked.

Anne stroked her daughter's head. "He isn't angry. He just has too many stories that he doesn't want to tell. Sometimes, that makes you unhappy."

"Why doesn't he want to tell?"

"I don't know. Maybe one day we'll find out."

One afternoon as David was dozing in his rattan chair on the balcony and enjoying the warm sunlight, something like a colourful cloud appeared in his head. It was magnificent in colour, holding him mesmerised and confused.

Is it leaves? A painting he and Marguerite had seen in some gallery? A firework? He finally realised: it was the multicoloured patchwork of tiled roofs over Wuping. He opened his eyes and stood.

Anne was sitting on the sofa reviewing an article she was considering for the magazine. Pierre was at work, the kids at school. When she saw her father through the window stand so quickly, she called out in surprise, "Ba, what's happened?"

David walked in, smiling, eyes gleaming, even his back

appearing straighter. He paced restlessly. "Marguerite, we need not stay in the hotel, let's go home. Pack some dumplings, we can take them with us. Paul and Anne love them."

Anne was used to these strange interactions with her father; he had often mistaken her for her mother in recent months. She used to correct him, but the doctor had advised her to follow along with him. "Anne is just getting ready," she told him. "Who is Paul?"

David smiled. "You're so forgetful. He's our son!"

"How old is he?" Anne asked, keeping calm.

"He was born on 12 September 1928. How have you forgotten?"

"In that case, he's fifty-seven years old."

"He can't be! I remember, he's so small. When we held him, his feet were shorter than my finger. His face was so thin. Where is Paul?"

"He's gone out, he'll be back soon." Anne resisted asking where Paul might be.

"Good. We'll all be together!"

David looked over to the clock. "The ship will set sail in three hours." He began to search for something, opening all the kitchen drawers.

"What are you looking for?"

"The tickets!"

Anne passed him a bookmark. David took it, inspected it, then placed it carefully into his pocket after nodding in satisfaction.

"Where's the luggage?" he asked.

Anne handed him a sofa cushion.

He secured the cushion under his armpit. "It takes a month to get there, the waves and winds are so strong at sea."

"It doesn't take a month to get to Lyon."

"Not to Lyon!" David shook his head.

"Then to where?"

"To where?" David asked himself, stunned as if he had been hit by a magic spell. His smile vanished. No, he could not go back to Wuping. Absolutely not. They will force him to stay if they see him. They will send Marguerite and the children back to France alone. There were too many of them, his parents, his siblings, the servants, he could not fight back. Even with Miss Lu pleading for his freedom, his father definitely would not let him go again. He remembered his father's letter: "Filial piety is the foundation of one's life, to be filial is to obey one's parents…" The cushion under his arm fell to the floor.

Anne tried to hold him but he pushed her away. "I'm not going any more!" he said harshly. He returned to the balcony, sat in his chair and turned sideways – his way of telling people not to bother him. He closed his eyes, his heart pounding. The colourful cloud was now gone; only darkness remained.

Time is running out, he said to himself. It's time to dispose of all those things that needed to be gone, leaving not a trace behind. He reached for the branches of the geranium beside his chair. His heart settled as he touched them, as if he were holding Marguerite's hand. After a while, he fell asleep.

Anne looked at him helplessly. "Ba," she muttered, "where is it you wanted to go?"

46

As always, the children's bedtime was chaos. With great difficulty, Pierre gave Noah a bath and took him to bed. Anne tucked Sophie in and kissed her on the cheek. "How about the story of Pinocchio tonight?"

"I want the story of the fisherman and the fish."

"But I told you that story just last week."

"I told it to Grandpa yesterday. He said he liked it."

"What else did he say?"

"Nothing, just that he liked it."

"So you want to hear it again because he liked it?"

Sophie did not respond. Blinking, she asked, "Can the magical fish really grant your wishes?"

"It granted a lot of wishes for that greedy grandma, didn't it?"

Sophie sat up at once. "Let's go to the sea tomorrow and find it."

"What do you want to find it for?"

"I want it to fulfil a wish for me."

"What do you wish for?"

"I don't want palaces or to become a queen. I just want Grandpa to get better."

Anne hugged Sophie and stroked her head. "Don't worry. He'll be fine."

Sophie yawned, snuggling back under her quilt. "I want to hear the Chinese song Grandpa sings."

"*Changting wai, gudao bian, fangcao bi liantian...*" Anne began to sing the lullaby she remembered from when Baba would sing her to sleep. "Outside the pavilion, beside the ancient road, the grass is green.." Her voice was soft.

Once Sophie fell asleep, Anne went to Noah's room to say goodnight. He was already asleep, and so was her husband. Pierre leaned against Noah's bed with *The Little Prince* still open in his hands, his snores rumbling. Since David had moved in, Pierre had taken on more of the chores in addition to work and picking the kids up from school, giving Anne more time with her father. Anne kissed his forehead guiltily, not wanting to wake him.

She had not been sleeping well lately. She often woke in the night and went to check on her father, making sure he was still breathing. He slept soundly, sometimes until noon. The doctor said that drowsiness was a common symptom of Alzheimer's patients. Still, Anne had to hear the rhythmic sound of his breathing before she was reassured enough to leave.

Anne was wide awake in her living room, watching television absentmindedly as she flipped through the day's newspaper. She was waiting for Clara, who had called her at two that afternoon.

"You're not going to believe what I've found," she had

said in an urgent voice. "I can't explain over the phone. I'll come over after class tonight."

Clara arrived at eleven, colourful as ever in a yellow jumper and red skirt. She was carrying a large folder in her arms.

"How's your dad?" she lowered her voice to ask.

"He was quiet today, just reading the paper. His appetite was pretty good at dinner."

"Has he been willing to talk?"

Anne shook her head. "Not much. When I talk to him it seems like he's listening, but I can tell he's thinking of something else, or nothing at all. It's like there's a screen between us. A few days ago, he asked me to take him back to his apartment but wouldn't tell me why. I think he misses Maman."

Clara pulled out a book from the folder and flicked it open to the first page before handing it to Anne. There was a Chinese newspaper clipping in the centre of the page, a black-and-white photograph of a ship crammed with Chinese people, all wearing the same cotton-padded clothing, a few with soft felt hats. Some faced the camera with smiles, confusion or downright alarm. Armed soldiers seemed to be guarding them. It was difficult to make out the soldiers' faces, but they were obviously white.

Clara explained, "These Chinese men are labourers recruited by the British government to be sent to France. There were a hundred and forty thousand of them. This picture is from 1917, and there are more."

Anne was stunned. "1917? That's the year Baba came to France."

Clara told her about the article, which had been translated for her by one of her Chinese-speaking colleagues.

"The photographs were taken by a Canadian, Tom Harris. He was working with the labour corps as a translator and lived with the labourers for two years. His grandson found all these after Tom died. He sent them to a French newspaper, which passed them to Luther, a colleague of mine who specialises in Asian history. I went to him when you told me about your dad. Luther wondered why I'd be interested, said that this stuff had been at the bottom of his research stack for years."

"So Baba could have been one of these Chinese labourers."

Clara nodded. Anne continued to run through the pages. All the photographs were in black and white. One showed the labourers stripped, washing in wooden basins. In another, they lined up in camps surrounded by barbed wire. Some showed labourers carrying weapons, repairing tanks, digging trenches, fixing railways or airfields, flying kites and stilt walking, pitching tents... One photograph was taken in a munitions factory. French women in smocks were carrying a cartridge box together with the Chinese labourers. A man in a Western suit and bowler hat looked on, expressionless.

She turned the page. A photo showed a British soldier whipping a bare-chested Chinese man, whose hands were tethered behind a wooden stake. The Chinese man looked on the verge of death. His eyes were closed and his head was tilted sideways, his body covered in welts.

Anne's heart tightened. She began to understand why, if her father had been one of these labourers, he would not want to mention his past experiences.

"They were locked up like criminals," Clara whispered.

Turning to the last page, Anne stared at a photograph in

the lower left corner. It showed two people sitting on the ground. The one on the left was handsome, with bright eyes and thick black hair. He smiled as he read a book. The other was bald, frowning as if he had just decided to do something important.

"It's Baba," she cried out. "The one on the left is Baba!"

Clara's gaze followed the tip of Anne's finger. "You're right, it's him."

"I'm so sorry, Anne," Clara said. "If I'd got hold of these earlier, maybe you'd have been able to get your father to talk about his past."

"No, I should thank you, not blame you. The mystery is finally solved."

"I've been studying the First World War all these years, and this is the first time I've realised there is still so much we don't know," Clara said. "During the war, more than a hundred and forty thousand Chinese labourers, 1.5 million Indian soldiers and labourers, and a hundred thousand from Africa and elsewhere all supported the Allies' war effort. Many came to fight or work in Europe. Some died here, some stayed, but most returned to their own countries. My professor in Cambridge told me that the First World War was a European affair that had nothing to do with the rest of the world." She shook her head in self-mockery. "I don't know what he'd say if he saw these photographs."

"Probably that they aren't worth mentioning." Anne laughed bitterly.

"When I was in England, I visited loads of war memorials, but there were none for the Chinese labourers. Not a trace of them on the memorials in France, either. They may not have fought on the battlefield, but without their labour we may never have won that dreadful war. At the least, the fighting would have continued for much longer."

"Does Luther do this sort of research?" Anne asked.

"He says he considered it once. He looked up material in the national archives, but in the end decided there were more important projects, and that this one wouldn't benefit his career."

"Clara, I found something in Ba's room, a bracelet with a number on it. It seemed to mean a lot to him."

"Luther mentioned bracelets. He said that each labourer had one, with his own identification number used for wages and rations. The officers and foremen who managed them would address them by their numbers, not their names."

"So that's what it is." 58909 was Baba's number. Sadness welled in Anne's heart.

Clara left the folder with Anne. After she departed, Anne went into her father's room. He had forgotten to close the curtains, moonlight flowed in through the window. Sitting on the edge of her father's bed, his hand in hers, she studied his weathered face. She imagined him as a strong young man labouring in the trenches, on the railways, in the factories.

"Why didn't you tell me, Baba?" she asked softly.

He muttered to himself as if about to open his eyes, but then just rolled over in his sleep. She drew the curtains and closed the door delicately behind her, heading for her son's bedroom. Pierre was still sleeping soundly beside his son, the book had fallen to the floor. She leaned over to nudge him awake.

Coming slowly to consciousness, he mumbled, "I dreamed Clara was here."

"She was, she just left."

"What was she doing here at this hour?"

Anne lay beside him, resting her head on his warm arm. She could not tell whether she was excited or exhausted. She felt as if she had just returned from a long journey.

"It was important," she said, after a while. "I'll tell you tomorrow."

47

It had been a month since David passed away.

The geranium's late summer blooms were fading, the rattan chair was empty. He had spent a dozen hours a day there in his final weeks, watching the sky with the occasional smile appearing on his face. By then, he was so weak that he needed a cane even to get around the house. Mr and Mrs Wang had visited again, but David never spoke, as if they did not exist.

Anne was consoled by the knowledge that he had slipped away in his dreams. He was lying with his hand over his photo album when she found him, his lips a faint smile, the page turned to a picture of him and Marguerite at their wedding.

The phone rang, breaking Anne's thoughts. She was working from home and was due to collect the kids from school in a few hours.

"Hello, is this the residence of Mr Zhang Delun?" The caller spoke with a thick Chinese accent.

"It is. This is his daughter, Anne."

"Ah, I've finally found him!" The voice jolted with excitement.

"Who is this?"

"I am Zhang Dekai, in Paris from China on a business trip... I, my grandmother's name is Lu Wenjia. She died last year. I say 'grandmother', we weren't blood relations but she adopted my baba, we all lived together until she died."

Anne listened in confusion. "I'm sorry, who is Lu Wenjia?"

"She and your father were once married. Your mother even wrote letters to her."

Anne's head was swimming. She didn't know what to say. The caller also fell silent, apparently realising that Anne had no idea what he was talking about.

Anne spoke first. "My father died last month."

"Oh, really? That's such a shame." He sounded deeply disappointed.

"Where are you?" she asked.

"A hotel near Notre-Dame. It was hard to find this number. I went through the Parisian Chinese Society." Anne had contacted the telephone company to forward all her father's calls once he moved in.

"You're near my place," Anne said. "Do you have time to come over? Or I can find you."

He said he would arrive within the hour. When the doorbell rang, Anne opened it to a young man of medium build wearing black spectacles and a jacket. He smiled shyly at her.

They sat in the living room and exchanged pleasantries. The young man said that his company had a trading partner in France, and he had come over for training. His eyes fell on a black-and-white photograph on the coffee table. "My grandmother mentioned this photograph of you all at the beach."

"Did she have this photo?" asked Anne.

"She did, once. Your mother sent it to her, but during the Cultural Revolution she burned everything, all the photos and letters. Red Guards were raiding people's houses, so she was afraid that all those foreign things would make her look guilty. She only told me about this stuff a few years ago, from her hospital bed. She never mentioned it before that." His vocabulary and grammar were good, despite his heavy accent.

"Your French is excellent," she said. "Did you study it in China?"

He nodded. "My grandmother suggested I learn French in college. I thought it was strange advice at the time, but I liked French literature, so I applied to the French department. Only later, when she told me the story of her and your father, I realised why she had given me that suggestion. She wanted me to find him."

"You said that they were married once. How could that be?"

"It's what she told me. She said he left her on their wedding night–"

"Wait, wait, you say my father abandoned your grandmother on their wedding night?"

"She never said the word 'abandoned'. She just said he left her. She said their wedding was outstanding, that the whole Zhang family mansion was alive with guests and decorations."

"Zhang family mansion? You're saying my father wasn't an orphan?"

"An orphan? Your father's family were practically the local nobility, rich and powerful. The same could be said for my grandmother's at the time. She told me that she was sitting on their wedding bed when your father told her that he was going to take a walk outside. She thought he was just nervous. She waited for him all night, but he never came back. Two weeks later, she received a letter from him saying he was leaving for France."

Anne showed him Clara's folder. He flipped through it carefully, saying that it was the first time he had seen these images. She showed him the bracelet, too. David had tried to throw it away before he died, but she had spotted it in the bin and saved it. She said, "My father also had two letters written in Chinese vertical script."

"Where are they? Could I take a look?"

"Unfortunately, he destroyed them before he died. I think they were from his family. He had treasured them for so many years, but in the end he decided to destroy them. The only explanation, I think, is that he just didn't want me to see them."

"Maybe so." The young man sighed.

"Do you have a picture of your grandmother?"

"I do." He pulled a small photo album from his backpack and handed it to Anne.

The first photograph showed around a dozen adults and children clustered around an old, white-haired woman sitting at their centre. The old woman was around eighty, with a round face and large eyes, her hair combed into a bun behind her head. She was smiling. Her feet seemed exceptionally tiny, only about a third of the usual size.

"This is my grandmother with her adopted children and their families," he explained. "She died not long after this was taken. My parents are back there." He pointed to the back row. "And I'm here, on grandmother's right side."

"Did your grandmother remarry?"

"No." He took a white box from his backpack. He opened it to reveal a yellowing envelope bearing a French postmark. With utmost care, he extracted a few sheets of paper, unfolded them and spread them over the coffee table. "It wasn't quite true, what I said about Grandma burning all the letters from your mother. My father took this one and hid it in a tree trunk sealed in wax, just because he liked the postmark. During the Cultural Revolution, the Red Guards went through her house many times, convinced that this rich, unmarried lady with relatives in capitalist France must be hiding treasure. They even brought shovels to dig up the garden. When they found nothing, they shaved her head, poured ink on her face and dragged her through the streets with chains around her neck. I was only two or three so I don't remember, but my father told me about it later. It was only last year that he dared take this letter out of the tree. He was surprised how well it was preserved. I've translated it into French." He handed another folded piece of paper to Anne.

Anne read intently.

Dear Miss Lu,

Hello.

Please pardon me for writing to you without permission. I am Delun's French wife, Marguerite. I know that Delun has mentioned me in his letters to you. Thank you for agreeing to break off your marriage to him – I can only imagine how hard it must have been for you. I think of you often and I feel guilty for the pain I have caused you. Please accept my most sincere apology.

I cannot speak Chinese. I wrote this letter in French and asked a Chinese friend who knows French to translate it for me, so this handwriting is his, not mine.

I considered writing to you for a long time. I have not told Delun that I have decided to do so, not because I fear he would oppose it but because I feel this should be a secret between the two of us. I was nervous about this letter, wanting to burn it several times. I've been guessing how you might react when you see it. Maybe you will burn it without opening it. Or maybe you won't be able to resist your curiosity about what this French woman who caused you so much trouble would want to say.

Delun mentioned that you are well-educated, that you read, write and paint. He was never trying to escape you, just the marriage his parents arranged. He told me that in China, arranged marriages are common for families like yours and his. This sounds terrible to me as a Western woman. Love should be free. But I have no right to dictate Chinese customs. The unfortunate thing is that you have been hurt by it, and Delun has lived in guilt since he left.

When I met Delun, I did not know he was married. Of course, this does not lighten my own guilt about the harm I have caused you. He and I met at the same factory, and I was fond of him the moment I saw him. I was captivated by his conscientious, hard work, his shy smile, his eagerness to learn, his courtesy.

I started paying attention to the news about China when I met Delun. I began reading books about China, too. I knew so little about the country. I marvel at China's ancient civilisation, and I loathe China's treatment at the hands of France and the other Western countries. Delun and I fell in love after a few months, so deeply that I would sleep poorly at night if I had not seen him that day. The look in his eyes when he saw me satisfied all my vain ideas about love. I tell you this not to be boastful, but because I want you to know that he and I are truly in love.

He talks often about his family. He worries about his parents' health, his siblings' futures. I would love to meet them, if it is ever possible. But I know that his family would never accept this Western woman, just as some French people refuse to accept my marriage to Delun.

He talks about you, too.

You must be in a difficult position. This grieves me. I'm not religious, but I pray for you and your happiness. I cannot dare hope for forgiveness; I would be satisfied if only you do not hate us.

I would like to hear back from you. I know this is selfish of me because if you write back, my heart will be lighter. If you prefer no connection with me at all, I will understand, too.

What's more, I read in the paper about a great famine in the north of China. Delun and I are very worried. We sent a few boxes of food and clothing last month, did you receive them?

Sincerely yours, Marguerite
5 February 1925

Slowly, Anne put down the letter. 1925... Maman and Ba had still been living in Lyon.

It had been almost seventy years since Ba had arrived in France, and this was the first time she had ever learned about his family in China. Maman, too, had her own secrets to hide.

She looked at a photograph of her parents on the wall. They were young, standing hand in hand in the shade of a blossoming tree. Baba was standing straight, with his usual subtle smile. Mama, lacking her typical vigour and vivacity, looked solemnly into the camera. Their hands were clasped, but their bodies were apart. They had taken few photographs when they were young. Only after Anne was born had they begun to take more family pictures. Anne had never studied that photograph before, but she could tell now from their expressions and postures that they were facing heavy odds.

"Did your grandmother ever mention something my mother had said in these letters?" asked Anne.

"She said your mother told her many things, both national affairs and family matters. She said that your mother wrote to her when their first child died, just after birth."

That must have been Paul, Anne thought.

"Did your grandmother write back?"

"She said that she wrote many letters, but never sent one."

"Why?"

The young man pushed his glasses higher up his nose. "She said that for a long time she couldn't stay calm enough to write to your mother. Later, she couldn't send a letter abroad or receive one because of wars and political struggles. I asked her if she would like me to give a message to your parents if I ever met them. She said that she just wanted to let them know that she had lived a good life."

"Lived a good life..." Anne repeated to herself, lamenting the gravity of it all, filled with a deep veneration for this lady whom she had never met. "So, did she forgive them after all?"

"I think that she never blamed them in the first place."

"And my father's family, are they well?"

He shook his head, remorseful. "Grandmother told me that they all died during a war in the late twenties."

"Do you know what his hometown is like now?"

"Wuping is still there, it's where I grew up. Though it's nothing like the town your father would remember. Many old buildings were destroyed in the wars in the thirties and forties, then in the sixties and seventies even more were demolished. Little of the past is left. Grandmother's old house was converted into a government office."

"Do you know what became of my father's house?"

"It's now a three-storey department store. A middle-school classmate of mine works there. There's a big stone lion outside the entrance that Grandmother said was left behind from the house. She said that there used to be two."

"Do you know anyone else who might remember my father?"

"Quite a few, actually. Last year, a local newspaper interviewed a centenarian named Xie Changqing. He was the Zhang family housekeeper for many years, and he mentioned your father in the interview. A few elderly people also remember him from childhood. He left quite the impression on people back home."

"Would it be possible," said Anne, her voice eager, "for

you to take me to see Wuping? My husband and children would also love to visit."

He nodded. "I'd be delighted. I have time off for the Spring Festival in three months. How about then?" They talked a bit longer and decided on a date when they would see each other again. It was only after he left that Anne suddenly realised that he shared both her last name and a part of her father's. Truly, Miss Lu had never forgotten him!

She stood, restless, pacing her living room. Wuping Town, a name she had never even heard before, had become a real, concrete image. A Frenchwoman with the surname Zhang was suddenly related to a small town in Shandong, thousands of miles away.

She looked up again to the photograph of her parents on the wall.

"Baba," she said to him softly. "That's where you wanted to go, right? You meant Wuping Town. I'm going to fulfil your wish for you, OK?"

Then she looked to Marguerite. "Maman, you're going to be so glad, aren't you?"

Afterword
Three Years Later

A group of second-grade students rushed out of a bus in their school uniforms. They were chatting and laughing together excitedly. Outings are always a fun adventure for inner-city school kids.

Anne went over to greet their teacher. The children all regarded her and the other volunteers behind her with curiosity. They were wearing French military uniforms from the First World War with steel helmets on their heads. Anne was sweating, her clothes sticking to her skin. It was a hot, still day, and she sighed that she could not keep up with the other volunteers physically. They were college students who wanted to experience a soldier's life.

She smiled at the children gathered around. "Welcome everybody! Today is World War One Armistice Day, and we're excited to tell you all about it."

She had been volunteering in this small town in the province of Pas-de-Calais for the past three years. These children were her final set of visitors for the day before she had to rush back to Paris to prepare for a lecture she and Clara were giving at the Saint-Genevieve Library that evening. Their topic was the work and life of Chinese labourers in France, her father's personal story included. She was excited and nervous that the pictures and materials she had collected during her three visits to China would be made public for the first time.

After they had visited the museum, the children looked over the nearby lawn. A mixed-race girl raised her hand. Her lips were pursed shyly, reminding Anne of herself at that age.

"Do you have a question?" Anne asked her kindly.

"Why are there so many craters in the lawn?"

"That's a great question," she replied. "More than seventy years ago, there was a battle fought close by. There were countless bombs, and some of them caused these big holes. During the war, a few villages were so damaged by artillery fire that they couldn't even be rebuilt. I'll take you all to see the traces of the fighting soon, including some trenches that have survived. There's a special, large stone over there with Chinese words carved onto it, and Chinese flowers and birds."

Several children raised their hands at the same time, speaking simultaneously:

"Did the Chinese people do the carvings?"

"Did Chinese people live here back then?"

"Could they speak French? Why did they come here?"

Anne smiled. "Don't worry, I'm going to answer all of your questions in time."

Clear, melodious birdsong sounded from the nearby grove. The old trench was in that direction. Anne took a deep breath, then led the children towards the trees.

Notes

Chapter 3

1. A literary magazine published in the early 20th century, founded by Chen Duxiu, a moderniser and founder of the Chinese Communist Party

Chapter 11

1. A *mu* is approximately 666 square metres

About the Author

Fan Wu is a bilingual writer, with her work published in more than ten languages. Born and raised in China, she travelled to the US for graduate studies and later worked in Silicon Valley's high-tech sector. She holds an MA from Stanford University and now lives in California. She is the author of three novels and her short fiction has appeared in numerous publications, such as *Granta* and *Ploughshares*, and has been nominated for the Pushcart Prize. Fan is also a co-founder of the Society of Heart's Delight, which promotes interracial and intercultural dialogue, as well as a trustee and leader of Mothers' Bridge of Love. She is the creator of the "Chinese Immigrants in Silicon Valley and Beyond" photoblog.

About the Translator

Honey Watson is a science fiction writer and translator living in Las Vegas, Nevada. She is a translator of both fiction and non-fiction from Mandarin into English, holding degrees from University College London and Peking University, Beijing. Her debut novel, *Lessons in Birdwatching*, will be released by Angry Robot in August 2023

About Sinoist Books

We hope you enjoyed this story about identity and memories of the Chinese Labour Corps.

SINOIST BOOKS brings the best of Chinese fiction to English-speaking readers. We aim to create a greater understanding of Chinese culture and society, and provide an outlet for the ideas and creativity of the country's most talented authors.

To let us know what you thought of this book, or to learn more about the diverse range of exciting Chinese fiction in translation we publish, find us online. If you're as passionate about Chinese literature as we are, then we'd love to hear your thoughts!

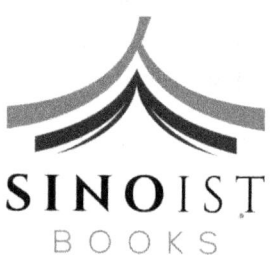

sinoistbooks.com
@sinoistbooks